Kat,

INCORRIGIBLE

STEPHANIE BURGIS

ATHENEUM BOOKS FOR YOUNG READERS
New York London Toronto Sydney

Atheneum Books for Young Readers

An imprint of Simon & Schuster Children's Publishing Division

1230 Avenue of the Americas, New York, New York 10020

ATHENEUM BOOKS FOR YOUNG READERS is a registered trademark of Simon & Schuster, Inc.

For information about special discounts for bulk purchases, please contact Simon & Schuster Special Sales at 1-866-506-1949 or business@simonandschuster.com.

The Simon & Schuster Speakers Bureau can bring authors to your live event. For more information or to book an event, contact the Simon & Schuster Speakers Bureau at 1-866-248-3049 or visit our website at www.simonspeakers.com.

The text for this book is set in Scala.

Manufactured in the United States of America

0311 FFG

First Edition

10 9 8 7 6 5 4 3 2 1

Library of Congress Cataloging-in-Publication Data

Burgis, Stephanie.

A most improper magick / Stephanie Burgis. — 1st ed.

p. cm. — (The unladylike adventures of Kat Stephenson ; bk. 1)

Summary: In Regency England, when twelve-year-old Kat discovers she has magical powers, she tries to use them to rescue her sister from marrying a man she does not love.

ISBN 978-1-4169-9447-3 (hardcover)

[1. Magic—Fiction. 2. Sisters—Fiction. 3. Family problems—Fiction. 4. Great Britain—History—George III, 1760–1820—Fiction.] I. Title.

PZ7.B9174Mo 2010

[Fic]—dc22   2009032543

ISBN 978-1-4169-9878-5 (eBook)

For Patrick,
whose love and faith
are the truest kinds of magic I know

One

1803

I was twelve years of age when I chopped off my hair, dressed as a boy, and set off to save my family from impending ruin.

I made it almost to the end of my front garden.

"Katherine Ann Stephenson!" My oldest sister Elissa's outraged voice pinned me like a dagger as she threw open her bedroom window. "What on earth do you think you're doing?"

Curses. I froze, still holding my pack slung across my shoulder. I might be my family's best chance of salvation, but there was no expecting either of my older sisters to understand that. If they'd trusted me in the first place, I wouldn't have had to run away in the middle of the night, like a criminal.

The garden gate was only two feet ahead of me. If I hurried . . .

"I'm going to tell Papa!" Elissa hissed.

Behind her, I heard groggy, incoherent moans of outrage—my other sister, Angeline, waking up.

Elissa was the prissiest female ever to have been born. But Angeline was simply impossible. If they really did wake the whole household, and Papa came after me in the gig . . .

I'd planned to walk to the closest coaching inn, six miles away, and catch the dawn stagecoach to London. If Papa caught up with me first, the sad, disappointed looks I'd have to endure from him for weeks afterward would be unbearable. And the way Stepmama would gloat over my disgrace—*the second of our mother's children to be a disappointment to the family* . . .

I gritted my teeth together as I turned and trudged back toward the vicarage.

Angeline's voice floated lazily through the open window. "What were you shouting about?"

"I was not shouting!" Elissa snapped. "Ladies never shout."

"You could have fooled me," said Angeline. "I thought the house must have been burning down."

I pushed the side door open just in time to hear my brother, Charles, bellow, "Would everyone be quiet? Some of us are trying to sleep!"

"What? What?" My father's voice sounded from his

bedroom at the head of the stairs. "What's going on out there?"

My stepmother's voice overrode his. "For heaven's sake, make them be quiet, George! It's past midnight. You cannot let them constantly behave like hoydens. Be firm, for once!"

I groaned and closed the door behind me.

Like it or not, I was home.

I squeezed through the narrow kitchen and tiptoed up the rickety staircase that led to the second floor. When I was a little girl and Mama's influence still lingered in the house, each of the stairs had whispered my name as I stepped onto them, and they never let me trip. Now, the only sound they made was the telltale creak of straining wood.

The door to Papa and Stepmama's room swung open as I reached the head of the first flight of stairs, and I stopped, resigned.

"Kat?" Papa blinked out at me, peering through the darkness. He held a candle in his hand. "What's amiss?"

"Nothing, Papa," I said. "I just went downstairs for some milk."

"Oh. Well." He coughed and ran a hand over his faded nightcap. "Er, your stepmother is quite right. You should all be in bed and quiet at this hour."

"Yes, Papa." I hoisted the heavy sack higher on my shoulder. "I'm just going back to bed now."

"Good, good. And the others?"

"I'll tell them to be quiet," I said. "Don't worry."

"Good girl." He reached out to pat my shoulder. A frown crept across his face. "Ah . . . is something wrong, my dear?"

"Papa?"

"I don't mean to be critical, er, but your clothing seems . . . it appears . . . well, it does look a trifle unorthodox."

I glanced down at the boy's breeches, shirt, and coat that I wore. "I was too cold for a nightgown," I said.

"But . . ." He frowned harder. "There's something about your hair, I don't quite know what—"

My stepmother's voice cut him off. "Would you please stop talking and come back to bed, George? I cannot be expected to sleep with all this noise!"

"Ah. Right. Yes, of course." Papa gave a quick nod and turned away. "Sleep well, Kat."

"And you, sir."

I tiptoed up the last five steps that led to the second-floor landing. The doors to Charles's room and my sisters' room were both closed. If I was very, very lucky . . .

I leaped toward the ladder that led up to the attic where I slept.

No such luck. The door to my sisters' room jerked open.

"Come in here now!" Elissa said. I couldn't make out her features in the darkness, but I could tell that she had her arms crossed.

4

Oh, Lord.

"'Ladies don't cross their arms like common fish-wives,'" I whispered, quoting one of Elissa's own favorite maxims as I stalked past her into their room.

Elissa slammed the door behind her.

"Give us light, Angeline," she said. "I want to see her face."

Angeline was already lighting a candle. When the tinder finally caught and the candle lit, the sound of my sisters' gasps filled the room.

I crossed my arms over my chest and glared right back at them.

"You—you—" Elissa couldn't even speak. She collapsed onto her side of the bed, gasping and pressing one slender hand to her heart.

Angeline shook her head, smirking. "Well, that's torn it."

"Don't use slang," Elissa said. Being able to give one of her most common reproofs seemed to revive her spirits a little; the color came flooding back into her face. With her fair hair and pale skin, I could always tell her mood from her face, and right now, she was as horrified as I'd ever seen her. She took a deep, deep breath. "Katherine," she said, in a voice that was nearly steady. "Would you care to explain yourself to us?"

"No," I said. "I wouldn't." I lifted my chin, fighting for height. I was shorter than either of my sisters, a curse in situations like this.

"What is there to explain?" Angeline said. "It's obvious. Kat's finally decided to run off to the circus, where she belongs."

"I do not!"

"No?" Angeline's full lips twisted as she looked at me. "With that haircut, I don't know where else you hoped to go. Perhaps if you hid behind all the other animals—"

"Shut up!" I lunged for her straight across the room.

Their bed was in the way. I hit my knees on it, then flung aside my sack and crawled across the bed to get to her. Angeline's taunting laughter made my vision blur with rage. I landed on her, punching blindly, and kept on fighting even after she'd shoved me down onto the bed and wrapped her arm around my neck, half strangling me.

"Stop it!" Elissa shrieked.

Something heavy hit the other side of the wall: Charles signifying his displeasure. Across the stairwell, a door opened. Footsteps approached. A firm knock sounded on the door.

We all froze. We knew that knock.

"You've done it now, haven't you?" Angeline whispered into my ear.

"Cow," I whispered back.

"What's happening in there?" our stepmother demanded, through the door.

Angeline shoved me off the bed and onto the floor. When I tried to stand up, she put one hand on my newly short hair and pushed me straight back down. "Stay where you are!" she hissed. "She mustn't see you like this." She looked across the bed at Elissa. "You try to fob her off."

Elissa was already moving for the door, her face suddenly angelic and serene. "I'm coming, Stepmama," she called. "Just a moment." She stopped just short of the door and whispered, "Put that light out! Quick!"

Angeline blew the candle out and threw herself back into bed, pulling the covers up to her chin.

I huddled on the cold floor in the darkness while Elissa opened the door.

"What do you think—"

"We are so sorry for the noise, Stepmama," Elissa murmured. "Angeline had a fright and fell out of bed."

"All that screaming . . ." Stepmama's voice drew nearer. I could imagine what was happening, even though I couldn't see it: She was poking her sharp nose into the room, peering around in hopes of mischief. It was her never-ending quest: to prove to Papa how incorrigible we all were. Just like our mother had been.

"Angeline had a terrible nightmare," Elissa said, and I was amazed by how well my saintly sister could lie when she was properly motivated.

"Perhaps I should come in and look things over," Stepmama said.

"Ohhh . . . ," Angeline moaned from the bed. Angeline, unlike Elissa, never found any difficulty in lying. "Oh, my poor stomach . . ."

Stepmama sighed and started forward. "If you're ill, I'd better—"

"I *was* ill," Angeline said. "All over the floor."

"Oh." Stepmama came to an abrupt halt. "Where—?"

"Do watch where you step," Elissa said sweetly. "I haven't had a chance to clean it up quite yet, so—"

Stepmama's feet shuffled back hastily. "Well," she said. "Well. I'm sure that you'll feel better after a good night's sleep, Angeline. But see that you girls take care of the mess first. And no more noise!"

The door closed, and her footsteps moved away. I stayed frozen until her bedroom door had opened and closed again on the other side of the stairwell. As I finally moved, my hand slipped on the wooden floor and slid across two familiar, oddly shaped books hidden just beneath the bed.

I knew those books. They weren't supposed to be here. They were supposed to be locked away with the rest of our mother's keepsakes, where Papa and Stepmama hoped we would all forget that they had ever existed. Just like Mama herself.

I started to pick them up, then stopped. Now wasn't the time to ask either of my sisters provocative questions.

"Whew." I stood up and stretched to relieve my cramped muscles as Angeline relit the candle. "Well, I'd better go up to bed and sleep now, as Stepmama said, so—"

"Don't even think about it," said Angeline. Her arm

shot out and grabbed the back of my jacket, pinning me to the side of the bed. "Open up her pack, Elissa. Let's see what Kat was planning to take away with her."

"I'm not a thief," I muttered.

Angeline threw me a look of amused contempt. "I never thought you were, ninny. I just wondered what sort of practical provisioning you'd made to prepare for your journey."

"Journey?" Elissa said. Her voice came out in a gasp. "What journey?"

"Oh, for heaven's sake," said Angeline. "What else did you think she was doing, dressed up as a boy and heading out in the middle of the night? She was running away, weren't you, Kat?"

I gritted my teeth and stood silent under her grasp.

"You couldn't—why—" Elissa collapsed onto the bed. "Whatever would make you do such a thing? How could you even think—?"

"I didn't have a choice!" The words burst out between my gritted teeth. "It was the only way I could stop you from being an idiot!"

"Me?" Elissa stared at me.

"If you're trying to fool us with one of your wild stories—," Angeline began.

I glowered at her. "And you. You were going to let her do it!"

"Do what?" said Elissa. "What is she talking about?"

"I heard Stepmama!" I said to Elissa. "She was positively

gloating about it to Papa. All about how she'd managed to save the whole family by selling you off to some horrible old man. And you hadn't even told me! You two never tell me anything! I knew if I tried to argue, you wouldn't pay any attention, so—"

"Oh, Lord," Angeline said. "I knew if she found out—"

"At least I was going to do something about it." I swung on Angeline. "You were just going to let her sacrifice herself."

"And what exactly was your plan?" Angeline asked. "Once you'd fitted yourself out like a monkey—"

"I was going to London," I said. "I knew if I ran away, there would be such a scandal that Stepmama wouldn't be able to sell Elissa off. And once I was there . . ." I half closed my eyes, to see my dream past my sister's skeptical face. "There are thousands of jobs a boy can get in London. I could sign on to a merchant ship and make my fortune in the Indies, or I could be a typesetter at a newspaper and see every part of London. All I'd have to do is get work, real work, earning money, and then I could send part of it home to you two, so at least you could both have real dowries and then—"

"Oh, you little fool," Elissa said, and the words came out in a half sob. "Come here, Kat." Angeline let go of me, and I crawled over the bed to Elissa's warm embrace. She wrapped her arms around me, and I felt her tears land on my short hair. "Promise me you won't ever do anything so rash and unnecessary ever again."

"But—" My voice came out muffled against her night-gown.

Angeline spoke from behind me. "How long do you think you would have survived in London on your own, idiot? And who do you think would have hired you, coming from the countryside with no references, no one who knows you to give you a good word, no skills or experience—"

"I have skills!" I said.

"Not the sort that get young men hired," Angeline said implacably. "And when they found out you weren't really a boy . . ."

Elissa shuddered and tightened her arms around me. "It isn't to be thought of," she said. "The danger you would have been exposed to—"

"The danger she would have walked straight into, without even thinking twice," Angeline corrected her.

"I could have taken care of myself," I said. "Charles taught me how to box and fence last year when he was sent down from Oxford for bad behavior."

"Charles is a fool," said Angeline, "and I wouldn't be surprised if he isn't half as good at boxing or fencing as he claims to be."

The three of us sat for a moment in depressed silence, acknowledging the truth of that.

Elissa sighed. "But the point is, darling, it isn't neces-sary for you to save me."

"Who else is going to do it?" I struggled up out of her

embrace. "I am not going to let you sell yourself off just so Stepmama can buy us all dozens of new gowns and seasons in London and—"

"And keep our brother from being sent to debtors' prison," Angeline said evenly.

I snorted. "You should know better than to listen to Stepmama's moans. She's just hysterical about—"

"It's true," said Elissa. "I saw the evidence myself. Papa borrowed everything he could to pay off Charles's dreadful gambling debts, but he couldn't cover all of them. If we can't come up with the money to pay the rest within two months, poor Charles will have to go to debtors' prison."

"'Poor Charles,' my foot," said Angeline. "Going to debtors' prison is exactly what Charles deserves."

I looked from Angeline to Elissa. "But surely—"

"If Charles goes to debtors' prison, we will all be ruined," Elissa said. "None of us would ever receive an eligible offer of marriage after that. You know our family is already considered . . . well . . ." She bit her lip.

"I know," I said. Stepmama was only too ready to remind us, anytime one of us forgot. There were plenty of people in Society who would always look at us askance just because of our mother, no matter how properly we behaved or what our dowries were. It was one reason why I had decided long ago not to bother behaving properly. "But that can't be enough to make you marry an old man! Whoever he is."

"Sir Neville Collingwood," Angeline said. "One of the wealthiest men in England. You can see why Stepmama chose him, can't you?"

"He's not so very old, Kat," Elissa said. She clasped her hands together and looked down at them. "I don't think he can be above forty, and—"

"Forty!"

"And Stepmama says he is supposed to be quite handsome."

"Supposed to be? She hasn't even met him herself?"

"We've been very fortunate even to gain this one opportunity." Elissa's voice sounded strained. "Stepmama has good relations, you know."

"Ha," I said.

"Well, she has connections, at any rate," Elissa said. "It was through them that she found out that Sir Neville is coming into Yorkshire—and that she arranged for us to meet him."

"Sir Neville will be part of a monthlong house party at Grantham Abbey, thirty miles from here," Angeline said briskly. "Stepmama has arranged for all of us to be guests there as well, because everyone knows that Sir Neville is looking for another wife."

"Another?" I repeated. "What happened to his first one?"

"That doesn't matter," Elissa said. She was knotting her fingers so tightly together now that her knuckles had turned white. "It's a wonderful opportunity for me. For all of us. Sir Neville is . . . he is . . ."

"He is so wealthy, he could pay off all Charles's debts for the rest of his life, without even noticing," Angeline said. "And since Papa and Stepmama can't keep Charles locked up in the house forever, it makes a great deal of sense for at least one of us to have a husband like that."

"I don't mind, Kat. Truly," Elissa said. "I always wanted to marry a man who could help my family. Sir Neville is a great man in Society."

I frowned at her. "Then why do you look so miserable?"

"Never mind that." Angeline put one hand on Elissa's knotted fingers, and for a moment I felt completely shut out as they looked at each other with sympathetic understanding.

"What is it?" I said. "What aren't you telling me this time?"

"Nothing, darling," Elissa said. "Just go up to bed now. We're all too tired to talk properly. Come back in the morning before breakfast, and I'll fix your hair. And please, don't worry about me anymore. I am perfectly happy. Truly."

"But . . ." I stood up slowly, still frowning at my two sisters and trying to guess the secret I could feel hanging between them. "If you marry Sir Neville, do you think he'll give Angeline a dowry?"

"I hope so," said Elissa.

"It doesn't matter whether he does or not," Angeline said, and flashed me a dangerous smile. "I have my own plans for that."

Ha. At least that gave me one clue.

Perhaps Angeline and Elissa wanted to play at keeping more secrets from me, but I would wager anything that there was one secret Angeline hadn't dared to share with our sweet, proper oldest sister.

I'd recognized the books hidden underneath Angeline's side of the bed. They were Mama's old magic books.

Now all I had to do was figure out what Angeline was planning to do with them.

Two

If my plan had worked, I would have woken up the next morning in a stagecoach heading toward London, with a whole new life waiting to unfold before me. I would have breakfasted on apples and cheese with the passengers around me, heard all their stories, and been halfway adopted as an honorary nephew into all their families by the time we reached London.

Instead, I had to face my own family.

I walked into the breakfast room at eight o'clock, and Stepmama's jaw fell wide open, exposing a mouthful of mashed toast.

"Katherine Ann Stephenson!" she uttered in a dreadful tone. "Whatever have you done to your hair?"

I dipped a curtsy to Papa and made my way to the sideboard, where bread and jam and kippers were laid out. "I like it," I said. I did, too, especially now that Elissa had straightened out the crooked edges. After one morning without the bother of hairpins, I was ready to keep my hair short for life.

"I thought something was different," Papa said, with quiet satisfaction. "Good morning, dear."

"George!" Stepmama flung down her napkin. "For heaven's sake. Your daughter has just chopped off all her hair. Is 'I thought something was different' really all you can say?"

"Not all her hair, surely." Papa peered up at me from behind his book. "Ah, no. No, there's still a bit left. It's rather . . ." He frowned thoughtfully. "It's rather boyish, actually."

"Quite," Stepmama said. "That is exactly my point. Aren't you going to ask her how she could do such a thing without even asking your permission?"

Papa said tentatively, "*Did* you ask my permission, Kat?"

"Kat's new haircut is quite stylish, don't you think?" Elissa said softly. "She looks just like the model in the *Mirror of Fashion* now."

"But with a rather higher-cut décolletage," Angeline said dryly. Mischief sparked in her eyes as she slid a glance at our stepmother. "What did you think of that latest style, ma'am?"

"Oh!" Stepmama shook her head. "None of my step-daughters will ever appear in public with such low-cut gowns as I saw in that journal. It is absolutely shocking what young ladies in London nowadays are up to. In my day . . ."

"Shocking indeed," Angeline murmured, and winked at me.

You might have thought, if you didn't know my sisters, that I could have just asked Angeline straight out about Mama's magic books.

But I knew better. If Angeline even suspected that I knew about the books, she would find them a new and better hiding place before I could even get the question out of my mouth. Then she'd devise one of her diabolically cunning punishments for my nosiness, and that was the last thing I wanted. No, I'd have to work the mystery out for myself.

Luckily, Stepmama took Elissa and Angeline out directly after breakfast to shop for fabric for new gowns— to impress Sir Neville, I supposed. There was only enough room in the gig for two people to travel with her to the fabric shop in the village, and no one asked if I wanted to be one of them. They knew better.

As soon as the gig rattled out of sight, I hurtled upstairs, hiking up my skirts and taking the creaking old steps two at a time. Charles let out a groggy roar from his room at the noise, but I ignored him. I headed straight for Angeline and Elissa's bedroom.

They ought to be gone for at least two hours. But if

anything went wrong . . . I imagined Angeline's expression if she caught me reading the books. I shuddered.

I would have to hurry.

I darted into the room and over the bed to Angeline's side. When I passed my hand underneath, all I felt was the bare wooden floor. Where had they gone?

I lay down to peer under the bed. *Aha.* She'd only pushed the books deeper in. I wriggled underneath, choking on dust, and emerged a moment later, holding them both. Victory!

A sneeze caught me by surprise. Then another one. I almost dropped the books. When I finally stopped sneezing, I glanced down and groaned. I was completely covered in dust, all the way across the front of my white gown. If Stepmama saw me like this, she'd throw a fit. And if Angeline saw me . . .

If Angeline saw me, she would know exactly what I had been up to. Curse her! Had she planned it this way? No, surely not—even Angeline couldn't be that devious. But still, whether she'd planned this warning system or not, I knew I'd just lost half an hour from my reading time. First I'd have to put the books back exactly where I'd found them. Then I'd have to change my gown and wash the telltale dust from this one, all before the others came home from their shopping trip.

I gritted my teeth and ran out of the room before I could lose any more time.

I didn't go to my own windowless attic room. That

wouldn't be nearly safe enough. Instead I hurried back downstairs and out the back door, heading for my favorite lookout spot—the old oak tree behind the vicarage, overlooking the graveyard. From my perch in the tree, I'd be able to spot Stepmama's gig from half a mile off as it came circling back up the winding road from the village.

I clambered up the wide, knobbly trunk and settled comfortably into the crook of one of the big central branches. My legs dangled in the air, and I kicked off my shoes, letting them fall to the grass. Through the ground-floor window of the vicarage, I could see Papa reading one of his hundreds of old books. A fresh breeze ruffled the leaves of the oak tree and set the yew trees in the graveyard to swaying gently. The road beyond was empty beneath the bright blue summer sky.

I adjusted my shoulders against the rough bark of the tree trunk and opened the first book.

A Diary of Magick, I read, in looping purple handwriting. *Olivia Amberson's Own Book.*

Amberson had been Mama's maiden name. That was one of the only things I knew about my mother. She'd died ten days after I was born, and a nursemaid raised me for the first few years, until my sisters were old enough to take over. I would have been more grateful to them if it hadn't left them so smugly convinced, no matter how old I grew, that I was still a mere child.

Papa never talked about Mama. It wasn't until he'd married Stepmama, though, that I'd realized Mama had been a disgrace. It was the first time I'd ever felt close to her memory. I was always in trouble, too.

Stepmama always said that it was a great trial to be the wife of a clergyman, especially one with such a poor income as Papa. She only hated it for the lack of money, though, which meant the lack of fashionable clothing, London townhouses, and scandalous gossip at close hand. It must have been even harder for Mama to be a clergyman's wife, since she was a witch.

Elissa wouldn't talk about Mama anymore—she had been seven years old when Mama died, but the memories still made her too melancholy, she said. Angeline told me once, though, about the disaster that happened when Papa's patron, Squire Briggs, was invited to tea at the vicarage, two months before I was born. Angeline was only five at the time, but she said she had never forgotten it.

"Mama got distracted as she poured the tea," Angeline told me. A smirk pulled at her full lips as she remembered. "Papa and Elissa were both so appalled, but I thought it was hilarious."

"What did she do? Did she spill the tea?"

"Oh, no. Nothing like that." Angeline leaned close to whisper the words in my ear, even though Papa and Stepmama were safely occupied with the accounting books in the next room. "Mama was trying so hard to concentrate on making polite conversation with Squire Briggs, because it was so important for Papa's future, that she forgot to use her hands to pour the tea!"

"You mean—"

"The teapot just rose up in the air all on its own and poured for everyone while she talked. You should have seen Squire Briggs's face! He turned purple and started to choke. And Mama still didn't realize . . ." Angeline bit her lip, holding back a laugh. She was meant to be tutoring me in French, as a punishment for both of us, so we couldn't let Stepmama hear us giggling together.

"Poor Mama," Angeline said. "She was trying so hard to help Squire Briggs stop choking, and Papa started stuttering hopelessly, he was so horrified, and that teapot just kept on pouring absolutely perfectly, without a single spill, until Papa lunged forward and grabbed it himself, and then the tea spilled all over his lap and the floor and . . . I laughed so hard, I thought I would die."

"And then what happened?"

Angeline's face hardened. "After that, Squire Briggs wouldn't come back to tea again as long as Mama was alive. He had already offered to give Papa a second living, but after that teatime, he changed his mind. And Mama . . ." Angeline looked away, setting her jaw. "Mama wept for a week."

I shivered in the oak tree now, remembering Angeline's story as I looked at my mother's lovely, looping handwriting.

There used to be a miniature portrait of Mama in the sitting room, when I was a little girl, but Stepmama had locked it away with the rest of Mama's things, magical or otherwise, in a cabinet none of us were allowed to open. *There's no use in reminding the neighbors of old problems*, she'd said. She had already cut down all of Mama's roses from the back garden by then; they were a scandal too. Apparently, roses weren't supposed to be able to bloom red all year long. But I had loved them anyway. My sisters used to take me out to sit underneath the oak tree on fine days when I was little, and the rich, sweet fragrance of the roses had filled the air with magic.

I hadn't remembered Mama's roses for a long time.

I took a deep breath and turned the page.

I have decided to begin as I mean to go on, no matter how Ominous the Dangers, my mother had written. *Tho' it must be kept Secret from my closest companions and even my own Colleagues, I cannot let Ignorance, Prejudice, or Pride hold me back any longer from exercising all the Talents I have been given. I shall teach myself first how to enchant Inanimate Objects.*

Well, I understood why she'd meant to keep her witch-craft a secret—if it hadn't been for the fact that she'd married a clergyman, she would have been completely cast out of Society for it, and as it was, she had still caused a scandal. Marrying her had ruined Papa's career. But that was because she hadn't kept the magic a secret after all. From all the stories I'd heard, she hadn't even tried very hard. Surely someone who really wanted to keep her witchcraft secret wouldn't have blatantly enchanted the roses in her garden, would she? And what on earth had she meant by "Colleagues"? Mama's family might not have been wealthy, but she had definitely been a lady—and ladies, as Elissa was always ready to remind me, did not work for a living, no matter how dire their circumstances.

I let out a long breath and turned the page. I didn't have time to waste worrying about any of that, no matter how tempting it might be. I was after my sister's secrets right now, not my mother's—and enchanting inanimate objects, like Mama's self-pouring teapot, wouldn't get Angeline her dowry.

I skipped through the pages of Mama's first failures and final successes, as she experimented with creating her own spells. She'd learned more and more difficult tricks as she'd progressed, but nothing practical like turning copper to gold. Half of Mama's spells were meant to make herself look prettier or to make her twice-turned, hand-me-down gowns look new. I even found a love spell—and next to it, circled and surrounded by tiny hearts, a name: *George.* My father's name.

I flicked quickly past that page, feeling my cheeks heat up.

It had been at least an hour since I had begun to read, and the sun had risen high in the sky above me. I couldn't see the gig in the distance yet, but I knew I didn't have much time left. I flipped faster and faster through the pages.

I was concentrating so hard, I didn't even notice the footsteps coming toward me from the graveyard.

The first I knew of it was when my stockinged feet, swinging in the air, brushed right against a man's beaver hat and knocked it to the grass. I almost fell off my branch in surprise. Both of Mama's diaries dropped from my hands, six feet down onto the grass, next to a moving pair of dirt-covered Hessian boots. My gaze went up past the boots, up mud-spattered pantaloons and a dark blue coat that looked like it had once been expensive, before it had all been covered in dirt. The man who wore the clothes—and the dirt—was a complete stranger.

"Who are you?" I asked. The words blurted themselves out of my mouth. If Angeline had been there, she would have said something smooth and courteous and subtly amused in greeting. If Elissa had been there, she would have been too proper to speak to a strange gentleman at all without a proper introduction. Then again, neither of my sisters would have been caught off guard in the first place by sitting in a tree without her shoes on.

The man underneath me had kept walking forward even after I kicked his hat off. He hadn't even paused to look up at me, or to pick up his hat. But when I spoke, he stopped walking and shook himself as if he were shaking off a cloud of gnats.

"I am Frederick Carlyle," he said in a strange, flat voice. He was still looking straight ahead at the vicarage, so I couldn't see his face, only the back of his dark blond hair. He was dressed like a gentleman, but from the look of his hair—not to mention the state of his clothing—it had been some time since he'd seen a valet, or a comb. "Here to study with Miss Angeline Stephenson's father," he said.

"With An—you mean with Papa? Mr. Stephenson?"

He still didn't turn. "Here to study with Miss Angeline Stephenson's father," he repeated. "I have brought my first quarter's payment with me."

"Ah . . . good?" I slid down off the tree. It was awkward, since I couldn't let my skirts ride up in front of him. I landed hard on a sharp stone, stumbled, and barely missed stepping on Mama's books. I snatched them up and tried to flatten the crumpled pages with one hand. Later I would probably panic about the damage, but right now I was too curious to feel scared.

"How do you know Angeline?" I asked the back of the gentleman's head.

He swung around, and I saw his face for the first time. It was alight with hope. "Is Miss Angeline truly here? Are you Miss Angeline?"

"No!" I said. "Of course not. I'm just Kat." I stared at him. He was young—about the same age as Charles, I thought, so probably no more than twenty. Handsome, too, I supposed, if he hadn't looked so vacant. I frowned, looking at his blank blue eyes. Maybe "vacant" wasn't the right word, after all. Maybe "entranced" would be more accurate.

Something about that started an ominous tugging in the back of my mind. *Entranced* . . . But before I could think it through, I heard a rattling sound behind me and something worse—familiar voices floating through the still air. I spun around.

"Oh, the devil!"

I had been the one too entranced to think straight. I hadn't been keeping my lookout.

Stepmama's gig was on the road just beneath us, less than two minutes' drive away. Even as I watched, it turned onto the final curve.

The full implications hit me with a thud. I stared down at the books in my hands. Half the pages had been bent in the fall, and the whole middle section of the first diary was crumpled. Even if I put both books back exactly where I'd found them, Angeline would never be fooled. She would know the moment she opened them exactly what had happened.

I wondered if it was too late to run away after all. The boys' clothes were still in the attic, where I'd left them. Maybe, if everyone else was absorbed in greeting our strange visitor, they wouldn't even notice I was missing. And this Frederick Carlyle, whoever he might be, certainly seemed to be excited about meeting Angeline, so that should distract her at least a little while, until . . .

"Is Miss Angeline in that gig?" he asked hopefully.

"Yes," I said unhappily. "So I really need to go and—no, wait! She'll be here in just a moment. You don't need to go chasing after it, Mr. Carlyle—Mr. Carlyle! Stop!"

I threw myself in front of him to hold him back. He walked straight into my raised arm, heading for the hedge around our garden that overlooked the road, a full fifteen feet below.

"It's too high!" I said. "You'll break your legs if you jump that. What's your hurry, anyway? It's not as if you've ever even met her, so—"

Oh. Suddenly it all clicked into place. Mama's magic books tingled in my hands as I regarded them with new-found respect.

"Miss Angeline Stephenson," Frederick Carlyle murmured. He sounded like a bleating calf being led to the slaughter, but a blissful smile curved his lips.

Now I knew why he had seemed entranced.

"Come inside," I said soothingly. "Why don't I bring you a cup of tea? Then you can brush yourself off before you meet Angeline. You want to make a good impression on her, don't you?"

He frowned, as if it were a difficult concept to grasp. "Miss Angeline is coming here? Inside this house?"

"She is," I said. "I'll show you in. I want to be there with you when she arrives."

I couldn't hide the books from Angeline, or keep her from finding out that I'd looked at them. But I had something better than secrecy now.

I had the perfect opportunity for blackmail.

Three

Stepmama was the first one into the house. According to her many, many friends, who clutter up the drawing room every Tuesday afternoon and cluck over her difficulties in life, Stepmama is still a great beauty even at the ancient age of eight-and-thirty (although she pretends to be three years younger whenever she can get away with it). They all agree every week over tea and cakes what a cruel injustice of Fate it was that she could never find a husband in a higher rank of life to support her in the style she deserved.

None of them, of course, ever bring up the fact that, based on all the social rules Stepmama herself taught us, as a spinster of three-and-thirty, she was lucky to be offered marriage by any gentleman, no matter what his income or social status . . . which was exactly why she'd accepted Papa the very moment he'd offered, despite all her fine words now.

When Stepmama stepped inside the front hall and found me waiting for her with my hands held carefully behind my back, her whole face pinched up so tight with exasperation that she could have cut paper with it.

"What on earth have you done to your poor gown this time? It's filthy!"

Angeline came up behind her, holding a pile of parcels, and looked over Stepmama's shoulder at the dust that covered the front of my gown. Her dark eyes narrowed. It was one of her most dangerous expressions.

Stepmama was still ranting. "Do you never take any thought for the most basic tenets of propriety and ladylike behavior? Or the embarrassment you might bring upon your poor sisters? Only imagine if we had had a caller, what they would think—"

"But we do have a caller," I said. "He's in the drawing room right now. He was most anxious to meet Angeline's family."

Angeline's eyes narrowed even more.

Stepmama stared at me. "This is an inappropriate moment for a joke, young lady. If you—"

"I gave him tea," I said. "Isn't that what I ought to do with visitors? Especially when they might be eligible suitors? After all, you're always saying that we'll all die old maids if we don't work very hard for ourselves."

Elissa let out a sound of pain from behind Angeline. "Did you make the tea yourself, Kat?"

"Well, of course I did. You know Mrs. Watkins always visits the market on Monday mornings, so—"

Elissa closed her eyes in an expression of pure agony. "Perhaps I can find some of her biscuits in the cupboard," she said. "They might take the taste of the tea from his mouth, if I'm quick enough." She hurried past the others, heading for the kitchen without even taking off her bonnet or pelisse first.

"Well, really," I said. "I must say—"

"You have already said quite enough." Stepmama unbuttoned her own pelisse with quick, angry gestures and shoved it at me. "Hang this up and change your gown before you show yourself in the drawing room."

I had to bring my right hand forward to take the pelisse before it could fall on the floor. Mama's thick magic books slipped precariously in my left hand. I pressed them hard into my back and edged toward the wall. "He's already seen my dust. I don't think—"

"I don't care. Angeline, follow me as soon as you've straightened your hair."

Chin up, Stepmama sailed toward the drawing room like a fully armed navy battleship heading for an unsuspecting French privateer.

Angeline waited until the drawing room door closed behind Stepmama. Then she shook her head.

"That," she said, "was very, very foolish."

I smiled innocently up at her, my fingers straining around the hidden books. "I don't know what you mean."

"Who is it, really, in the drawing room? A farmer's boy? The milkman? I'm sure I'll be terribly amused by whatever joke you've prepared for me."

"Maybe," I said. "Or maybe only I will."

She nodded at my dusty gown. "Did you find out what you wanted to know when you went nosing around under my bed?"

"You mean in these?" I brought my left hand out from behind my back to show her the magic books. "Oh, I didn't need to read these to find out what you've been up to."

"No?" She raised one perfect eyebrow, a gesture that usually drove me mad with frustration. I could never imitate her, no matter how hard I tried. "Enlighten me," Angeline said. "I'm truly curious."

"Oh, you'll find out," I said. "Just step into the drawing room and see who's waiting for you."

"Fine. I shall."

Angeline took off her pelisse. She patted down her dark hair as she gazed into the murky mirror that hung beside the parasol stand. She twitched the puffy shoulders of her gown into place and smiled at me sweetly. "I do hope you're enjoying this moment very much, darling Kat, because I promise you will pay for it."

"Just go into the drawing room," I said.

Then I threw Stepmama's pelisse onto its hook and

chased after Angeline as, for once, she actually followed my orders.

Inside the drawing room, we found Stepmama glowing with satisfaction. That had to come from the news of Mr. Carlyle's first-quarter payment, I thought. Only the promise of money ever put such pleasure in her eyes. She was in such a good mood that she barely even grimaced when she saw me still wearing my dirty gown.

"Girls," she purred. "May I introduce your father's new student? Can you imagine, he has come all the way from Oxford, on foot, to study with your father! Mr. Carlyle, may I present my husband's two younger daughters? These are Miss Angeline and Miss—"

She broke off as Frederick Carlyle burst to his feet, shoving aside his full cup of tea so hard it sloshed and spilled all across its saucer.

"Angeline?" he said. "Miss Angeline? Is it really you?"

"I . . ." Angeline paused, licking her lips nervously. I had never seen my arrogant sister so discomposed. "I am Angeline, yes," she said. "But sir—"

He shook his head. His dark blue eyes were wide and wondering. "I've come so far," he said. "I would have walked forever."

In three quick strides he was across the room, knocking elegant little tables aside. Stepmama's brand-new Wedgwood teapot, delivered all the way from London, went flying to the ground. The sound of its crash, as it shattered, mingled with Stepmama's moan of pain. Two vases followed, splashing water and lilies across the carpet as they broke. But the clatter of breaking china never slowed Mr. Carlyle in his path.

He threw himself down on one knee and grasped Angeline's hand. "Miss Angeline," he said. "Marry me. Please. I beg you."

Stepmama's voice came out as a shriek. "What in heaven's name—?"

Angeline opened her mouth and closed it again. Color rose in her cheeks until they were a deep, dusky red.

Frederick Carlyle bent his head to kiss her hand passionately. It made a disgusting, wet, sucking sound. I might have gagged if I hadn't been trying so hard not to laugh.

Elissa opened the door behind us, holding a plateful of Mrs. Watkins's best biscuits, and froze in openmouthed astonishment.

"My goodness," I whispered into Angeline's ear. "It's almost like . . . magic!"

Angeline found me in my attic an hour later. I'd been ordered up there by Stepmama the very moment she'd regained her breath, so I'd missed the rest of the entertainment. I would wager anything that Elissa hadn't been dismissed like a child. At least I still had Mama's diaries with me. I read more of them on my bed while I ate one of the apples I'd packed in my bag for last night's journey.

Spells for love . . . spells for whispering secrets across

a great distance—not much use, since I hadn't managed to run farther away from home than our own boring front garden. What I could have used was a spell for eavesdropping on secrets from far away so that I could hear the conversations downstairs.

When the trapdoor swung open, I wasn't surprised to see Angeline's glossy, dark head rise from the opening.

I closed the book and set it on my lap. "Well?" I said. "Did you say yes? That was the whole point of your spell, wasn't it?"

Angeline glared at me. "That was the single most embarrassing moment of my entire life," she said. "What a relief it is to know that you, at least, found it amusing." She clambered up onto the wooden floor and swung the trapdoor shut. "Give me one of those apples," she said as she crossed to the bed. "I need something to restore myself."

I passed her an apple and a hunk of cheese. "At least you've been kissed now," I said. "Even Elissa can't say that much."

"You think not?" Angeline arched her eyebrows at me and bit into her apple as she sank onto the bed.

"Really?" I stared at her, lowering my apple. "No. She wouldn't! Who was it? When? On the hand or on the mouth?"

"Wouldn't you like to know." Angeline smirked. "I'll tell you when you're old enough."

"Hmm," I said. "I wonder how old Stepmama would

have to be before she was ready to find out how Mr. Carlyle really found us."

Angeline put down her apple and narrowed her eyes. "That is not going to happen."

"No?" I narrowed my eyes back at her and tried to arch just one eyebrow. It didn't work. So I just had to make my voice as cool as hers had been. "Wouldn't you like to know that for certain?"

"Is this blackmail?" Angeline sighed. "Come now, Kat. We both know you aren't going to tell Stepmama anything. She'd tell Papa, and then . . ."

We both winced at the same time. It was too terrible to even contemplate. Stepmama would fill the house with her outrage and horror at the discovery—and her vindication. It was exactly what she'd been waiting to see ever since she'd first stepped into the house five years ago and seen the three of us standing in front of Mama's miniature portrait, still on shocking public display.

And the way Papa's face would sag in defeat as he listened to her . . . I couldn't bear the thought of it.

"Of course I won't tell her," I said. "I'm not a fool."

"No? You do act like one sometimes."

"Cow."

"Ninny."

"I don't have to tell Stepmama," I said. "I know someone else who doesn't know the truth. Elissa."

Angeline's dark eyes flashed. "You wouldn't!"

"I would," I said. "I really would, and you know it. Just

think how shocked she would be. How many weeks she'd spend lecturing you if she found out."

"You little traitor!"

"I'm not the one who's a traitor," I said. "I'm not the one shutting you out. Ever since you entered Society last year, you and Elissa have both been treating me like a child."

Angeline sneered. "You are a child."

I grabbed hold of my temper before I could throw my apple core at her. If Stepmama heard us fighting, I'd never get my way. Instead I said, "I'm not too young to understand that you laid a spell on Frederick Carlyle to make him love you and walk all the way across the country against his will, just to find you."

She flushed. "It wasn't against his will."

"How do you know? He doesn't even have a real will of his own anymore, does he? All he wants now is you, and he never even met you until today."

"That isn't . . ." She scowled down at her half-eaten apple. "You make it sound as if it's a terrible thing."

"Well . . ." I thought about it. "It is, isn't it? I mean, it would be one thing if you only put yourself in his way and let him fall in love with you naturally, but to make him fall in love . . . well, that's like cheating at cards, isn't it? It's dishonorable. Even Charles wouldn't do that."

"It might help if Charles did cheat," Angeline said. "Then he might not lose so often." But I could tell by the look on her face that I'd won. "I didn't mean it to happen that way," she said. "I cast a spell to bring my true love to me. I thought he'd arrive riding a great black stallion, or driving a fine carriage through the village, and he would see me quite by accident and fall in love. I didn't expect him to be already so"—she gestured helplessly with her apple—"so stupidly besotted. And I certainly didn't expect him to be one of Papa's students, for heaven's sake!"

"Well, you can't get rid of him now," I said. "He's already brought his first quarter's payment, and Stepmama knows it too."

"Oh, Lord. She'll never let him go!"

Suddenly we were laughing together, for the first time in ages—the first time since she'd started going to balls with Elissa and gossiping in secret, when everything had changed between us. Angeline reached across the bed and grasped my hand. "Kat, you little wretch. What on earth am I going to do about him?"

"You could always marry him," I said doubtfully. "If the spell was meant to summon your true love . . ."

"There was some mistake," said Angeline. "There had to be. I'm not even surprised—it was the first spell I ever made up by myself, so it's no wonder it brought me the wrong man. This one isn't even old enough to get married."

"He's older than you are."

"He can't be more than twenty! His family would have a fit. They'd say I'd bewitched him."

"You did."

"Not intentionally. Why would I? He's completely witless! All you have to do is talk to him for two seconds to realize that."

I said, "Maybe once you take away the spell . . ."

"I don't know how to take it away!"

"Oh," I said. I bit my lip, but I couldn't keep the laughter from leaking out. "Can you imagine what mealtimes will be like? Stepmama can't stop both of you eating together. He'll propose to you three times a day!"

"Papa probably won't even notice," Angeline said. "Anyway, it will wear off eventually. It has to. And in the meantime . . ." She sighed. "In the meantime, Papa can earn a bit more money than usual, and Mr. Carlyle will have a very good tutor."

"But what are you going to do?" I asked. "If you won't marry Mr. Carlyle—"

"I wouldn't marry a fool like Frederick Carlyle even if he had ten thousand pounds a year," Angeline said. "It's completely out of the question."

"Well, then, what will you do instead?"

"I'm certainly not going to sit here waiting for Stepmama to fix on an eligible suitor for me, I can tell you that much." Angeline snorted. "Elissa may sigh all she likes about family loyalty, but I won't let it take me that far."

"Elissa." Finally we'd come to what I'd meant to ask all along. "What wouldn't you two tell me last night? What's wrong with Sir Neville?"

Angeline sat back. I could see her face shuttering

against me—the "secrets" look I'd learned to hate. "Would you expect anything to be right about a man picked out by Stepmama?"

"You know more than that," I said. "You're just not telling me."

"Well, there's the fact he's twenty years older than her, for a start."

"You said Frederick Carlyle was too young."

"There's a difference between a handsome man of five-and-twenty—or even thirty—and one who's old enough to be your father," Angeline said tartly.

"So that's all it is? Sir Neville is too old for her? That's what I tried to say last night, but you both—"

"That's not bad enough to stop the marriage," Angeline said.

I studied her face. Her expression was as bland as the watered wine Stepmama gave me at dinner . . . but I knew her too well to be fooled. I picked up Mama's magic books.

"It won't wash," I said. "If you don't think I'm old enough to understand, that's your decision, but if you don't tell me the truth, you'll have to listen to Elissa being horrified by your behavior for the next three weeks at least." I raised my voice to imitate Elissa's soft, lilting tones. "'I just don't *understand*, Angeline. How could such a thing ever *occur* to you? How could you possibly *dream* of such a wickedly improper, immoral—'"

"Enough!" Angeline threw her apple onto the bed. "Fine. I'll tell you exactly what I don't like about Sir Neville. But if

I tell you, you can't let anyone else find out that you know, and you absolutely *may not* think up some mad scheme to interfere. Elissa has made her decision, she is determined to follow Stepmama's orders, and there is nothing *you* can possibly do to stop her."

"Fine," I said. "But you needn't tell me that Elissa's as stubborn as a mule. She's my sister too."

"I know. That's exactly what worries me." Angeline took a deep breath. "Very well," she said. "Sir Neville Collingwood was married once before, as you know. And . . ." She closed her eyes, frowning in concentration as if she was trying to think of exactly the right words.

"And?" I said. "What happened to his wife?"

Angeline opened her eyes and looked straight at me. "He murdered her."

Four

"He what?" I stared at her across the bed. The apple suddenly felt very cold and clammy in my hand.

"You heard me." Angeline set her jaw. "Elissa won't admit it, and Stepmama says it's all pure, unfounded gossip and speculation that young ladies should be ashamed to repeat, but it's the truth. Mrs. Watkins's niece works in the village where it happened, and she told me all about it two months ago."

She leaned closer to me, lowering her voice to a whisper. "Sir Neville Collingwood was so jealous of his first wife that he locked her up as a prisoner in a tower room, and she died of grief. Now that he's looking for another victim, we're all supposed to hope and pray that his eye falls on Elissa, so Charles can be rescued from his own folly and the rest of us can escape social ruin." She pointed her finger at me like a weapon, her voice rising. "But I will be *damned* if I sit by and let her marry him!"

"What can we do?" I tossed my apple aside, half-eaten. I had lost my appetite. "Why didn't you say any of this last night? Why did you chime along with Elissa when she said what a wonderful thing her marriage would be for all of us? How could you—"

"What good would it have done?" Angeline said. "You know Elissa. I tried everything I could three days ago, when I first found out. I told her we don't need the money that badly. Good God, let Charles go to debtors' prison for a month or two and actually feel the results of his idiocy! Let the whole family be ruined in Society and none of us ever make eligible marriages. Let us be whispered about and pointed at in the streets, if it comes to that! I'd rather we all become outcasts from good Society than sell her into slavery."

I winced. "You didn't say all that to Elissa."

"I did."

"Whispering in the streets? Social outcasts?"

"I was angry!" Angeline scowled. "But of course it didn't work."

"Well, of course not," I said. "Elissa would die of humiliation if even one person pointed at her in a public street. I think she'd *rather* die than have that happen."

"Well, I wouldn't. But of course she got completely up-in-the-air about it all and said if I had any hint of propriety I would never say such wicked things or put my faith in wild rumors that sound like dreadful gothic novels."

"That is unfair," I said. "Elissa's the one who reads gothic novels."

"She adores them," Angeline said. "And I'm starting to think she has a fancy to become a gothic heroine. You should have seen how noble she looked as she was saying it. I'm sure she was already picturing herself in her shroud, looking beautiful and being wept over by all the peasantry."

"We can't let it happen," I said.

"*I* won't," said Angeline. "*You* need to stay well out of it. I mean it, Kat. I only found my way back into Elissa's good graces by finally pretending to agree with her and repent my bad behavior."

"But if Mrs. Watkins told her—"

"I told Elissa exactly what Mrs. Watkins had said, and Elissa just told me that that was what came of Gossiping with the Lower Orders."

"What a prig! As if she didn't gossip with Mrs. Watkins all the time!"

"Just try telling her that," Angeline said. "Or, rather—don't. Truly. Don't tell her anything, don't argue about her decision, and especially *do not* run away or come up with any other nightmarishly bad schemes for her rescue. I have everything in hand, and the last thing I need is for you to interfere."

"What are you going to do?"

Angeline scooped up the magic books. "I'm going to find myself a wealthy fiancé," she said, "and well before Sir Neville works up the breath to propose."

I frowned at her. "Mr. Carlyle—"

"A wealthy fiancé with a brain and a sense of humor, who happens to be old enough to be married," Angeline said firmly as she stood. "We won't leave for Grantham Abbey for at least another week and a half. That's plenty of time to get started. And once we're there, it should be at least another month before Sir Neville proposes, no matter how much Stepmama flaunts Elissa before him. With Mama's magic to help, I shouldn't have any difficulties. Once I'm betrothed to a man just as wealthy as Sir Neville, there won't be any reason for Elissa to accept his offer, no matter how much of a martyr she longs to be."

I eyed her warily. "Maybe we can take Mr. Carlyle along with us, just in case."

Over the next week, I grew less and less convinced that Angeline did have everything in hand. It was bad enough that Frederick Carlyle slid out of Papa's study at every opportunity to follow her around the house and gardens. No matter how rude she was to him, he still made moon-eyes at her to an extent that Stepmama said was positively shocking. Even having to share a bedroom with Charles hadn't dimmed Mr. Carlyle's ardor for Angeline, which was ample proof in itself that a magic spell must be at work.

But none of Angeline's other spells were working. Oh, she didn't say so, but I knew that look on her face. The way she snarled at me the fifth time I asked was every bit as good as an outright confession. It was all very well for Angeline to say she could manage everything herself. Angeline always knew best, according to Angeline. But Frederick Carlyle wasn't the first evidence of one of Angeline's mistakes . . . and the storm-cloud look on her face as she bent over the new gown she was sewing for our trip was all I needed to know exactly how her great plans were proceeding.

Three days before we were due to leave for Grantham Abbey, I decided I had waited long enough. Elissa might be the prissiest female in all of England, but she was still my oldest sister. She was the one who'd carried me out to the back garden to play near Mama's roses when I was only a baby. She was the one who'd made up a thousand excuses to Stepmama over the years to keep me out of trouble, no matter how sternly she'd lectured me afterward. If she was to be saved from Sir Neville, there was only one thing to do. It was time for me to take the situation in hand.

I waited until midnight and then crept out of bed. I hadn't heard any noises for the past hour and a half, but that didn't mean I was safe. Angeline slept like the dead, but Elissa could wake up at the sound of a pin falling outside her door. If Elissa found out what I intended to do, I would never hear the end of it. And if Stepmama heard me, or guessed what I was up to . . . well, I just wouldn't let that happen.

I balanced carefully on the balls of my feet for silence as I crossed the room.

I eased open the trapdoor that led down from the attic, using both hands. It was too dangerous to carry a lit candle; if I wasted one hand juggling it, I might do something foolish like letting the trapdoor slam shut and wake everybody up.

There was one thing I had to carry with me, though. I'd slipped Stepmama's hidden key out of her bedroom that evening after dinner while she was still downstairs drinking her final cup of tea. Now I gripped it between my teeth as I stepped down into total darkness.

My feet felt for the steps beneath me. I breathed as quietly as I could while I gently lowered the trapdoor, wincing at every creak.

When I reached the landing outside Angeline and Elissa's room, I had to take a moment to orient myself. I closed my lips to breathe through my nose, listening through the darkness for any telltale squeak or whisper. The key in my mouth tasted metallic and dangerous, like forbidden secrets taking root inside me.

I felt for the banister of the stairs.

Angeline had found a new hiding place for Mama's magic books. I'd searched her room through and through every day for the past two days and hadn't found a hint of them. For all I knew, they might be hidden by another of her spells.

But Mama's magic books weren't the only magical items in our house. And if Angeline could dare to break the most powerful rules in our family, then so could I.

I made my way down the stairs, through the drawing room, and into the sewing room, where we'd all sat for hours that afternoon working on tedious dressmaking for the upcoming house party. I'd hidden a candle, a tinderbox, a candlestick, and two paper spills in the window seat.

It took me three minutes of trying and a set of scraped knuckles before I finally managed to light the tinderbox and transfer the flame over to my candle. Its pale glow flickered across the chairs and our folded gowns-in-progress, casting shadows from the cabinets that lined the walls. I only cared about one of the cabinets: the one that none of us were ever allowed to open. The one that we were all meant to pretend didn't exist.

The key in my mouth seemed to swell, pressing out-ward, as I crossed the room.

I spat it into my hand and knelt down on the floor. The key slipped into the lock as easily as if it had never left.

I took a deep breath and turned the key. The cabinet doors swung open.

At first I couldn't make anything out from the jumbled piles that filled up every shelf. They'd been tossed inside without order or reason, and in the flickering candlelight, they all seemed to merge into unified shapes: Mama's past, just waiting for me to make sense of it.

Then I made out the shape of a small, rounded frame.

Mama's miniature portrait sat on the top shelf.

She looked like Angeline. I knew I didn't have time to linger—at any moment Stepmama might decide to come downstairs for a late-night cup of tea, or Elissa might wake and hear me—but I couldn't stop myself from picking up the miniature, just for a moment. Mama had Angeline's dark, curling brown hair and deep, dark eyes, but she had Elissa's sweet smile. She smiled up at me from the painting with pure delight. My vision blurred in the candlelight.

I despised weeping females. So I swallowed hard as I put the miniature back on the shelf.

Stepmama had thrown all of Mama's possessions in here five years ago, three months after marrying Papa and moving into our house. The teapot had refused to pour for her, the cups had spilled themselves before they met her lips, and when she'd touched Mama's harp, it had sung the name "Olivia" until she'd sliced out all its strings. I still remembered her voice raging at Papa through their bedroom door afterward while Elissa held me tight.

At seven years old, I'd watched Stepmama sweep through every room in our house, gathering up all the familiar pictures and cups and plates, while Angeline and Elissa held my hands and glared at her. She must have used up all her dowry in replacing everything she'd packed away. I still didn't know what had stopped her from destroying it all. Perhaps Papa had put his foot down and refused to let her.

Or, just as likely, perhaps the neighboring pigs had all begun to fly.

I sorted through the jumble as quickly as I could. The teacups rustled hopefully as my hands brushed past them. Did they recognize me as Mama's daughter? My fingers trembled at the thought.

I stopped and closed my eyes, gritting my teeth with frustration. I wasn't some missish, nitwit heroine from one of Elissa's gothic novels, ready to swoon at the slightest shock. There was no reason to ruin my midnight adventure by going all teary-eyed and sentimental. I'd never even met Mama. All my memories were of my sisters. I was here to save Elissa, not myself.

There had to be some magic in this cabinet that could help me. I just had to stop daydreaming and search harder.

I opened my eyes and dug deeper in the shelves of the cabinet. When the teacups bumped themselves along the shelf to rub against my hand, I set my jaw and pushed them aside.

What I needed was another magic spell. Surely Mama hadn't written them all down in just those two books? Or a magical object would work just as well, if I could find the right one. Maybe I would find a wand to compel the truth, so I could force Sir Neville to publicly admit what he had done to his first wife. Or an enchanted ring to force obedience. Or . . .

My hand passed over something smooth and round and tinglingly warm to the touch. An electric thrill shot through me. Every inch of my skin prickled with alertness. My fingers closed around the palm-sized metal circle. I could barely breathe. I had to know what it was.

How could anything metal in this cabinet be warm?

Maybe it was an amulet of power or protection. Maybe . . .

I sat back on my heels, holding the candle high, and opened my hand to see what lay inside.

It was a gold-encased, folded-up travel mirror.

I could have screamed with frustration—at myself. Of course it was only a mirror. What else could it have been? All of Mama's spells in her magic books had been about love and clothing and foolishness—the same girlish witlessness every female in the world was supposed to care about. Well, not me. I should have known better than to have even hoped that anything in this cabinet could save us.

In my head, I repeated every curse word I'd ever learned from Charles as I reached up to put the mirror back in the cabinet where it belonged.

My hand wouldn't let it go.

I tried to open my fingers and drop it back into the

jumble. They wouldn't open. It was as if someone had attached the mirror to them with thick paint.

Warmth tingled against my palm and spread. The golden mirror heated up, hotter and hotter, until it burned against my skin. I had to bite down hard on my lower lip to keep from crying out at the pain. Surely this hadn't happened to Stepmama when she'd first put it in here. If it had, she would have destroyed it no matter what Papa had said. So what had I done wrong?

I set the candle down on top of the cabinet, breathing hard with the pain. I used my left hand to pry open the fingers of my right hand. It felt like peeling off layers of my own skin. I was surprised not to see any blood when I finally managed it. But what I did see instead was even more frightening.

The mirror was glowing in the dark, casting golden light across my palm and fingers. The light came from inside the folded mirror. With the light, I heard voices, faint but unmistakable, just at the edge of my perception. Either the mirror itself was alive, or there were people somehow trapped inside it.

I stared at it, breathing hard.

The sensible thing would be to peel it off my hand, fling it back into the cabinet, and lock the door as fast as I could. Even Angeline would tell me that. Only a ninny would do anything else.

But if I put it back, I would never know what might have happened.

It was Mama's own mirror, after all. It couldn't be that dangerous.

I snapped open the clasp and flipped the case open to reveal the mirror inside.

Golden light exploded in my chest, and I lost consciousness.

Five

Unfamiliar voices battered against my aching head. As my mind cleared, I started to pick out words in the jumble of sound, and two distinct voices.

"She doesn't look like Olivia, I must say," said a woman.

There was a hesitant male cough that sounded like disagreement. "She came through Olivia's mirror. I should call that indisputable evidence."

The woman let out an irritated huff of air that blew directly against my prickling, uncomfortable skin. "What a very odd outfit she is wearing. Do you think she often wanders around in public in her nightgown? There always were some signs of instability in Olivia's family, you know. That might account for her ridiculous hairstyle as well."

There are some things that cannot be tolerated, even inside a magic mirror. I forced my eyes open with a scowl.

As my vision cleared, I saw two faces peering down at me—a lady and a gentleman, kneeling on either side of me—both illuminated by a deep, golden glow that didn't feel like candlelight. As they examined me, both of their faces pursed into exactly the same expression Stepmama always wore when she was inspecting a particularly inadequate sample of my embroidery.

I directed my scowl at the lady and spoke clearly, even though every word hurt my head.

"I was not intending to go out in public," I said, with all the hauteur Angeline herself could have summoned. "I am wearing my nightgown because I am in my own house, and so are you. This is my mother's magic mirror we're all inside, so you might care to show a little more respect."

"Well!" The lady drew back from me, scowling. She was very elegantly dressed, with a dark green gown every bit as low-cut as the pictures in the *Mirror of Fashion*, and bright jewels sparkling in her black hair. And she was every bit as good as Stepmama at looking down her nose at me.

I pushed myself up to my feet, setting my teeth so I couldn't let out any humiliating whimpers of pain. Everything inside me felt as if it had been scalded with fire. When my head finally stopped reeling, I turned pointedly away from the others to look around me. I was determined not to show any signs of surprise or awe, but it was more difficult than I'd expected.

I'd never in my life seen so huge a room, nor one so strange and empty. There were no candles to account for the bright light that flooded through the hall. The floor and walls were smooth and gold, like the outer casing of the mirror had been, and the rounded ceiling above us arched almost as high as the sky itself. I couldn't see any doors or windows, no matter how hard I looked.

"Welcome to the Golden Hall, my dear," the gentleman said. "As Olivia Amberson's daughter, you are most heartily—"

"Olivia Stephenson's daughter," I corrected him, and turned back to face them both. "She was only Olivia Amberson until she married Papa."

The lady let out a disdainful crack of laughter and turned away.

"Mm. Yes. Well, the less said about that, the better," said the gentleman. He drew a handkerchief from his pocket and began to polish his spectacles with quick, exact movements. The lenses glittered distractingly in the golden light. Meanwhile, he peered at me from pale, washed-out blue eyes. His thin brown hair was specked with gray, and he was beginning to go bald; I thought he must be even older than Papa. "What's done is done," he said, "and we cannot change the past now, even if we might wish to."

I lifted my chin. My head still hurt, but outrage helped me ignore the pain. "Why exactly would you wish to change that?" I asked. "Are you by any chance insulting my papa?"

"Humph." His eyes narrowed; I thought I saw the corners of his lips twitch, but it happened so quickly, I couldn't be sure. "No need to take offense, my dear—ah—what is your name?"

"Kat," I said, and then thought better of it. "Katherine Ann Stephenson," I said, as haughtily as I could.

"Her youngest daughter, then."

"Yes." I frowned at him, but he looked away, folding his pocket handkerchief.

"Am I to understand, Katherine, that you believe we are all inside your mother's, er, magic mirror at this very moment?"

"Yes," I said. "Of course we are. I heard your voices coming from the mirror. That's why I opened it—I could tell someone was trapped inside. I was going to help you escape."

The lady rolled her eyes in a very unladylike fashion, but the gentleman smiled.

"A kind instinct, my dear. But, fortunately for all of us, it is entirely unnecessary. Neither of us was trapped here any more than you are now."

I glanced around me at the vast, empty hall. If there was a way back to my family's sewing room, I couldn't see it.

The gentleman followed my gaze and said, "No, the way

57

out is not marked any more than the entryway was. But you may take comfort in the fact that anyone who could not find their way safely back out would never have found their way inside in the first place."

"I'm not afraid," I said. But I wasn't sure I was relieved by his words either. I hadn't found my way into the mirror; I'd been swept inside and knocked flat out of my wits as it happened. I decided it was safest not to admit that, though.

If there was one thing that growing up with two older sisters had taught me, it was that the best defense in any dangerous situation is a good, vigorous attack. So I narrowed my eyes at the gentleman and said, "If neither of you is trapped here after all, then what exactly are you doing in my mother's mirror?"

"Oh, for heaven's sake," said the lady. "Aloysius, will you please do something?"

"Why, there is only one thing we can do in these circumstances," the gentleman said. "I believe it is time for us to welcome a new member."

Her eyes flared wide in shock. "You must be jesting. After what her mother did?"

I blinked. *What?* But before I could ask any questions, the gentleman replied.

"Miss Katherine is not her mother. You know we always planned that when the time came for Olivia's child to take her place—"

"I do not recall ever joining into any such unlikely

plans," the lady said. "What I do remember is that Olivia Amberson's famous curiosity was exactly what started all her mischief in the first place. And thus far, her daughter seems to take after her exactly in that regard." She swept me with a scathing glance and then turned back to the gentleman, dismissing me. "Olivia was the worst thing that ever happened to our Order, even before she went quite mad. You can hardly—"

I gasped. "Mama was not mad!"

"No, of course she was not," the gentleman said. "Really, Lydia, such extreme language . . ."

"Not mad?" She arched her narrow eyebrows. "Whatever else could possibly have caused her to behave in such an outrageous manner? If her daughter is even half so mischievous and irresponsible—"

"Stop insulting my mother!" I shouted.

Her eyes flared open. "Good Lord, what vehemence! Whoever's attempted to teach you manners—"

"Ladies!" The gentleman's cough this time sounded like a crack of thunder. "Disputes about the past may wait until a more appropriate moment. In the meantime, only one third of our introductions have been made. Katherine—Miss Katherine Stephenson, that is—I hope you will allow me to present you to Lady Fotherington, who joined our Order in the same year your own mother did."

"Charmed," Lady Fotherington snarled.

I only glared at her. I did not curtsy. Elissa might claim

that manners always mattered, but having to listen to people be rude about Mama even inside her own magic mirror was beyond what could be borne.

"I," the gentleman said, "am Mr. Gregson. I was your mother's tutor."

"No, you weren't," I said. "Mama didn't have a tutor. Her magic books say—"

I stopped myself with a gulp as my mind caught up with me. Just because these people happened to be inside Mama's magic mirror didn't mean they were trustworthy. For all I knew, they might not have dared even to come in until she was safely gone. So I started again, backing up slightly so that I could keep an eye on both of them. "I mean—"

"Her magic books," Lady Fotherington repeated. Her lips curved into the most unpleasant smile I had ever seen. "Good heavens, Aloysius. Your would-be protégée is already following exactly in her mother's footsteps. Are you still so certain you wish to induct her into our Order?"

"You've found Olivia's books of spells?" Mr. Gregson frowned. "Miss Katherine, I must know. Have you actually been studying your mother's magic books?"

Studying them? Well . . . I'd read them, anyway. Or at least, I'd skimmed the first half of the first book, and Angeline had read the rest. So, "Of course I have," I said, and met his gaze square-on. "I am Mama's daughter. Why shouldn't I?"

"You will have to stop. Yes. Immediately." Mr. Gregson's wispy eyebrows drew together into a scowl of concentration. "That was very, very foolish of you. But if you truly repent your actions and promise never, ever to do so again—"

I could feel my cheeks heating up as they both studied me, Mr. Gregson with worry and Lady Fotherington with contempt. "I don't see why I should," I said. "You two are doing magic, aren't you? You couldn't even be here otherwise. So why shouldn't I?"

"We," said Lady Fotherington, "would rather die than carry out disgusting witch magic of the kind your mother practiced. And so would anyone of quality."

I stared at her. "What other kind of magic is there?"

"None, obviously, that you are fit to learn." She stalked pointedly away from both of us, her slim back vibrating with outrage.

"Lydia . . ." Mr. Gregson shook his head and sighed. "We should have found you earlier," he said to me. "I had hoped—that is to say, I had expected . . . no. It is too late for recriminations. But what you must understand immediately is this: Witchcraft is not the only kind of true magic. The second type, which has never been made public, is far more rare and remarkable." He adjusted his spectacles and fixed me with a look so intent it made me step back. "The power of a Guardian can be inherited by only one child in each generation of a family. Your mother was born a natural Guardian, one of the most powerful magic-workers in the nation—and you, my dear young lady, by coming here tonight, have proven yourself to be her heir."

My head was whirling. Heirs . . . magic Guardians . . . I fastened on what I knew he had gotten wrong. "But Mama was a witch! Everyone knows that."

"Her family, unfortunately, had both bloodlines running through it. She was a Guardian by birth and by talent, and she did great work for her country as a member of our Order—but yes, she did, tragically, also inherit a talent for witchcraft. It was that inheritance that ruined her in the end."

"She certainly made no secret of it, once her betrayal was finally exposed," Lady Fotherington said. She didn't bother to turn back to us as she spoke, but I could hear the scowl in her voice anyway. "Flaunting her spells until even the most obtuse of her neighbors must have noticed—for all of our protection, she should have been pacified for good, and you know it!"

"What do you mean, 'pacified'?" I said.

Mr. Gregson waved away the question impatiently. "Olivia was no menace to any of us. No matter what mistaken choices she may have made, she was still a Guardian and our own former colleague, even after she was exiled from our Order."

Colleague. That was what Mama had meant, in her diary, when she'd spoken of keeping her witchcraft a secret from her colleagues. But it hadn't worked. And Lady

Fotherington had wanted her "pacified" . . . for exactly the same witchcraft that she'd passed on to Angeline.

My hands curled into fists at my side.

"All of that is ancient history," said Mr. Gregson. "It can do nothing for us at this point but rake up painful memories. The only point of interest now is that Miss Katherine cannot be blamed for breaking rules she did not even know existed. As she was not yet a member of our Order when she committed her acts of witchcraft, she cannot be banished from the Order for doing so. I am sure she will never be so foolish as to do so again, now that she knows better."

"Mm," I said. My nails bit into the palms of my hands.

"In the meantime, though, she may have inadvertently put herself into some danger, and I must look into . . . hmm . . . Yes." His voice strengthened with decision. "Katherine, you will have to bring Olivia's books to us for safekeeping. There is no other choice."

"No other choice but to give you my mother's magic books," I repeated. Elissa would have been proud of me. I didn't hit anybody, scream, or run, and I even managed to keep my voice as cool as if we were discussing the weather at one of Stepmama's endless tea parties. "And why is that, exactly?"

"If someone sensed your workings, if they felt that particular combination—no, there isn't enough time to explain the whole matter now," Mr. Gregson said. "I must hurry to our library to begin my research. If I stay there until dawn . . ." His words dropped to a worried mutter underneath his breath as he turned away. "Yes, yes, we may still be able to avoid . . ."

He might just have walked away and left me then, except that Lady Fotherington spoke. "You truly have forgotten Olivia, haven't you, Aloysius?" She swung around to face us. "Do you really imagine that this . . ." Her gaze raked up and down my nightgown and short hair, and I had to resist the impulse to smooth down the tufts I knew were sticking up. Her lips twisted. "This young *lady* is going to prove so biddable as to fetch you her mother's most intimate belongings simply on your say-so?"

Mr. Gregson turned back, blinking. "No? I have told you, Katherine, I was Olivia's tutor. I shall be your tutor as well, you know, now that you have found us."

"Shall you, indeed?" I said, as icily as Lady Fotherington herself might have done.

But he looked too distracted to notice. "Yes, yes. I train all our new members, you know. I am the historian of our Order. But I don't have time to explain matters fully to you tonight. I have an appointment early in the morning, and there is much to consider beforehand. I must go to our library now, before I lose any more of the night hours. Yes." He nodded. "You may go home now, my dear. Come back tomorrow night with the books, and we shall have our first proper lesson. I'll explain it all then, I assure you."

If he had known Angeline, he would have known how

dangerous it was to trust an innocent smile. I smiled as innocently as I could. "Very well," I said.

"Oh, Aloysius, you fool," said Lady Fotherington. She shook her head. The smile that spread across her own face was insufferably smug. "If we don't have time for explanations, you'll need far more security than her word."

"What do you mean?" Mr. Gregson asked. For the first time since I'd mentioned Mama's magic books, he seemed to emerge from his abstraction. Worse, he looked decidedly uneasy. "What are you intending, Lydia?"

"Security," said Lady Fotherington, and started toward me.

I jumped back. "Stay away from me!"

"I think not." Lady Fotherington gazed at me with green, catlike eyes. "I think if we let you go now we may never see you again. I believe you might even be intending to hide your mother's magic books from us, for your own nefarious purposes."

"You're wrong," I said. I shot a glance around me at the vast, empty hall. No doors. No signs of any escape route, and I hadn't had the wits to memorize a single one of Mama's spells. Mr. Gregson was only watching us, his eyes unreadable. "I wouldn't do that," I told them both. "Believe me!"

"Believe you?" Lady Fotherington tilted her head to one side, considering me as she paced across the golden floor, her silk skirts swishing around her legs. Her smile deepened. "You forget, my dear. I am prepared for you. After all, I knew your mother—which is more than you yourself can claim. And I can tell you, she was quite a devilish little trickster."

That did it. I lunged straight for her smug, smiling face.

I caught her off guard. She threw up her hands, but I barreled straight into her and knocked her backward. We fell together onto the smooth golden floor. I landed on top.

"I told you," I panted. "Do not insult my mother!"

I slammed my fist into her nose just as Charles had taught me in his boxing lessons. It made a horrible crunching noise, and it hurt my hand.

She screamed. Her hands flew up to her face. Mr. Gregson was making distressed noises as he hovered to one side.

I kept my fist up and ready, even though it hurt like the devil.

"Let me go," I said to both of them. "Now!"

"My dear girl—," Mr. Gregson began.

Lady Fotherington's eyes narrowed. She stopped screaming. She squeezed her eyes tightly shut in concentration.

Pressure built in the air around me until it felt thick and heavy, prickling at my skin. It tingled against my wrists, like a warm, thick cloud of smoke. Then it wrapped around my hands, creeping upward. I tried to bat it away. It came higher.

"Lydia . . . ," Mr. Gregson said.

She shook her head. Blood was flowing down from her

nose to her lips, but she was smiling, her eyes still tightly shut. I hadn't seen her recite any spell, but I suddenly understood what was happening.

Magic was one thing I couldn't fight with my fists.

I lurched off her and onto my feet. My hands felt numb, and the numbness was traveling higher, up my arms.

I had to get away. But there weren't any doors.

What had Mr. Gregson told me before? *Anyone who could not find their way safely back out would never have found their way inside in the first place.*

I didn't trust a word that either of them had spoken, but I had no choice. I had to try.

Even if the doors back to the outside world weren't visible, they had to exist. And if I couldn't see them with my eyes, I'd have to find them some other way.

I shut my eyes and ran straight across the Golden Hall. The pressure followed me, growing stronger all the time, until it felt like I was trying to run through thick jelly. My upper arms tingled. The numbness was moving to my shoulders. What would happen to me when it reached my head?

I whispered as I ran, stupid, hopeless pleas that couldn't help me, but I couldn't seem to stop. "Please, Mama, please, Mama, please . . ."

My shoulders went numb. The tingling sensation crept up to my neck.

"Mama, please!"

All I wanted was my home, and my sisters, and my

mother's cabinet of forbidden memories, and my brother who'd taught me how to fight even if he was useless in every other way, and my sweet, helpless father, and even—

The tingling reached my chin.

I opened my eyes. I was barreling straight toward the golden wall, much, much closer than I'd realized. I was going to hit it if I didn't turn back. But if I turned back, Lady Fotherington would have me.

The tingling rose up my jaw. Chills raced across my scalp. My mind was slowing down, my thoughts scattering.

I closed my eyes and fixed the image of home in my mind with all my strength. I flung myself forward, bracing myself for the collision that would come if I was wrong—

And I fell, in a flash of golden light, tumbling hard onto the carpet of the sewing room, just in front of a pair of slippered feet.

Someone was waiting for me.

Six

After all I'd been through, it should have been a relief to see only Elissa waiting for me. But I had never seen my oldest sister so angry.

"How could you, Kat?" She kept her voice low, too quiet to wake anyone upstairs, but it vibrated with rage. "I never thought you could be so wickedly hurtful. *How could you?*"

Oh, Lord. It was the fit of prissiness I'd known would happen if Elissa ever found me or Angeline meddling with magic. I sighed and pulled myself up to my knees. The tingling had disappeared, but my head ached worse than ever, and my right hand hurt like blazes. As usual when he was being helpful, Charles had neglected to mention that there was a flaw to what he was teaching me: Hitting people *hurt*.

"I didn't do anything so terrible," I said. "So you needn't look at me like that. But I have to tell you—"

"Not so terrible?" she said. "It's not only that you must have stolen Stepmama's key, which is bad enough. It's not even that you were clearly playing with magic, which is far worse than anything I could ever have believed you would do."

I rolled my eyes. "Elissa—"

"What?" she said. "What are you going to say to try to fob me off this time? What mad scheme? What wild story to excuse yourself?" Her cheeks flushed as she pointed past my shoulder. "Is there anything that could possibly excuse *that*?"

I turned, following the direction of her pointing finger—and lost my breath.

A whirlwind had torn through Mama's cabinet, flinging everything in its wake. Her picture frames had broken. Her single strand of pearls had exploded across the floor. And her teacups had shattered. They lay in lifeless, unmoving shards across the carpet before the open cabinet. The same teacups that had tried to brush up against my hands for petting . . .

Something welled up in my throat so hard I almost choked.

"I didn't—this wasn't—"

"It wasn't you who did it?" Elissa asked. "Can you really

bring yourself to say such a deceitful thing when I've seen the evidence with my own eyes? Would you actually lie to me right now?"

I shook my head. I couldn't look away from the blue and white shards that were all that remained of Mama's teacups and teapot—the same teapot I'd heard about in Angeline's stories. It must have been my passage back and forth between here and the mirror world that had done it. I couldn't deny that to Elissa or myself, no matter how desperately I wanted to.

Instead I said, "I didn't mean to." My voice cracked as I spoke. "I didn't know it would happen!"

Elissa shook her head. For the first time I could remember, I couldn't see a single speck of love or forgiveness in my oldest sister's face. "You've been careless before," she said, "but never so cruelly."

Her voice swelled on the last word, her face tightened, and I finally realized she was trying not to cry.

I leaned forward hastily to start picking up the scattered pieces and hide my face. But Elissa said, *"No,"* and took them out of my hand.

"I'll take care of them," she said. "I don't want them hurt any further."

I shuffled back, still on my knees. "Please," I said. "It was an accident. What happened was—"

"Not now," Elissa said. She didn't even look at me as she spoke.

"But Elissa, I have to tell you—"

"Just go, Kat. Please. I can't even talk to you right now. I'm too ashamed."

Her hand curved around a shard of blue and white china as tenderly as if she were cradling a newborn baby. A sob broke from her throat. I saw her lips form a word she didn't speak out loud: *Mama.*

I jumped to my feet and fled the room. But when I crawled through the trapdoor into my attic, I realized I hadn't managed to escape after all.

Mama's golden mirror lay on my pillow, waiting for me.

When I went down to breakfast the next morning, I could see in Angeline's face that she knew what had happened. The cabinet was closed and locked again, and to an outside eye—to Stepmama and Papa and Charles and Mr. Carlyle—it must have looked as if nothing had happened.

But I knew better.

Elissa was as cool and reserved at the breakfast table as if I were one of Stepmama's most unfortunate guests, who had to be tolerated even if they couldn't be liked. Angeline was even worse. She didn't glare at me or narrow her eyes or whisper threats in my ear, the way she had a hundred times in the past, the way that I'd expected. She couldn't even bring herself to look at me.

Both my older sisters' faces were puffy from crying. For me, Mama's cabinet had been full of mysteries and secrets to be puzzled out, like an adventure. For them, it had been full of memories. And I had broken all of them.

I didn't weep, but as soon as breakfast ended, I lunged straight out of the house before Stepmama could stop me. I didn't come back until it was dark and well past dinner-time. It was almost a relief when Stepmama sentenced me to stay in my room for the last two days before our trip. At least that way I didn't have to see my sisters.

But there was one thing I couldn't escape, no matter how hard I tried.

When I ran into the fields, I found the golden mirror lying on the stone I chose to sit on. I took it home and buried it deep in one of the boxes in my attic, where I wouldn't have to look at it and be reminded of what I'd done. When I woke up the next morning, though, I found it lying on the pillow beside my head. And on the morn-ing of our trip to Grantham Abbey, I found it lying on top of my packed traveling case.

It had belonged to Mama. But now it seemed to think that it belonged to me.

I tried very hard not to think about how easy Mr. Gregson and Lady Fotherington had said it was for them to leave the mirror . . . and how much they already seemed to know about my family. Maybe it was good that we were leaving for Grantham Abbey. At least they wouldn't know to look for me there.

Since it wouldn't allow me to leave it behind, I slipped Mama's mirror into the beaded reticule Stepmama had made me for Christmas. I hung the silly, dainty bag over my arm before I left the attic. Angeline and Elissa might raise their eyebrows at the sight of me actually carrying such a ladylike item, but that had to be better than any reaction they might have to the sight of Mama's mirror appearing suddenly on my lap in the carriage as we traveled, or at my place setting on the Grantham Abbey dinner table.

I had been careful to pack my boys' clothing, though, just in case. If worse came to worst, I could always fall back on my first plan . . . especially if I needed to make a quick escape.

We set off an hour later in Squire Briggs's rickety old second-best traveling carriage, loaned to Stepmama for the trip. It had once been painted a horrible shade of dying olive, but the paint had mostly faded on the outside. The cushions inside felt as thin as writing paper. I scrunched myself into an uncomfortable far corner with my reticule on my lap and tried not to meet my sisters' eyes as they took their seats across from me. I couldn't help noticing how pale and unhappy Elissa looked. Angeline's face was set in her most mulish expression.

At least Frederick Carlyle was staying at home with Papa and Charles, so Angeline would have a month's respite from his proposals. I didn't think she'd appreciate it if I pointed that out right now, though.

Stepmama came last and sighed as she settled herself beside me. Dozens of bandboxes and valises were already tied precariously to the top of the carriage, but our housekeeper, Mrs. Watkins, had to push several more underneath our feet and on top of our laps before Stepmama finally declared us ready to leave.

Mrs. Watkins shoved the door closed on our mountain of parcels, and with a crack of the whip, Squire Briggs's coachman started the horses off. The carriage rattled and shook us all the way down the drive and onto the winding main road.

As I peered back through the narrow carriage window, I saw Frederick Carlyle staring after us from the branches of the oak tree, as heartbroken as a lost puppy. From a distance—from far enough away that you couldn't see the blankness in his eyes—he really did look quite handsome. My lips twitched.

As I turned back from the window, my gaze crossed Angeline's. She'd been looking back at Mr. Carlyle too. Her eyes sparkled; for a moment, I thought we were about to share a conspiratorial smile.

Then her expression smoothed back into disdain, and she looked pointedly away.

I scowled and scrunched myself tighter into my corner, letting my head bang against the hard wooden panels of the carriage as it rattled down the road. We were on our way to Grantham Abbey.

As the hours passed and we drove deeper and deeper into the Dales, the landscape grew harsher and bleaker around us. In our house, and in our comfortable little village, despite how hilly it was, you could almost forget that we lived in Yorkshire. But the Dales were different. Wild. Dangerous. As massive, craggy hills rose high before us and a rocky chasm opened up beside the road, I managed to forget Stepmama's never-ending voice rising and falling beside me and even my sisters' simmering disapproval. A hawk soared over our carriage, letting out a high, piercing cry of defiance, and I wanted to jump out of the window and fly with it. When the carriage finally took a steep descent into a wooded valley, I had to bite down on disappointment.

But we drove deeper and deeper into the rolling, wooded valley, and I realized that it was just as wild and untamed as the barren hills above it. The thick woods made a dark, whispering wall to our left, full of secrets. A roaring river swept past us on our right, powerful enough to carry us all away.

Stepmama said, "There must be dreadful flooding every year. They shouldn't build these roads so close to the water. Really, it only takes a little common sense. . . ."

I hunched my shoulder away from her and kept my gaze on the rushing, foam-scudded river just outside my window. I wondered if it would ever be safe to swim in it . . . or, if not, how dangerous it would really be.

Elissa gasped and pointed out the window. "Is that it?"

I tore my gaze away from the river to look where she was pointing. Gothic stone arches rose in the distance, high above the trees.

"Grantham Abbey," Stepmama said. I could hear the

smile in her voice. "My second cousin, on my mother's side, will be our hostess. Lady Graves. She was fortunate enough to catch the eye of Sir John Graves after only one season in Town, and her sisters . . ."

I tried to ignore the rest of her lecture on the many fine connections her family had made. But I twitched when I caught her saying to Elissa, ". . . because they knew what was due to their family, who had taken care of them all those years without reward."

"Happiness, you mean?" I said, and turned around. "Maybe what was really due to their family was for them to make happy matches to men they truly cared for, so that their family could be happy for them." I narrowed my eyes at Stepmama in an imitation of Angeline's classic, most threatening look. "And that's exactly what their family wanted from them. Not financial reward. Because their family actually loved them, unlike some people."

Elissa said, "Kat—"

"You, young lady, are very ignorant," said Stepmama. Color mantled her cheeks as she glared at me. "If you think any young ladies in your situation can afford to wait for some fanciful notion of romantic love, you are blind to the ways of the world. And you should know better than to talk to your elders about things you know nothing about, particularly in such an impertinent manner."

"Why wouldn't I know what I was talking about?" I said. "I'm part of Elissa's family, aren't I?" *Unlike you,* I could have added, but I was old enough to know how much trouble that would have caused. "So I know exactly what Elissa's family really wants for her."

"It's all right, Kat," Elissa said quickly. "You don't need to—"

Stepmama opened her mouth to blast me.

Angeline drawled her words as lazily as if they meant nothing to her. "There's no use trying to quash Kat, ma'am. You know she's not old enough yet to understand that girls are only worth what they can bring their parents in their sale, like a milch cow or some other disposable possession."

My eyes flashed to Angeline's face.

Stepmama said, "That is quite enough from both of you! All of you!" She was breathing quickly. "You three girls may think yourselves very clever and ill-used, I daresay, but I don't see any of you paying your own room and board in my house, or finding yourselves any funds to support yourselves in the future."

"Indeed not," said Angeline. "But I had thought it was Papa's house, actually. And I don't see you paying room and board either."

"Everyone stop it!" Elissa shouted.

It was so unexpected, everyone fell silent and stared at her. Her pale cheeks were flushed, and her eyes shone bright with unshed tears.

"I know what I must do," she said more quietly. "And I will do it. For all my family's sake. But I can't bear all this lecturing and arguing and—" She broke off, putting one hand to her mouth. "I can't," she repeated. "Please. Just let us not talk about it!"

"But you don't have to do it!" I said.

"Katherine—," Stepmama began dangerously.

"*No*," Elissa said. "Just stop!"

And, to my amazement, Stepmama did.

Angeline took Elissa's hand and squeezed it, and Elissa rested her head on Angeline's shoulder. I stared at them both from my corner of the carriage and felt hot prickling behind my eyes.

"Oh, Lord," Angeline said. She sighed and reached across the piled boxes to take my hand, too.

I squeezed her warm, strong hand. Elissa leaned over to close her free hand around both of ours. The prickling sensation behind my eyes grew even stronger. I had to twist my back to lean across the bandboxes, but I didn't care. I could have sat that way forever.

"Humph," said Stepmama, and turned away to look out her window.

We rode the rest of the way in silence. But as we drew closer and closer to Grantham Abbey, down the narrow, winding road between the river and the dark wall of trees, Elissa's hand gripped tighter and tighter around mine and Angeline's.

We turned the last curve in the road and saw it all spread out before us along the opposite riverbank: Grantham Abbey. Great stone arches curved upward, filled with empty blue sky where stained-glass windows should have been. Tall stone walls formed rooms that were larger than Papa's whole church, but without any roofs left to shield them from the wind and rain. Even the outlying piles of medieval stone, where other walls had fallen, looked as massive as if a giant had been at work.

As I gazed, openmouthed, at the ruined abbey, my reticule began to itch and burn with heat against my lap.

I pulled my hand back from my sisters' grasp and wrapped both hands around the reticule. At any moment the little beaded bag might start to glow with dangerous golden light. Mama's magic mirror was excited by where we were. And my mouth was suddenly dry with sickly, horrible fear. I'd learned my lesson. I wasn't ever going back into that mirror world again. But I wasn't sure that the mirror itself would accept my decision.

Luckily, my sisters weren't looking at me.

"Look," Angeline said, as the carriage rattled onto the stone bridge that led across the river. "There's the house itself . . . if you can call it a house." She snorted. "The first owners certainly must have thought well of themselves."

"What on earth are you chattering about now?" Stepmama's frown eased into a smile of satisfaction as she peered through the window at the house beyond the abbey. "I would call that a very fine house indeed."

If Grantham Abbey could have fit two hundred monks within its walls, the manor house attached to it could have held a hundred more of the monks' closest friends. The peaked windows of the house had been built to mirror the arches of the abbey, and it sprawled nearly as far along the sides of the hill as the abbey ruins below it.

It was almost enough to take my mind off the dangerously hot reticule in my hands. "What do you think they do with all that space?"

Angeline arched one eyebrow and smirked. "Roll around in it and gloat, perhaps?"

"They most certainly do not," Stepmama said sharply. "My cousin Rosemary has done very well for herself indeed, and you girls would do well to take note of it. Her success certainly did not arise from impertinent humor."

"What a pity," Angeline murmured. "She could use a sense of humor, to live in a gothic monstrosity like that."

Elissa still hadn't uttered a word. Her face was as white as snow.

I frowned at her and freed one hand to reach out to her. She gasped at my touch.

"Why, Kat! You're burning hot. What's wrong with you?"

"Nothing!" I said. I pulled my hand back, too late. Angeline had already swiveled around to frown at me.

"She doesn't look feverish," said Angeline. "She is a little flushed, though."

"I'm fine," I said. I wrapped my hand back around my reticule, pushing it deeper into my lap, away from view. "Leave me alone."

"If you're not feeling well . . . ," Elissa began.

Angeline's frown deepened. "Maybe that's not it after

all," she said. "I know that look in your eyes, Kat. What have you got in your lap?"

"Nothing," I said. "Just a reticule, like yours."

"Hmm." Angeline leaned across the pile of bandboxes that separated us. "Let's see that—"

"Enough!" Stepmama said. "We've arrived." The carriage pulled to a stop in the long, circular drive in front of the house, where about a dozen footmen waited for us. "Angeline, Elissa . . . Kat . . ." She directed her most forbidding glare at me. "I trust you all to behave like proper young ladies. Or—!"

She left her threat unfinished as the carriage door sprang open. The footman's eyes widened as he saw how much baggage lay piled at our feet, but he bowed low anyway and offered his hand to Stepmama as soon as he'd cleared the way of bandboxes. She accepted his hand with a steely smile and stepped down onto the stone drive.

Beyond her, two figures stepped into the open doorway of the manor house. One of them was a tall, brown-haired woman I'd never seen before in my life.

The other was Mr. Gregson.

Seven

Mr. Gregson's gaze met mine. I shoved myself back against the carriage panels. If it hadn't been too late to hide, I would have thrown myself underneath the piles of bandboxes at my feet.

Then I caught myself.

Mr. Gregson and Lady Fotherington had insulted my mother and my parents' marriage. They had tried to attack me with magic—to make me do whatever they told me, like a magical slave. But I had escaped, despite their best efforts, and I was almost certain I'd broken Lady Fotherington's nose.

They were the ones who should be afraid of me.

I lifted my chin and glared straight at Mr. Gregson as I took the footman's hand and stepped out of the carriage as daintily as any duchess.

Mr. Gregson's lips curved into a smile.

"My dearest Margaret," Lady Graves cried. She swept across the drive to take Stepmama's hands. "It's been a positive age since I saw you last. How wonderful you look! Quite as young as ever. Sir John and I are so very pleased you could join our little house party."

She and Stepmama exchanged cooing cheek-kisses, and then she drew back to include the rest of us in her smile. It was meant to appear gracious, I supposed. I couldn't focus on it, though, not with Mr. Gregson hovering in the background and smiling so much more ominously.

"And these must be your charming stepdaughters," said Lady Graves. "What lovely young ladies they all are."

"Mm," Stepmama said, and coughed into her glove. "Ah, yes. Indeed they are. Rosemary, may I present my husband's daughters to you? Miss Stephenson"—she nodded to Elissa, who smiled wanly—"Miss Angeline, and . . ." She gave me an admonitory glare. "Miss Katherine."

Out of the corner of my eye, I saw Mr. Gregson's lips tighten as if he were holding back a laugh. Stepmama looked as if she'd just bitten into a sour apple. But she needn't have worried this time. I curtsied as politely as the others and smiled up at Lady Graves as sweetly as if I were the most angelic young lady in existence.

Stepmama's eyes narrowed. "Of course, Katherine is too young to participate in the house party, but I hadn't the heart to leave her behind." *Hadn't trusted Papa to keep me in order*, she meant. But I didn't correct her as she continued, "Perhaps she can stay in the nursery quarter with your own children, Rosemary, and—"

"Oh, no, my girls are in Scotland with my sister for the month, and the boys are off on a shooting party with their friends from Eton. You know how boys are. No, of course Miss Katherine mustn't be locked away while everyone else enjoys themselves. I'm sure she'll be no trouble, will you, child?"

"No, ma'am," I said in my meekest voice.

She smiled and touched my hair lightly. "What a very daring haircut you've been given. Rather like one of the ladies I met in London this past season, Lady Ca—but no, perhaps I'd better save that particular story for your stepmama and older ears than yours." She withdrew her hand, sliding a mischievous glance at Stepmama. "I must say, though, that style does suit you, for all its radicalism. Perhaps you'll be a Society fashion-setter one day too. You may practice tonight in my drawing room."

"Kat will do very well on her own," Stepmama said. "She—"

"Nonsense." Lady Graves stepped back, her smile quite as steely as any of Stepmama's own. "It is very good of you to try to look after me, Margaret, but I have made my decision, and I really will not be dissuaded. I'm certain Miss Katherine will make a charming addition to our party. It is always helpful for young girls to have some experience in the public eye before they are thrown willy-nilly into their London debut, you know. Now." She gestured toward the house. "Won't you all come in and refresh yourselves? Your rooms are prepared and waiting for you."

"Thank you, Rosemary," Stepmama murmured, in a tone of pure vinegar. "You are too kind."

It was the first time I'd ever seen Stepmama overruled by anybody. I would have enjoyed it more if I hadn't been so preoccupied with hiding my reticule from Mr. Gregson's keen gaze.

He bowed politely as we started toward the door, and coughed. This time it was a polite, harmless cough, the kind you might cough if someone had stepped on your toe by accident and you wanted to alert them without seeming rude. It stopped Stepmama in her tracks, and she looked to Lady Graves with a questioning arch of her eyebrows.

"Ah, yes. I'd nearly forgotten to make the introductions," said Lady Graves. "Margaret, this is my husband's cousin Mr. Aloysius Gregson, come all the way from London to consult Sir John's family library. Mr. Gregson is a highly regarded scholar, you know, as well as being quite the favorite among London's hostesses."

Mr. Gregson bowed, smiling, as I blinked at the idea.

"If you are a scholar, Mr. Gregson, I am sure you and my husband would have much to discuss," Stepmama said graciously. "Mr. Stephenson has quite the library of his own at our dear vicarage. Perhaps you may come and visit us one day."

"What a delightful idea," Mr. Gregson said. "I should be

happy to take up your charming invitation. Perhaps after Lady Graves's house party?"

I nearly gagged with horror. It hardly even helped to see Stepmama's gracious smile slip—clearly, she hadn't meant the invitation to be taken seriously. Have a fashionable London gentleman to stay in our rickety old house? Sleeping in Papa's study, perhaps, since Charles and Mr. Carlyle were already sharing a bedroom? It must have been almost as frightening a thought for her as it was for me, for entirely different reasons.

Still, she rallied, regaining her smile and saying, "We must consult our calendars, certainly. But for the moment . . ."

"Of course," said Mr. Gregson. "You will wish to refresh yourselves. Ladies." He bowed again. When he straightened, his pale blue eyes were fixed straight on me. "I shall look forward to speaking to you later."

Thank goodness, the manor house at Grantham Abbey was so huge that Elissa, Angeline, and I had all been given separate bedrooms, an unheard-of luxury. Before I could finally be alone, though, Stepmama had to read me Volume Three Hundred of her never-ending lecture on propriety and the behavior expected of young girls at respectable gatherings. The moment she finally swept off to her own room, I slammed the door behind her and threw the reticule onto my bed. I was surprised not to see the striped green and yellow bedcovers smoke and char at the contact.

I collapsed onto the bed next to the reticule and stared down at it. "Well, what is it, then? What's set you off this time? Was it Mr. Gregson, or . . . ?"

The reticule didn't answer me. I undid the beaded fastening and upended it over the bed. The golden mirror dropped out, small and—almost—harmless-looking, except for the warm glow that emanated from it.

I peered at it but didn't lift a finger to touch it; this time I knew better. It was the worst possible moment to be sucked back into the mirror world, just when Mr. Gregson was hovering nearby, waiting to capture me again.

Or . . . *was* it the worst possible time? After all, as a houseguest already in residence at Grantham Abbey, Mr. Gregson was probably in the company of all the other gentlemen of the house party right now, doing . . . well, whatever gentlemen did when they were alone together. All I could imagine was gambling, drinking, and boxing, but that was only because Charles was the only gentleman I knew apart from Papa, who didn't count. I was certain other gentlemen must have more varied forms of entertainment than Charles had, and certainly more than poor Papa, who would sit wrapped up in a book all day long if he was allowed.

The point was, Mr. Gregson was fully occupied, and as it was the middle of the afternoon, fashionable Lady Fotherington would probably be busy driving around one of London's parks or paying calls on her circle of terrorized friends.

Maybe now wasn't the worst possible time for an exploration, after all. Maybe it was the best. I wasn't expected anywhere until dinnertime, and Stepmama had absolutely ordered me not to step outside my room. The mirror was in the center of my room, wasn't it? So it wasn't even off-limits.

I reached for the mirror's clasp—

And the door to my room swung open.

I threw myself across the bed. Mama's mirror burned into my stomach as I stared at the open doorway, where Angeline stood staring back at me.

"What on earth are you doing?" she said.

"Nothing," I said. "Just resting. I was tired."

"Of course you were." She closed the door and advanced toward me. "That would explain why you leaped like a cat when I walked in on you. And why you're still wearing your shoes." She crossed her arms and smiled down at me. "Come off it, Kat. What are you really trying to hide?"

"Nothing," I said. I felt monumentally foolish, lying on my belly like a beached fish as I stared up at her, but I couldn't move or else she'd see the glowing mirror. So I tried to sound casual and perfectly at my ease as I spoke. "What are you doing here, anyway? Shouldn't you be assembling the perfect outfit for this evening? Or practicing your spells while Elissa can't see you?"

"Very good, Kat. But you can't distract me, and you know that perfectly well." Angeline sat down on the corner of the bed and fixed me with a glittering gaze. "So why don't you give up now and tell me exactly what you were up to in the carriage that made your hand feel so hot?"

"It was stuffy in there," I said. "Of course I was hot."

"Mm," Angeline said. "Perhaps that was it, after all. Or perhaps . . ."

She struck so quickly I couldn't prepare for it, slamming herself with all her weight against my shoulder.

"Get off!" I struggled and scratched and pulled her hair, but she was stronger and heavier than I was. She pushed me all the way off my stomach and onto my back.

". . . more likely," Angeline finished, panting, "it was this!"

She snatched up the empty reticule.

My breath came in harsh gasps. My shoulder felt bruised. But the mirror was safe, trapped inside the folds of my gown. I pushed myself up carefully, making sure to cover the mirror with protective muslin all the way.

Angeline turned the reticule upside down over her hand and shook it, hard. Nothing came out. She frowned down at her empty palm. Then she turned her narrowed gaze on me.

"Don't look to me for answers," I said. "You're the one coming up with wild ideas this time. Maybe it's because you already miss Mr. Carlyle so much. Maybe the agony of loss is making your mind disordered . . . if it wasn't already, that is."

"Very amusing." Angeline set the reticule back down on my green and yellow bedcovers. "So. You've already hidden it." Her gaze crossed the small bedroom consider-ingly. "It certainly doesn't smell like magic in here."

I blinked at her. "Smell? What does magic smell like?" I had a sudden image of Angeline sniffing the air like a hunting spaniel, and I had to stifle a snort of laughter. Luckily, she didn't notice.

"Flowery," she said. "Like lilacs." She gestured vaguely with her hands, still not looking at me. "There's a resi-due left in the air every time I cast a spell, and I don't smell it here right now. But still . . . that leaves us with one question." She turned back and narrowed her eyes at me. "What exactly are you up to?"

"Nothing," I said, and narrowed my eyes right back at her. "Why exactly are you so suspicious?"

"Hmm. Let me think. . . . Perhaps because I know you?" Angeline stood, smoothing down her dress. "I don't have time right now to pry the answers out of you. Elissa is expecting me."

"What a pity," I said. "Well, have a good time. Come back whenever you want to interrogate me again or come up with any more wild stories."

Angeline went very still. "Don't get cocky, Kat. You haven't forgotten any more than I have what happened three nights ago."

Mama's cabinet. Coldness crept inside my chest with the reminder. "And?" I said, with as much bravado as I could muster.

"I won't let you hurt Elissa any more than you have

already," Angeline said, and closed the door behind her.

I heard her footsteps retreat down the hallway, then another door open. Angeline's and Elissa's voices mingled for a moment in easy communion. Then the sound cut off with the snick of Elissa's bedroom door closing, shutting the two of them in cozily alone, together. As usual.

I snatched up the reticule and flung it against the door with all my strength. Beads showered off it in all directions.

"Devil take her," I whispered. "Devil, devil, devil!"

I jumped off the bed and paced around the tiny room. It wasn't big enough for proper pacing. There was barely any floor space outside the bed. I stalked to the broad windows and stared outside. Grantham Abbey rose up before me, massive and powerful even in its ruined state. My eyes traced the high, empty window arches, outlining the blue sky. My breath slowly began to even itself out.

I wondered what Angeline and Elissa were talking about right now.

I set my teeth together with a snap. It didn't matter what they were talking about. It didn't even matter what they thought of me. I didn't care.

But I had to get out of this room, into somewhere I could run. And there was only one place I could do that without being sighed at and lectured half to death.

I slid back onto the bed. Taking a deep breath, I picked up the golden mirror. It burned against my skin with familiar heat.

If Angeline had found it . . .

Wait. I jumped off the bed and hurried to the door. I didn't want any more nosy visitors while I was gone. I locked the door and set the little key safely on my bedside table.

There. Angeline and Elissa would have to stay right out of it. I was the only one in the world who knew where I was going, and my sisters had nothing to say in the matter.

I sat back on the bed, breathing easier this time. *Mama*, I thought, and closed my eyes as I clicked the mirror open.

Heat swept through my chest. A hot wind seized me and flung me inside out.

When I opened my eyes, I was sitting in Mama's Golden Hall. My head didn't hurt. I hadn't hit anything on the way. I laughed out loud with sheer delight.

I was getting better at this, and wouldn't Angeline be shocked to hear it!

I stood up and stretched luxuriously as I stared at the vast hall around me. I'd been scared and overwhelmed last time, but I'd also been right about one thing: It was a perfect space to explore. I couldn't wait to see what lay beyond it.

I had at least three hours before anyone would expect to see me. I could do anything I wanted.

I started across the empty golden room. There had to be doors hidden somewhere along these smooth, shining walls, I was certain of it. And I was determined to find out where every one of them led.

The only warning I had was a soft popping sound behind me.

I spun around, lifting my fists to the boxing position Charles had taught me.

"Oh, I do hope you won't choose to hit me, my dear," Mr. Gregson said. He straightened the glittering spectacles on his nose as he smiled at me. "I've been so looking forward to meeting you again."

Eight

"*How—?*" my voice came out as a croak. I swallowed and started again with more force. "You were supposed to be occupied with the house party!"

"I was," said Mr. Gregson. "But I left a warning signal in place to alert me as soon as you returned here. It was a very sensible precaution. After all, I couldn't waste my time waiting here for you to come back, could I? I would never get anything else done." He shrugged. "You showed remarkable restraint, though. I must admit that I did not expect you to wait so long."

"I'm not a complete fool," I said. Inside my head, though, I could hear both my sisters' voices in unison: *Kat, you little fool!* I'd known better than to come back at all, hadn't I? I'd sworn not to. But here I was again, and no one even knew where to look for me if I didn't escape.

I wasn't about to reveal my fear, though. Instead I looked pointedly past Mr. Gregson's shoulder. "Where is your friend? Was she too afraid to come back, after last time?"

"Lady Fotherington?" Mr. Gregson's eyebrows rose above his spectacles. "Both Lady Fotherington and I thought it best that she remain in London for the moment. She was, of course, able to heal the physical damage you had done. You needn't worry about her well-being."

"I didn't," I muttered. But I couldn't stop a small pang of relief from shooting through me. The crunching noise I'd heard when I hit her nose had made me feel sick every time I'd remembered it, even though she had completely deserved it and I didn't regret it at all.

"Mm," Mr. Gregson said, and coughed stiffly. "Regardless, I—we—felt it would be better if I came alone to Grantham Abbey, as your first meeting together had not gone so, er, pleasantly as one might have hoped."

"This meeting won't go pleasantly either," I said. "Especially not if you're planning to cast any more spells on me to let you steal Mama's magic books."

Mr. Gregson winced. "Please, my dear. Guardians do not cast spells. Guardians work magic. It is quite a different matter."

I kept my fists raised in boxing position. "Regardless," I said, "I didn't see you stopping Lady Fotherington from attacking me last time."

"Lady Fotherington is sometimes a bit impetuous, but she has only the best interests of our Order at heart, and, of course, your own best interests as well, my dear. If you had never come back through the mirror, you could never have been taught the full extent of your own powers. Fortunately, I, knowing your mother rather better than Lady Fotherington ever did, knew perfectly well that there was no need to work any magic upon you to bring about what we all desired. Your own natural curiosity, much like Olivia's—"

"Never mind that," I said. I didn't want to think about what my curiosity had led me into . . . or how horribly, unforgivably predictable it had been. I knew that even my own sisters would have agreed with Mr. Gregson about that, which made it even worse. "I'm not joining any Order with Lady Fotherington in it," I said. "Much less one that expelled my own mother. So if that's all you're here to talk about—"

"You have no idea what you are dismissing so cava-lierly!" Mr. Gregson took out his pocket handkerchief and wiped his forehead. "Really, Miss Katherine, I must ask you to be reasonable. You do not seem to have any notion of how fortunate you are even to have this opportunity! It is offered only to—"

"'Only one child in each generation of a family,'" I quoted. "I heard you last time."

"No," Mr. Gregson said. "That is not what I said at all."

I lowered my fists, frowning. "Yes, you did. You said—"

"Not every child who inherits the powers of a Guardian is offered the chance to join our Order."

I tried to raise just one eyebrow, like Angeline. They both came up together, so I had to settle for looking surprised instead of sardonic.

Mr. Gregson fixed me with a firm look. "Your family hovers on the edge of respectability in Society's eyes, and thus in the eyes of our Order. If they were but one step lower on the social scale—if your father had turned to trade rather than to the clergy; if your mother had married a merchant rather than a vicar—"

"Wait a moment," I said. "You said last time that my parents' marriage was the whole reason Mama was exiled from your snobby Order. Didn't you?"

He looked uncomfortable. "Not . . . exactly. The point is—"

"What could possibly have been wrong with Papa? He's a clergyman. That's the most respectable position there is!"

"The Church," said Mr. Gregson, "has never understood the necessity for any kind of magic, even the respectable and natural form that we practice."

"Hmm," I said, and thought, *Not that respectable, if you have to keep it a secret.* He kept going, though, his voice speeding up with agitation.

"One could hardly approve of any clergyman as a husband for a Guardian. And your mother—Olivia Amberson, of all women! The most powerful young Guardian I had ever trained!—was choosing not only to marry a man who could never appreciate her, but to bury herself in a community that would never accept who she was. It was the most phenomenal waste of ability I have ever seen in my life. I begged her to reconsider—we all begged her—but she would not listen to any of us. She was too young to understand the risks she ran, and too foolishly in love. And, to be fair, he did seem quite besotted with her at the time."

Besotted. I remembered the love spell in Mama's magic book, with Papa's name written beside it. Every sarcastic thought I'd been forming tumbled straight out of my mind. My lips formed an *Oh* that I didn't say out loud. Instead I asked faintly, "How long do love spells last?"

He cocked his head to one side like an inquisitive bird. "That depends on the strength of the spell. Sometimes, only a week. Others last for years."

"Oh," I said, and closed my mouth tightly.

"Why do you ask?"

"No reason," I said. "I only wondered."

I hoped Mama's love spell had lasted for years. I hoped it had lasted all her life. I hoped it had never faded away and left Papa blinking at her with blank surprise, wondering how he could ever have sacrificed his career for her sake.

My chest hurt. I blinked hard and set my jaw. "Why couldn't she stay in the Order after she married Papa? Did you expel her just because"—I could hardly even say

the words, they sounded so ridiculous in my mouth—
"because she married beneath herself?"

"Oh, no. Of course, it would have been difficult for
her to disguise her activities from your father and
everyone else in the community. A clergyman's wife
in a small country village has an extraordinarily public
position, and it all would have been dreadfully incon-
venient for everyone. But despite everything . . ." Mr.
Gregson sighed heavily, his shoulders slumping. "I had
no idea how far she had strayed from our path until
Lady Fotherington came to me. She had gone to your
mother, tried to make her see sense about that absurd
betrothal."

"Oh, I can imagine that meeting," I said.

"Humph," said Mr. Gregson. "Well, perhaps you
can. But it was much worse than any of us had antici-
pated. For during the course of their confrontation, Lady
Fotherington found evidence—quite incontrovertible
evidence—that your mama had betrayed us all." He lowered his voice as if he were speaking blasphemy. "Olivia
had actually been practicing witchcraft, as a Guardian!"

"So?"

"So?" He shook his head. "Young lady, it is the most
unbreakable law in our Order! We protect Society against
the misuse of magic—against rogue witches! It was witchcraft that nearly burned Parliament to the ground in 1605.
It was witchcraft that led to the Civil War, when Cromwell
and his associates turned against us all. Guardians were

burned at the stake because of the damage witchcraft had caused!"

I gritted my teeth. "Are you going to tell me that witches are the only people who have ever misused magic?"

He flushed. "Our membership requirements have changed in the last two hundred years," he said stiffly. "Nowadays, any Guardian who might misuse their powers would never be trained by us in the first place."

Ha! I thought. Any Order that would keep Lady Fotherington and expel Mama had no notion of reasonable membership requirements. But I had more important matters to pursue. I put on my most innocent voice. "And your Order pacifies witches. Isn't that what Lady Fotherington said?"

He shrugged. "If we must. If they use their powers against innocent members of the public, for instance, or if we deem them a significant threat to Society itself."

If they use their powers against innocent members of the public . . . As Mama had, with her love spell. And as Angeline had, only a week ago. Coldness crept through me at the thought.

"How exactly would I pacify a witch?" I said sweetly. "If they were misusing their magic? If I were . . . protecting Society?"

Lady Fotherington might have noticed the sharp edge hidden in my voice. Mr. Gregson only looked confused.

"Well, we do have ways of modifying a witch's magical powers, if necessary—of taking away even their most ingrained ability to use them. But that is of no matter now. It will be many years before you can control your own powers to that extent, and at any rate, that—"

"Taking away their powers," I repeated flatly, and gave up on sounding sweet. "Why didn't you do it to Mama, then? Wouldn't it have solved all your problems?"

Mr. Gregson suddenly looked much older. "Olivia had been my student," he said. "She was a Guardian. Expulsion was enough of a punishment for her. The process of pacification might have damaged her mind irreparably. To take such a risk . . . no." He shook his head. "No. The Head of our Order agreed with me. If you had seen Olivia's distress—if you had seen her reaction when her portal was closed, and she was shut out of our Order and the Golden Hall forever . . ." He took a deep breath. "Even Lady Fotherington could not have desired more than that. Not if she truly considered the matter."

You don't know Lady Fotherington at all, if you think that, I thought. I'd met her only once, but it had been enough to know one thing for certain: She had truly hated Mama. I would have wagered any sum that when she'd discovered Mama's witchcraft, she had been absolutely delighted. Even now, more than twenty years later, she was still seething that her revenge hadn't been complete.

"Thank you," I said politely, and started to turn away. "That's all I needed to know."

"I'm glad." He relaxed, smiling. "You've already discovered your portal, of course; otherwise you wouldn't be here."

I hesitated. "You mean the mirror?"

"Indeed. You thought we were inside the mirror itself at first, didn't you?" Mr. Gregson's smile turned into a smug grin. "Quite amusing, really, but entirely misguided. No, no, it is merely a portal to our hall. We all have them, under various disguises—my own is this pair of spectacles I wear, inherited from my father. I imagine the mirror displayed some strong reaction when you first touched it? It drew you toward it, in a manner that could not be resisted?"

"Well . . ." I hated to be so predictable, especially to him.

"Of course it did," Mr. Gregson said. "So, you see? The choice has been made." He beamed at me complacently. "Now all that remains is for you to begin your training. I believe the first step ought to be—"

"Thank you," I said. "But I think not." I slitted my eyes half-shut, trying to remember last time. When I'd left . . .

"I beg your pardon?" Mr. Gregson looked at me as if I'd suddenly started speaking Spanish. "What are you saying?"

"I told you," I said. "First you expelled Mama, which made her miserable, and then Lady Fotherington tried to make me her magical slave. I'm hardly going to join you after all of that, am I?"

I didn't mention the real reason I'd bothered to stay and

ask him so many questions—and the real reason I would never, ever join his pompous Order. I knew exactly what they did now, and especially what they did to witches. Mama had only escaped because of Mr. Gregson's fondness for her; Angeline wouldn't have any such protection if she was ever discovered by them.

"But you don't understand. The work of our Order— the urgency of our need! If you only knew how vital it was to—"

"I'm sure it is," I said. "So perhaps you should have thought twice about expelling Mama. Perhaps you should think twice about being so prejudiced in the first place." I closed my eyes. *There.* I had it: the thread of connection I'd found just at the last moment last time, when I'd run from Lady Fotherington and flung myself at the golden wall. I smiled.

"But my dear young lady—think of your own potential magical powers! If you don't join us, you'll be stunted— you'll never learn how to use them properly, you—"

Mr. Gregson's sputtering was the last thing I heard before I landed with a bounce on the green and yellow covers of my bed in Grantham Abbey. Sunlight streamed in through the windows, bright and clear and entirely different from the deep golden glow of the hall I'd stood in only a moment before. The bed was satisfyingly solid and real, there were no signs of whirlwinds or hurricanes in the room around me, and I was wonderfully, perfectly alone.

The mirror was back in my hand, closed and latched once more. I looked down at it and laughed out loud. Then I tossed it in the air and caught it again.

I was getting better at this. I was almost certainly safe, too. Mr. Gregson was far too proper to follow me out of the hall and into my own bedroom, no matter how irate he might be. He wouldn't be able to lecture me or work any magic on me in public, in full view of all the other houseguests, either. As long as I stayed away from the Golden Hall, I was safe.

Unless . . . Sudden discomfort coiled in my stomach. Lady Fotherington had stayed in London for the moment, Mr. Gregson had said. But if he gave up on convincing me through self-righteous lectures alone, would he decide to summon her? And then—

I stood up, closing my fingers tightly around the mirror. *Let her come.*

By the time we all went down to dinner, two hours later, I'd patched up the reticule just about well enough to carry with me. Stepmama gave me a definite Look, though, when she saw it looped around my arm with half the beads knocked off. She sighed and shook her head.

"Thank goodness no one will be looking at you, Kat," she said. "At least Elissa looks perfect."

Elissa really did look beautiful. Even her pale cheeks only set off her deep blue eyes and fair hair, and she was wearing her newest and finest gown, of pure white muslin, with puffy short sleeves, a modest round bodice, and a string of pearls around her neck—Stepmama's pearls, I realized. I bit down hard on my lower lip at the memory they brought back: Mama's broken pearls, lying scattered around her cabinet . . .

"Do hurry, Kat! We don't wish to be late, tonight of all nights," Stepmama snapped, and herded us all down the long corridor and grand flight of stairs.

As we reached the bottom of the stairs, Elissa's hand found mine and squeezed. I squeezed it back.

"Elissa," I began, in an urgent whisper.

"Hush," she said, and smiled at me more wanly and unhappily than ever as she let go of my hand.

"*Now,*" Stepmama said, and ushered us, smiling as fiercely as a general, into the crowded Long Gallery.

Nine

There must have been at least fifty people in the gallery, and at first all I could take in was a confused mass of gowns and coats and far, far too much high, trilling laughter ringing in my ears.

But Stepmama plowed straight through the crowd toward our goal.

"Smile, girls," she hissed through gritted teeth. "And Kat, if you say a single word out of place, I vow I'll see you locked in the nursery tonight no matter what Rosemary might say."

I didn't bother to grace that with a response. Even if I'd wanted to, I was too busy avoiding the hard male elbows that jutted out from the crowd around us, just asking to be knocked into, and the women's hands flung out for emphasis, glittering with rings. I'd never been allowed to attend a single dinner party back in our own village, and those parties only ever included six or eight families, all of whom I'd known my entire life. I'd never even seen this number of strangers before, let alone been required to mind my manners in front of them.

For a moment, the nursery actually sounded like an appealing option. But only for a moment.

I was concentrating so hard on avoiding the shift of arms and elbows all around me as I followed in Stepmama's wake, I completely forgot to look where my feet were going. So the first sign of disaster didn't come until it was too late.

I stepped back to avoid a swinging arm and landed on something soft. My right foot caught and slipped; my arms swung out, searching for balance; I pulled them back before I could hit anyone; and then I lost the battle altogether and fell flat onto my back in the middle of the crowd, knocking into at least three people on the way. My head hit the marble floor with a thud that was almost— but only almost—enough to drown out the ripping sound from around my feet, and the sounds of breaking glass nearby.

Nothing could have drowned out the shriek that came straight afterward. "My gown! What have you done to my new gown?"

I cringed and closed my eyes. Pain thudded through my skull. But there was no escape.

All the laughter and buzzing talk of the crowd vanished as if it had been sucked right out of the room. Then whispers erupted around us, and footsteps hurried toward me. I felt a cool, familiar hand against my cheek.

"Kat?" said Elissa. "Kat, can you hear me?" Her voice shifted as she spoke to someone else above me. "She did hit her head. Do you think she—?"

"Oh, she's not unconscious," Angeline said in a low, scathing whisper, from my other side. "She's only embarrassed. As well she should be. Come on, Kat, you might as well get up before Stepmama can pull you up by your hair."

I opened my eyes. My sisters both knelt beside me, and Stepmama was hurrying back toward me, rage in her eyes. Nearby, two footmen were cleaning up the remains of two broken wineglasses. I let Angeline help me up.

"I am sorry," I said to the crowd at large, and heard my voice waver pathetically. "I tripped—"

"I ordered this gown all the way from *Paris*," said the voice I'd heard before. It came from a tall, fish-faced blond woman who wore an enormous silk turban like a Turkish sultan. She pointed down at the train of her crimson gown. The flounces around the hem had been torn half off; they hung limply from her skirts, dragging against the marble floor. "This was the first time I'd even worn it!"

The whispers intensified. I felt the whole crowd staring at me.

"I'm sorry," I said again, and curtsied as well as I could.

It made my head spin horribly. "I didn't mean to, truly."

"We are all so sorry," Stepmama said. She gave me one of the most furious looks I'd ever seen from her. "Katherine is very young and inexperienced, and she will be—"

"You ordered that gown from Paris, you said?" Angeline repeated the woman's words with a slight frown, speaking as lightly as if she were only mildly curious. But I knew that look in her eyes. "Is that not illegal, ma'am? In a time of war against the French? In fact, I thought it had been specifically prohibited by His Majesty's government."

"Well . . ." The woman fluttered her fan higher as color mounted in her thin cheeks. "That is hardly—"

"You would have had to order the gown rather than go to Paris yourself, naturally," Angeline said thoughtfully, as Elissa's face went paler and paler beside her. "For only the smugglers ever actually cross—"

"That is quite enough!" Stepmama said. "Madam." She curtsied stiffly to the fish-faced woman. "You have our deepest apologies. From all of us. If you will do us the honor of having your gown conveyed to our apartments this evening, my own maid shall see to its repair." Of course, what that really meant was that Stepmama would stitch it up herself. None of us had a maid to do our sewing for us.

The fish-faced woman drew herself up haughtily, folding her thin face into fishier lines than ever. "*My* maid," she said, "is a genius from France, and she will take care of the matter herself, thank you very much." She cast one last simmering look at me. "And you should dismiss your own maid without references if she's the one who cut your daughter's hair. It looks ridiculous!" With a swish of her remaining skirts, she turned her back on us. Supported by two of her friends, she hurried across the room, back toward the stairs to the guest quarters. She was followed by whispers all the way, mounting into a full-out roar of delighted gossip.

Stepmama turned on me. She couldn't tell me everything she thought, of course; not now, under the pressure of all the eyes still upon us. But her face spoke for her.

"*Later,*" she said, and twitched her skirts away from me.

"Ah, Margaret." Lady Graves appeared. She was very nearly panting with exertion, in the most refined possible manner; she must have hurried all the way through the crowd to arrive so quickly. "And girls. I do hope you are all enjoying your evening so far."

I don't know what looks we gave her, but I saw her blink and step back an inch.

"I'm afraid Miss Katherine suffered a small injury to her head," Stepmama said, in tones that were trying to sound honeyed. "It would really be best if you excused her so she could lie down quietly in her room. Isn't that so, Kat?"

I gulped. Five minutes ago, I would have argued. But now . . .

"Nonsense," said Lady Graves. "A girl of her age can hardly miss dinner. Isn't that so, Miss Katherine?"

"Well . . ."

"There, now." She patted my arm. "Never mind, dear. Once you have a little wine, you'll think nothing of a mere headache, I can promise you that. But in the meantime . . ." Her smile broadened as she turned to Elissa. "There is someone who is particularly anxious to meet you, Miss Stephenson. And all your family, of course."

Lady Graves swept us with her, and the crowd moved aside to make way—whether in honor of the hostess in our midst, or out of fear that I'd go mad and attack them as well, I couldn't be sure. I was glad of it, though. If it had been up to me, I wouldn't have come face-to-face with another guest for the rest of our stay at Grantham Abbey.

All too soon, though, Lady Graves drew us up before an enormous painting of a morose-looking old gentleman in a really startling long red wig. In front of the painting stood two tall, dark-haired men in black coats, their heads turned away from us as they studied the painting—or, perhaps, just marveled at the painted wig. I couldn't believe anyone had ever been willing to wear such a monstrosity.

Lady Graves coughed delicately, and both gentlemen swung around to face us.

"My dear Sir Neville . . . and Mr. Collingwood," she purred. "May I have the pleasure of presenting my cousin, Mrs. Stephenson, and her daughters? Miss Stephenson, Miss Angeline, and Miss Katherine."

We all curtsied. But I was so busy peeking up under my eyelashes at the gentlemen, I nearly toppled over as I did it.

They looked very alike, both with hawk noses, dark eyes, and glossy black hair. But the older brother—Sir Neville—had harder eyes. I could actually feel the power vibrating off him as his gaze swept across us. The younger brother, Mr. Collingwood, smiled with what seemed to be real, friendly interest. Sir Neville looked as if he were measuring each and every one of us for a contest of strength. My skin prickled under his gaze, and I didn't like it. Worse yet, I felt a telltale heat against my leg as the mirror awakened inside my reticule.

Just perfect. If I had to guess the single thing most calculated to send Stepmama into a screaming, uncontrollable rage, even at the best of times, it would be exposing the shame of Mama's magic in front of an eligible bachelor. And to do it right now, just after publicly humiliating the entire family on the very first night of our visit . . . I gritted my teeth and closed my hand tight around my damaged reticule to keep any hint of golden glow from leaking out.

"Charmed," Sir Neville said, and smiled. It looked like a predatory snarl.

Elissa looked as if she might faint from sheer panic.

I stiffened my back and returned Sir Neville's smile with interest. His eyes widened.

"I say," said Mr. Collingwood. "Are you perfectly well,

Miss Stephenson? You look a bit under the weather, if you don't mind my saying so."

"No, no," Elissa murmured faintly. "I'm fine, truly."

"Are you sure?" He started forward, one hand held out as if to catch her arm.

"She is perfectly well," Stepmama said. "Honestly. Young ladies these days." She gave a trill of laughter. "I'm sure you gentlemen both understand. The honor of attending such a grand party as this, for an innocent young girl . . ."

Angeline looked sardonic. Elissa looked ready to swoon again, but this time from humiliation rather than nerves. Mr. Collingwood blinked and flushed and tugged at his cravat. He stepped back hastily.

"Of course," he said. "So sorry. I shouldn't have—"

"We are all delighted that she could be here," Sir Neville said. "And her charming sisters as well, of course." But his hard eyes were fixed only on Elissa now. "Will you do me the honor of allowing me to escort you into dinner tonight, Miss Stephenson?"

"Of course," Elissa murmured. Her eyelashes fluttered down to cover her eyes, and color rose on her pale cheeks. "Thank you, sir."

"Oh," said Mr. Collingwood. He looked like a little boy who'd just found out he couldn't have a puppy after all. "Erm." He set his shoulders. "Miss Angeline, would you—?"

"Thank you," Angeline said. "I would be delighted."

"Mm," said Mr. Collingwood, and gazed wistfully at Elissa.

"Excellent," said Lady Graves, and nodded to the butler who stood in the corner of the room, waiting.

He rang the bell with a jangle, and everyone formed into pairs to enter the dining room. I, of course, had to walk next to Stepmama. But still, I had an excellent view as Sir Neville led Elissa forward like a man claiming his latest and least important possession. Just like a milch cow, as Angeline had said earlier. My mouth twisted at the thought.

Just before they disappeared into the dining room, Sir Neville looked back at the rest of us. His gaze went straight to me.

I lifted my chin. He smiled and turned away. And the mirror in my reticule burned hotter than ever.

Just to make the evening complete, I ended up sitting directly across from the fish-faced woman, who wore a new and different gown, probably also from Paris, and hadn't let her change of gown change her mind about me. Of course, Stepmama had drilled it into me beforehand that I was only allowed to converse with my neighbors on either side and was never, ever to be so rude as to speak across the table, so Fish-Face and I wouldn't have had a chance to talk anyway. But sitting only a few feet away from me gave her plenty of opportunity for disdainful looks and sniffs whenever I picked up the wrong fork or knife or actually spoke to my own lawful neighbors. Luckily, that didn't happen often, as I was squeezed between two middle-aged gentlemen who were both completely intent on their own dinners and their gallons and gallons of red wine.

But Fish-Face surprised me by having a much more interesting conversation of her own across the table. The moment I heard the word "highwayman," I gave up even pretending not to listen.

"It is too shocking for words," she said to her neighbor, a pallid, thin young man who looked far too fashionable to move or even speak. "Lady Graves may tell us all she likes not to concern ourselves, but how can we help but worry with a dangerous highwayman on the loose?"

The pallid young fashion plate's only reply was a languid, "Um." He seemed more concerned with lifting the food on his plate and then gracefully replacing it, uneaten, than with any nearby highwaymen, dangerous or not. I wondered how he managed to survive without eating. Was he powered entirely by fashion?

Fish-Face's other neighbor, though, harrumphed loudly and shifted in his seat to glare at her. "Nonsense, nonsense! Only dangerous at night, Mrs. Banfield, no danger to you in the day. Just don't drive out at night and you'll be perfectly well. No need for flights of fancy here!"

"How ever can you say so?" Mrs. Banfield's fish face pursed with irritation, and she tossed back a glass of wine, emptying it to the dregs. I watched, fascinated. "One cannot remain forever confined to one small house for an evening. One would go mad!"

Small? I thought, and blinked. But she kept going.

"We can hardly let ourselves be trapped here, can we? And the miscreant might well take to harassing innocent travelers in the daytime, too, if we all stay safely hidden away from him at night."

"Then give your footmen a pair of pistols each," the harrumphing neighbor said. "Tell 'em to shoot the devil down at first sight. Only in danger then if you drive on a night without moonlight so you can't see him. You can bear to stay inside only on moonless nights, can't you?"

"There is no need for the moon to be hidden for him to hide from us. With that dreadful forest hanging over the road, no wonder he manages to stay hidden until the final moment every time! I should never feel safe for an instant—and my footmen are hardly trained shots, you know."

"Better stay inside, then," the harrumphing man said, and turned back to his veal and mutton as the twelve new dishes of the second course arrived.

"Well!" Mrs. Banfield said. "I never."

The pallid fashion plate beside her smiled dreamily, perhaps in sympathy, or perhaps just in a world of his own. Mrs. Banfield looked at him, gave another impatient sigh, and then looked across the table at me. I smiled in as friendly a way as I could manage. She shuddered and turned back to the lobster on her plate, her massive silk turban rustling with frustration.

Since her conversation seemed to have dried up, I decided to try again for my own. I turned to the man beside me, whose attention was focused intently on his plate of beef. "Is there really a highwayman in the area, sir?"

"Eh? What?" He blinked at me as if I'd only just appeared beside him. "Highwayman, you say? Deuced odd thing for a young girl to talk about, I must say."

"But if there really is a highwayman loose near Grantham Abbey—"

"Stories," he said dismissively. "You're perfectly safe here. The devils never come near the houses themselves. They'd be fools to risk it."

"But—"

But he had already turned back to his beef. I sighed and took a sip of my wine. It was a deep, rich red, and it tingled against my tongue. I'd never drunk unwatered wine before, and it made me a little nervous. I decided not to try flinging it down my throat yet, the way Mrs. Banfield had done, even though I was sorely tempted. After my misadventure earlier, it would be hard enough to convince Stepmama to let me downstairs again tomorrow night, even without spilling red wine all over Lady Graves's tablecloth now.

Maybe later tonight, safe in the privacy of my own bedroom, I would practice flinging a glass of water down my throat until I had the movements perfected.

By the end of the final course, my stomach was so burstingly full I couldn't even think about drinking more wine, or anything else that might shift the horridly delicate balance of my digestion. I watched my plate be taken away with pure relief and stifled a macaroon-flavored burp. Mrs. Banfield had finally drawn the pallid young fashion plate into, if not a real conversation, at least one that seemed to moderately interest him. She spouted her opinions on the latest fashions, and he roused himself enough to make noises that might have almost been taken to be encouragement whenever she paused. Her other neighbor's face had grown redder and redder with every refill of his wineglass. He was bellowing about hunting methods to the poor woman on his other side.

The noise levels had risen all along the long table, actually, into a not-so-civilized roar that bounced off the walls. Together with my over-full stomach, the din made me feel dizzy and a little nauseated. I swallowed hard and fixed my eyes on Lady Graves at the head of the table. Thank goodness, she was already starting to rise. As soon as she signaled, all the ladies would have to follow her out into the drawing room for tea and coffee, and then—

A footman approached Lady Graves and whispered into her ear. She frowned and looked at Stepmama, signaling down the table with her eyebrows. Stepmama was too engrossed in conversation to notice.

I saw Lady Graves's lips move in recognizable words. "What does he want?"

The footman's head was turned to her, so I couldn't make out his reply. But I heard the doors crash open, and I turned with everyone else at the table to stare at the intruder who hurried inside, cravat disarranged and hair disordered, panting from exertion. His own dark blue eyes, of course, went straight to Angeline, ignoring everyone else in the crowded room.

It was Frederick Carlyle, more agitated than I'd ever seen him.

"Miss Angeline," he said. "Thank God I've found you. Your house has been burgled!"

Ten

"*Burgled in broad daylight!*" Even half an hour later, Stepmama could not stop repeating it.

She sat in one of Lady Graves's most elegant drawing-room chairs with a bevy of older women gathered around her solicitously, plying her with tea and sympathy. For all their fussing, though, I could see the avid speculation in their eyes. Our family was providing plenty of fodder for gossip tonight.

"Did you hear to whom he addressed himself?" Mrs. Banfield murmured to her companion as they passed my corner of the room, on their way to refill their cups at the tea urn. "It was Miss Angeline he'd come to tell—not Mrs. Stephenson. I wonder if his mother knows how thoroughly he is being dragged into their toils, buried in that little country vicarage?"

Her companion giggled. "It is too delicious, isn't it? Perhaps a judicious letter really ought to be sent to Mrs. Carlyle's sister to pass on the hint. . . ."

I glared at both of them, but they didn't notice. They were too busy savoring the moment.

"But what could they even have wanted?" Stepmama moaned piteously to her supporters on the other side of the room. "We have nothing—that is . . ." She blinked and drew herself up, suddenly speaking more cautiously under the weight of so many measuring eyes. "We think of our possessions as absolutely nothing, of course, despite what some people might call their vulgar monetary value. . . ."

I curled in tighter upon myself in my corner. Elissa was holding off her own interrogators in another part of the drawing room, while Angeline, cheeks flushed, was held as captive audience by Mr. Carlyle, the only gentleman in the room, under the interested gaze of all the other ladies. But none of them knew as clearly as I what must have happened.

"It was while your father and I were on our daily walk across the hills," Mr. Carlyle had told Angeline at the dinner table, while all the other guests stared and whispered. "Mr. Stephenson's study was ransacked, and all the other rooms in the house gone over. But we could see nothing that had gone missing, so the burglars must not have found what they were looking for. Mr. Stephenson decided it would be best for me to be the one who came to tell you, as your brother was, ah, indisposed, and your father himself, er, well . . ."

Of course Papa couldn't have come to tell us himself. He was needed to keep an eye on Charles and make sure he came to no new trouble while we were gone. No matter what the rest of Lady Graves's houseguests thought, all of us in Charles's family understood that part without needing any further explanation. But as for the rest of it . . .

"What were they even looking for?" Stepmama wailed to her audience now. "And what if they should come back? Or come here to find it, whatever it is?"

"Nonsense, my dear," Lady Graves said. She cut through Stepmama's spellbound audience to pat her hand and smile bracingly. "This house is very well protected. A dozen servants would alert us before a single burglar could find his way to your rooms. I promise you, you are entirely safe here."

But I knew she was wrong.

The door to the drawing room opened, and the gentlemen arrived, spilling into the room in a rather unsteady fashion after their session of port swilling. Sir Neville and his brother both headed straight for Elissa; the pallid young fashion plate wandered idly to the rich velvet curtains to look out into the darkness; my neighbor from dinner headed straight to the farthest sofa in the room and promptly fell asleep.

But I only had eyes for one gentleman in the room.

Mr. Gregson smiled thinly at me as he seated himself with a neat flick of his coattails by our hostess's side.

Apparently Lady Fotherington wasn't the only ruthless one in their partnership after all.

I followed Angeline into her room that night, even though her face was still flushed with embarrassment and anger, and her eyes sparkled with a light that meant danger. I ignored all the signs and closed the door behind me.

"I'm too tired, Kat," she said, before I could utter a word. "If you want to talk, go find Elissa. I'm sure she's simply longing to sigh like a martyr in front of an audience right now. Heaven knows, inspiring two gentlemen to passion in one night is plenty of reason to feel sorry for yourself. It's practically a gothic tragedy."

"You're just annoyed because Frederick Carlyle followed you here and mooned over you in front of all the other guests," I said. I sat down on her bed uninvited and looped my hands around my knees. "There's no need for you to take out your bad mood on Elissa."

"I am so glad you decided to visit me tonight," Angeline said sweetly. "How fortunate I am indeed. Do you wish to spend any more time explaining my own motivations to me, or are you ready to be thrown out yet? Because I warn you, I haven't the patience to listen to much more of this right now." She yanked the pins out of her thick, piled-up hair and threw them down onto her dressing table. "Frederick Carlyle be *damned*," she said. "He had no reason to come chasing after us only because of a burglary in which nothing was stolen. An utterly pointless burglary, in fact. Perhaps he made the whole thing up. I shouldn't be at all surprised."

"He didn't," I said. Then my throat closed up before I could say what I knew I ought to say next.

"Well, there's no need to sound so certain about that," said Angeline. "You may think you're quite the expert at guessing all my secrets, but you might be surprised to know how often you're wrong about other people."

I thought of Mr. Gregson and didn't argue. Instead I said, "Where have you put Mama's magic books?"

"Oh, for heaven's sake!" She whirled around, scattering hairpins in her wake. "Do you really think that now is the time to pester me for those? Go to bed, Kat. We'll talk about it in the morning . . . if I'm in a better mood by then."

I didn't stand up. "Are they safe? Have you really hidden them?"

She closed her eyes and breathed deeply. "Yes. Yes, yes, yes, they are safe. And no, you still can't have them. There!" She opened her eyes and glared at me. "Are you satisfied?"

"No," I said, but I stood up and left the room anyway.

When I stepped out into the candlelit corridor, though, I realized I wasn't alone. I closed Angeline's door with a jerk. "Mr. Carlyle!" I hissed. "What are you doing here?"

He jumped back guiltily. "Nothing," he said. "Only . . ."

I stared at him. "You wouldn't—you couldn't think of trying to go into Angeline's bedchamber!"

"Of course not!" he said. He didn't have the right kind of skin to blush. But he looked positively ill with horror at the thought. "I would never! I have the uttermost respect for Miss Angeline, I swear it. I only . . . it's just . . ." He blinked soulfully at me. "I only wanted to be near her for a little longer. Just to know that she was close."

"Oh, for heaven's sake!" I said, as sweepingly as Angeline herself ever could. "She is in an absolutely foul mood right now. If she had any idea that you were out here . . ."

But I could see my words weren't getting through.

It was all too much. My head was ringing with exhaustion and frustration and the wine I'd drunk at dinner and the fear I'd felt ever since he'd brought the news from home. I could feel the golden mirror burning against my leg through the reticule, making everything worse. I looked him directly in the eye and spoke as clearly as I could. My voice came out in a throbbing, muffled shriek.

"Stop it!" I said. *"You don't really love her anyway. Don't be ridiculous!"*

There was a muffled pop in the air around us, like an explosion. The candles in their wall sconces flickered, sending shadows flying through the air. We both stumbled back. I spun around, holding my reticule like a weapon. If Lady Fotherington had just appeared in midair behind me—

But the long corridor was empty except for us.

I turned back to Mr. Carlyle. He looked as if he'd seen a ghost. His eyes were wide and shocked, and he was breathing hard.

I said, "Are you all right? I don't know what—"

"Where am I?" Mr. Carlyle said. He blinked at me. "And who are you?"

In the end, I had to knock on Angeline's door. I couldn't think of what else to do.

She appeared a minute later, wrapped up in her dressing gown and with her dark hair already plaited in a braid for the night. "I might have known it was you, Kat. What do you want now?" Then she saw Mr. Carlyle. "Oh, Lord! No more. Not tonight!"

She started to close her door. I pushed it back open. "Wait!"

"I do beg your pardon," Mr. Carlyle said. He grinned easily and swept a bow. "It's an awkward moment for a meeting, I understand. But I appear to be in a bit of a fix, and your sister thought you might be able to help."

"You *what?*" Angeline frowned at him. "Kat, what's going on?"

"He doesn't know what he's doing here or who we are," I said. I was proud of myself for keeping my voice so steady as I said it. I added, as lightly as I could, "It's almost as if he'd been under a spell until just now."

Mr. Carlyle laughed. "Well, I'm not sure I would phrase it quite so thrillingly. I'm sure there's some more tedious explanation for it."

"Oh," Angeline said. *"Oh."* Her dark eyes widened. She took a deep breath and stepped out of the room. "You don't remember anything? About any of us?"

"I'm afraid not," he said. His lips curved into a startlingly mischievous grin as he met her gaze. "But I must say, I rather wish I did."

I couldn't believe it. Angeline blushed.

I said, before he could get completely the wrong idea, "You've been studying with our father, Mr. Stephenson."

"Really? They sent me down from Oxford for a term?" He frowned. "Why would they? I haven't gotten into any trouble, have I? I was doing quite well, I thought."

I took the coward's option. "We wouldn't know anything about that," I said. "You arrived on our doorstep about a week and a half ago, with your first quarter's payment, and that's all any of us know about you."

"Hmm. Well, lucky me." He smiled again at Angeline. She stared back at him, looking completely unlike herself.

"I'm Angeline," she blurted. "I mean, my name. Angeline Stephenson. Since you've forgotten."

"Miss Angeline." His smile deepened. "A pleasure to meet you. Again."

I said, "If anyone hears us talking out here, we'll all get into enormous trouble. Don't you think you should go to bed, Mr. Carlyle?" I glared at Angeline to reinforce the message.

She said weakly, "Yes, perhaps that would be a good idea."

"Perhaps it would, after all," he said. "And who knows?

Perhaps when I wake up, I'll remember everything."

Angeline looked as if she might swoon with horror at the thought.

"We shall all hope so, for your sake," I said firmly.

He bowed to both of us. "Well, I am sorry to have disturbed both of you. But there is just one more small problem . . ." He paused, tilting his head questioningly. "Do either of you know where my bedroom is?"

·✶·

I was the one who saw Mr. Carlyle to his bedroom door. Angeline was still behaving extremely oddly. Perhaps it was the strain of having her spell broken that had thrown her off balance. Whatever it was, I didn't like it.

As soon as Mr. Carlyle was safely stowed away, I hurried down the corridor to my own room. But I heard another door open first.

"Kat?"

It was Elissa's whisper. She stood in her own doorway, her blond hair unpinned and falling around the shoulders of her light pink dressing gown. "I thought I heard your voice," she said. "Who were you talking to?"

"Mr. Carlyle," I said. I frowned at Angeline's door beyond, but it didn't budge. "He seems to have suffered a loss of memory. He doesn't remember the past week and a half."

"Oh, no! That's terrible." Elissa's face softened into distress. "The poor man. Perhaps it was the shock of the burglary."

"Perhaps," I said. "But at least it looks like he'll stop mooning around Angeline now."

Elissa's lips twitched. "I shouldn't laugh," she said, "it's too unkind. But thank goodness all the same. He's been driving Angeline wild. She must be so relieved."

I narrowed my eyes at Angeline's closed door. "Let's hope so."

"Don't go to bed yet," Elissa said. "I wanted to talk to you. Why don't you come inside for a few minutes? You can braid my hair, if you don't mind."

"All right." I followed her in, and she closed the door behind me.

Only one slim candle, sitting on a table beside the bed, lit Elissa's room. Her bedroom was as small as my own, but needless to say, it was much tidier. I didn't see scattered beads anywhere on her floor, or any piles of clothing. In the shadows, only her combs and pins glittered on her dressing table, and a copy of *The Mysteries of Udolpho* sat half-open on her bed. She must have sat up reading again. Without Angeline nearby to complain about the candlelight, Elissa could read gothic novels all night long.

I sat down on the bed next to her book, and she brought me her hairbrush and sat down in front of me, curling her legs up neatly underneath her. I liked the soft, silky feel of Elissa's hair in my hands, and the swish of the brush through it, throwing sparks into the air.

I brushed her hair in silence for a few minutes, enjoying the peace. The room was perfectly quiet and still except for the creaks of the old house around us. Then Elissa spoke, so softly I could barely hear her.

"Mr. Collingwood was very gentlemanly, wasn't he?"

"Who? Oh, Sir Neville's brother. Yes, I suppose so." I set down the hairbrush and started to divide her fair hair into three sections across her shoulders, frowning with concentration. "Certainly not as bad as his older brother, anyway."

"I thought he was very kind."

"Well, he did spend the whole night mooning after you, just like—well, almost as badly as Mr. Carlyle used to moon over Angeline," I said. "So I'm not surprised you liked him."

Elissa didn't say anything. But I heard her sigh.

For once, Elissa had actually chosen me, instead of Angeline, as her confidante. So I tried to think of something more sympathetic to say. "Couldn't you marry him instead of Sir Neville?" I asked. "If his family is so wealthy—"

"He's a younger son," Elissa said. "Sir Neville inherited all the property as well as the title. Stepmama told me very clearly that Mr. Collingwood has no fortune of his own. Even though . . ." Her voice softened into wistfulness. "Their mother had an independent fortune. If she had wanted to, she could have left both of her sons wealthy men. Everyone expected her to divide her fortune between her sons . . . but she never left a will, so it all went to Sir Neville." Her voice dropped to a whisper. "Mr.

Collingwood is a completely ineligible prospect."

"Oh." Suddenly the little room didn't seem so peaceful anymore. The weight of Elissa's melancholy felt like a smothering cloak, lying across both of us. I said, "Maybe he'll come into some money of his own soon."

"How?"

"Well . . ." I was thinking so intently, I didn't take enough care with my braiding. Elissa let out a stifled gasp, and I realized I had yanked her hair so tightly that the braid was pulling at her scalp. "Sorry!" I said. "Sorry." I loosened the strands and saw her shoulders relax. I sighed. "Maybe he'll inherit money from an eccentric great-aunt who doesn't like his older brother. I wouldn't blame her for it either. I didn't like Sir Neville one bit."

"No?" Elissa turned her head to look at me, pulling the half-finished braid out of my hands. Her blue eyes were shadowed in the darkness. "Truly, Kat? Why not?"

That feeling of brooding, dangerous intensity, like a malevolent shadow creeping across me . . . I held back a shiver and tried to think of how to say it properly. "He looked as if he wanted to own everybody in the room. Or as if he already did, and just took that for granted."

She sighed and turned away, looking down at her clasped hands. "He's a wealthy man. That's how they all are."

"Mm . . ." I wasn't so sure, but I couldn't argue. Until tonight, I'd never met anyone wealthier than our own local squire. The only way you could call Squire Briggs "brooding" was if you meant it like a brooding hen, fat and lazy. But I supposed he wasn't wealthy enough to count. So I only said, "He made me nervous."

"You? Nervous?" Elissa's lips curved into a smile. "I don't believe it. You've never had a nervous moment in your life. My brave Kat."

You'd be surprised, I thought. But I didn't say it out loud. The last thing I wanted to do right now was admit to my oldest sister what I'd been doing with Mama's magic mirror—or what my meddling had brought about. And I didn't want to even think about what had happened in the corridor just now.

So I stayed quiet until I finished the braid and tied it off. "There," I said. "All finished."

"Thank you." But Elissa didn't look up from her clasped hands.

I frowned at her. "What is it? Is it only Mr. Collingwood, or—?"

"Don't worry," Elissa said. "It's only foolishness, I know it. Please. Forget that I ever mentioned Mr. Collingwood."

"But—"

"And please," Elissa added, "don't mention it to Angeline. She wouldn't understand."

"All right," I said. I wasn't at all sure that I understood either. "But if you truly prefer Mr. Collingwood to Sir Neville—"

"It doesn't matter what I prefer," Elissa said. Her face

looked drawn and noble in the candlelight, and I remembered Angeline calling her a would-be gothic heroine. "What the family needs from me now—"

"Oh, Lord," I said, and stood up fast, knocking *The Mysteries of Udolpho* off the bed. I left it lying on the floor as I glared at her. "Just because Stepmama's been pouring family duty into your head doesn't mean that you have to listen. Someday you could try thinking of what you need from yourself instead. Then maybe you'd have to stop being such a perfect martyr and actually let yourself be happy for once!"

I was panting with outrage by the end, but Elissa didn't even blink.

Instead she sighed wistfully and gave me a sad, sweet smile of ineffable love and forgiveness. "You'll understand when you're older, dear," she said.

I ground my teeth and stalked out of the room.

Eleven

The first person I saw when I walked into the breakfast room the next morning was Mr. Gregson. He stood near the big bay windows, bathed in sunshine and spearing ham and pheasant from the sideboard as calmly as if nothing in the world could worry him. It was infuriating, especially after I'd spent half the night awake and vibrating with tension.

I stalked straight across the room to him, ignoring the guests already sitting at the breakfast tables. "What do you think you're playing at?" I hissed.

He bowed courteously and gestured to the stack of dishes by the sideboard. "You had better take a plate, Katherine, or the other guests will wonder what you're making such a fuss about."

"A fuss?!"

But he was right. If we'd been alone I would have let him have it, but there were six or seven people eating at the breakfast tables behind us, conversing (the ladies) and reading the morning paper (the gentlemen). If I embarrassed myself in public again, even Lady Graves might give in to Stepmama's way of thinking. Seething, I snatched up a plate and turned my gaze to the piles of food waiting on the sideboard, as if I were simply trying to make up my mind among them.

I'd had all night to transform my first fear into outrage, though, and I wasn't going to let myself be distracted now. "You're not going to get away with it!" I whispered.

"With eating breakfast, you mean?" Mr. Gregson murmured back. "Or are you referring to our little discussion yesterday? I can hardly claim to have 'got away with' anything at that point, as I recall, since you ran away before I even had time to marshal my arguments."

"I did not run away," I said. "I'd heard everything you had to say that was of interest to me, so I chose to leave."

"Hmm." He bent over the sideboard, reaching for the pot of raspberry preserves. "If you say so, my dear. It would be most improper for me to contradict a lady, even when her story does sound remarkably unconvincing."

"I did not—" I cut myself off as I realized the nearer houseguests were already turning around to look at us.

Mr. Gregson only smiled beatifically at our audience,

his spectacles glinting in the sunlight. I speared a hard-boiled egg, breathing hard.

"I wasn't talking about yesterday afternoon, anyway," I whispered, once I had my voice back under control. "As you know perfectly well, I was referring to the burglary!"

"Ah. Well, you will recall that I did warn you at our very first meeting. If you will continue to meddle in things you do not understand—and to reject perfectly rational advice on the matter—then you must, I'm afraid, be prepared to face the consequences. I trust you do have the books safely hidden now? Somewhere nearby—in this very house, I would imagine?"

I breathed deeply and restrained myself, with great effort, from throwing a plate of eggs right into his smug face. "They are not only hidden, they are protected. So there's no use in trying to take them from me!"

He coughed delicately. "And yet it might, however, be for the best—for the sake of everyone concerned—if you did give them to me of your own free will, as soon as possible."

"Or?" I slammed down my knife with a clatter. "Or else? What will you do?"

"I am merely thinking of your own safety, my dear. And the safety of your whole family, of course."

I gasped and swung around, forgetting all about the other guests. "Are you actually trying to threaten—?"

"Why, Miss Katherine!" said a familiar voice behind me. "Good morning."

It was Frederick Carlyle, looking well-rested, fresh, and

impossibly different from the man I'd known for the past week and a half. Even the graceful way he bowed now was different from the way he'd moved until last night, and the look of intelligent amusement on his face was a transformation. Even as I thought that, his eyes narrowed, and the amusement vanished from his face. He moved smoothly to place himself beside me in what looked astonishingly like a protective position.

"And are you perfectly well this morning, Miss Katherine?" he asked me blandly—but his gaze was fixed on Mr. Gregson.

"I'm fine," I said. "Thank you." Since the two men were still looking measuringly at each other, I added, "Mr. Carlyle, Mr. Gregson," as an introduction.

"We've already met, just last night," Mr. Gregson said, and frowned at me.

"Umm . . . ," I began, and then caught a ghost of a conspiratorial grin on Frederick Carlyle's face. I decided not to mention his amnesia. Mr. Gregson didn't deserve an explanation, anyway.

More guests were pouring in now behind us, starting with three fluttering young ladies in pastel shades, all giggling and blatantly making eyes at Mr. Carlyle. It was obvious that nothing was going to be sorted out now, so I only gave Mr. Gregson one last warning look and left the sideboard without bothering to curtsy. It was a good thing Stepmama wasn't down yet, or she might have had a Spasm at the oversight.

I didn't have long to sit and simmer on my own, though. Ten minutes later, a plate slammed down across from me so hard I was surprised it didn't crack.

"What's wrong with you?" I said.

Angeline's back was ramrod straight, and her cheeks were flushed. "Nothing in the world is wrong with me," she said. "I'm not the one making a fool of myself."

"What did I do?" I set down my knife and stared at her as she sat down. "I haven't even—"

"I wasn't talking about you," Angeline said. She enunciated her words as clearly as bullets from a dueling pistol, and bit off each one with distaste at the end.

"Who, then? I don't—"

"Oh, for heaven's sake, why don't you turn around and see for yourself?"

If Elissa had been there, she would have told us both that it was entirely improper for a lady to stare, or even to look directly at any person she wasn't partnering in conversation. Luckily, Elissa wasn't there, so I turned in my chair and looked around without bothering to hide my interest. But I didn't see anything worth looking at, no matter how hard I tried. Mr. Gregson was reading the morning paper; various guests I didn't know were gossiping and eating; Mr. Carlyle was laughing and talking to the three young ladies who'd been eyeing him earlier; they were all giggling at everything he said. . . .

"You see?" said Angeline. "He's making a complete fool of himself."

"Really?" I said. I squinted and looked harder, trying to understand.

As we watched, one of the young ladies reached out and tapped him on the arm. "La, Mr. Carlyle! You are wicked!"

They all exploded into giggles. I turned back to Angeline—then scooted my chair backward. "What?" I said. "They don't seem to mind whatever he's telling them."

"Ha." Angeline stabbed a kipper and glared at it. "I'm sure they do not."

"Then . . ." I eyed the knife in her hand warily. "What is the problem?"

"Well, if they wish to waste their time flirting with a hardened rake, then I see no problem whatsoever," Angeline said. Her knuckles whitened around her knife. "Why should there be any problem with that? I'm sure I don't mind at all."

"Good?" I tried. I scooted my chair back another inch as her glare scorched me. I tried again. "Why would you?"

Another explosion of giggles sounded behind me. Angeline's hair nearly shot out sparks. Out of the corner of my eye, I saw Mr. Gregson turn another page of his newspaper.

Inspiration struck. I pushed my chair all the way back from the table and jumped up. "I'll see you later," I told Angeline. "If Stepmama asks where I am . . ."

But I could tell she wasn't listening.

I tiptoed all the way down the final corridor of the guest wing, ready to run and hide at the first sign of Stepmama's approach. Other groups of ladies bustled past me on the way, looking askance at my tiptoeing walk and whispering to one another as they passed, but I didn't care about any of them. All I cared about was getting into Angeline's room undetected by the rest of my family.

It was the perfect opportunity. Mr. Gregson had only just begun reading his morning newspaper—an occupation that, so I'd heard, could take some gentlemen up to an hour every single morning—and Angeline was busy eating breakfast and enraging herself over Mr. Carlyle's flirts. I might not understand what had come over her to make her so bothered by them, but I knew Angeline, so I knew one thing for sure: She wouldn't leave the breakfast room until all three of the other young ladies did. Anything else would be an admission of failure.

As I passed Stepmama's door, I heard the unmistakable rustling sounds of preparation. I ran the final six feet and turned Angeline's doorknob just in time. Even as I slipped inside and closed the door behind me, I heard the next door in the corridor start to open.

Footsteps sounded outside. They paused just in front of the room I was in. A light knock sounded on the door. I froze, holding my breath.

"Angeline?" Elissa said. "Are you in there?"

The doorknob began to turn. I looked around wildly,

searching for something—anything—the closet? I prepared myself to leap—

Stepmama spoke in the corridor outside. "Good morning, my dear. I heard Angeline go down to breakfast some
time ago. Shall we meet her there?"

"Oh," said Elissa. "I suppose so." She sounded wistful,
and I wondered if she'd been hoping for a private chat
with Angeline, away from Stepmama's listening ears. If
she was hoping to get sympathy from Angeline over Mr.
Collingwood and her Tragic Dilemma, she'd chosen the
wrong morning for it. I hoped Angeline would give her
a good withering scold for her idiocy. Not that it would
make any difference—once Elissa had made up her mind,
no one could ever convince her otherwise.

"Pinch your cheeks, child," Stepmama said. "You're
pale as death. Sir Neville may be at the breakfast table,
you know, and you must look your best."

"Yes, ma'am," Elissa murmured, and their footsteps
moved away together.

I stuck my tongue out in their direction as they went.
Then I turned to survey the territory before launching my
attack.

I would have known Angeline's room anywhere, even
without the long strands of thick, dark hair caught in the
combs on the dressing table or the familiar rose-colored
dressing gown that had been flung across the chair in
front of it. There was already something about the whole
feel of the room that made it Angeline's, even though

she'd occupied it for less than four-and-twenty hours. Two years ago, Charles had borrowed an electrifying machine from one of his friends and brought it home to show us. Angeline, Elissa, and I had all linked arms, and he'd shot an electric current down the whole row of us, flying from one person to another in the chain. It had happened only once, but I'd never forgotten the sensation, the exhilaration and the fear of it. Now I was feeling it again.

A faint, flowery smell tickled my nose. Electricity crackled through the air, sparking off my skin as I moved. Even as I looked around, noting the tall closet with its potential as a hiding place, and Angeline's four valises piled in the corner, the electric sparks pushed against my skin, stinging me and pushing me backward. Maybe now wasn't the best time to do this after all. Maybe I should come back later, when Angeline was here to help me. Maybe if I went to Angeline and told her what I was doing . . .

What? I shook my head hard, sending the sparks flying. I could actually see them now, ghostlike in the corner of my vision as they flashed past.

This wasn't just the force of Angeline's personality, frightening though that could undeniably be. No, this was magic. She hadn't only been practicing love spells after all.

The sparks settled in around me again as I went still. They clustered around my face like buzzing insects. I ought to leave now, immediately. I ought to forget about this. There was nothing to look for in here, anyway. . . .

"Balderdash!" I said, as forcefully as I could. But the word came out surprisingly weakly from my mouth. It sounded uncertain.

Really, what was the point of searching Angeline's room? I'd wanted to find the magic books, to keep them safe from Mr. Gregson; but my lie to him had turned out to be the truth. They were protected. No one could touch them. No one even knew where they were except for me; and even as I thought that, I became less and less sure of it. Maybe she didn't have them here after all. Maybe I'd only imagined it. Maybe . . .

"Oh, no, you don't, Angeline," I said, through gritted teeth. "Not this time."

I pushed forward through the spark-filled air. My leg seemed to weigh at least two hundred pounds. It moved sluggishly, leadenly, through air that was much too full to let it pass. I stopped, panting. I hadn't progressed a single step. The sparks buzzed against my ears and eyes and the bare skin on my arms, pushing me backward, toward the door.

It was useless. I should just give up. I should . . .

Never. I was so dizzy and angry I could barely see. Magical pressure built around me. The sparks pushed against me. My head was throbbing. But I didn't care.

Angeline could set all the spells she wanted. She could try all her tricks. She could intimidate or make a fool of anyone she chose. But I was her own sister. I knew her better than anyone else in the world, and I would not give in.

"I will not be fooled!" I shouted.

The air exploded around me.

I blinked and staggered back, my ears ringing. The sparks were gone. The pressure had lifted. My head was suddenly, furiously clear. It felt as if it had been scalded on the inside. It *hurt*.

I sucked in deep lungfuls of air. Slowly, gradually, I regained my balance. I stepped forward. Nothing stopped me.

"Ha!" I said, as firmly as I could. "You see?"

But I looked around nervously as I said it.

Surely Angeline wouldn't have gone to all that trouble to set a spell that would just go away on its own if someone waited long enough. Surely? Maybe it was a trap. Maybe it was meant to lure me further.

I didn't care. I'd come too far now to give up. And I was not going to let Angeline have the upper hand. She couldn't chase me away no matter how many spells she threw at me.

I was Mama's daughter too. I had every bit as much of a right to her magic books as Angeline.

I stalked across the floor and started my search.

The magic books weren't in any of Angeline's valises. They weren't under her bed. But when I opened the tall closet, it took less than a minute of poking around before I found them, hidden underneath a single pile of thin chemises. She must have depended upon the spell she'd set to hold off any investigators before they came this far.

Why hadn't it worked on me?

I set my teeth as I reached for the magic books, waiting for the stinging sparks to return in a full attack. All I felt was the frayed leather binding of the books underneath my hand. The spell had truly disappeared.

I would have to think that through later. But not yet. Right now, it was time for me to do what I should have done more than a week ago, the first time I came across the magic books. It was my fault that Mr. Gregson and Lady Fotherington and their Order were after Mama's magic books. So it was my duty to learn how to protect them— and protect them properly this time, not just with a spell that anyone could break through sheer stubbornness. I had a nasty feeling that Lady Fotherington—and even Mr. Gregson, for all his mild way of speaking—might prove to be at least as stubborn as I was, and just as unwilling to give up what they wanted. I really didn't want Angeline to be in their way.

But I didn't have much time. I couldn't count on those three young ladies to hold on to Mr. Carlyle forever, and as soon as they left the breakfast room, Angeline would too. So I had to find a good spell, fast.

I flipped through the books, vibrating with impatience. Love spells, spells for beauty and fashion—you'd think someone who'd been part of a great and mysterious Order meant to protect the nation would have had more impor- tant things on her mind than clothing, but maybe that was why she'd turned to witchcraft. Spells for scent and taste and—

Footsteps sounded in the corridor outside, breaking my concentration. They came to a halt just outside the door. There was no knock. The doorknob didn't turn. But the footsteps didn't move away.

Someone was standing just outside. Listening.

My hands clenched around the book I was holding. If it was Angeline, I would be in so much trouble. If it was anyone else—someone looking for these books, for example—then things could be much, much worse.

I glanced down at the page the book was open to. Useless. All I saw was a spell for changing one's appearance. Nothing about protection, or fighting, or . . .

Wait. Changing one's appearance . . .

I barely breathed as I scanned the page. Mama's lovely, looping handwriting spelled out all the steps for me. The incantation itself was easy, and then all I had to do was focus on exactly what I wanted to look like. Or rather, *who* I wanted to be . . . It had to be someone safe. Someone eminently proper. Someone even Angeline wouldn't attack for being here and looking at these books.

The footsteps outside still hadn't moved. I took a deep breath and closed my eyes. As I whispered the words of Mama's spell, I focused hard. *Elissa,* I thought. *Elissa, Elissa, Elissa . . .*

The doorknob began to turn. What if it wasn't Angeline? What if it was Mr. Gregson? What if, even worse, it was—

My whole body burst into flame. I bit back a scream. My poor scalded head shifted and stretched. My legs lengthened, shooting fiery pain through my joints. My hair burned against my scalp as it grew suddenly heavier. Dark strands fell around my face. The sharp, sweet scent of fresh raspberries filled the room.

I dropped the books from my lap onto the floor as I jerked backward, flailing—

The bedroom door flew open.

"Good God," Mr. Gregson said. "Lady Fotherington? What are you doing here?"

Twelve

I stared at Mr. Gregson. He stared back.

"I thought we had agreed that you would stay in London unless I called for you," he said. His shocked stare was rapidly becoming a grim scowl.

I pulled myself up to a sitting position on the floor and swallowed hard. Even my throat felt different. Longer. Thinner. And my chest . . .

I blinked and shifted my shoulders to adjust myself. Lady Fotherington had a very different shape from what I was accustomed to. I felt as if I were carrying weights on my chest just by breathing. My—her—chest was only barely covered by the same dark green, low-cut gown she had worn when I saw her several days ago. I hoped Mr. Gregson was too much of a scholar to take notice of the fashion mistake. I was almost certain that anyone as elegant as Lady Fotherington would never dream of wearing an evening gown at eleven o'clock in the morning, at a country house party.

Even as I thought that, I caught sight of Mama's books in the corner of my vision. They had fallen to the ground just by the bed, hidden from Mr. Gregson's line of sight. I lunged forward, swept out my arm, and shoved them all the way under the bed as I pushed myself up off the floor, hoping that the whole movement looked natural. From the way Mr. Gregson's eyes widened, I hadn't succeeded in looking anything but deranged. I tossed my head back, flinging the fallen hair out of my eyes and trying to look coolly dangerous and invulnerable.

"I decided to come and see for myself," I said. "Quite understandable, don't you think?" I smiled as thinly as I could, trying to replicate Lady Fotherington's customary sneering smile. The problem was, I hadn't actually seen her smile much at our meeting. When I smiled, Mr. Gregson blinked and stepped farther into the room.

"Are you quite all right?" he asked. "You look rather . . ."

"I fell," I said. I rose to my full height, which was quite a bit taller than it had been five minutes earlier, and smoothed down the front of the green evening gown, resisting the urge to tug up the bodice. I felt as if I were about to spill out of the top of it. How on earth did she manage it? Surely, no matter how low-cut the current fashion might be, it wasn't possible for even the most stylish gowns to entirely escape the bonds of gravity.

"I can see that," said Mr. Gregson, and it took me a moment to realize that he was talking about my fall. He frowned, looking back through the open door. "This is not a safe place for us to be discovered. Shall we find somewhere more private for our discussion?"

My absurdly overextended chest clenched at the very thought of it. But I didn't see any other choice.

"What a good idea," I said.

I would have to hope that this spell, at least, wouldn't disappear without warning, like its forerunners.

Mr. Gregson held the door open for me, and I swept past him into the corridor, my head held high and my shoulders back, the way Stepmama said all elegant ladies should walk. I wasn't doing it to be elegant, though. It was the only practical way to keep the gown from falling off my chest.

As Mr. Gregson closed Angeline's door behind us, I spared a thought for her probable reaction when she arrived to find her closet door wide open and Mama's magic books flung beneath the bed. But I didn't have any energy to spare for worrying about that prospect. All my nerves were fully reserved for the interview ahead of me.

"This way," Mr. Gregson said, and ushered me down the corridor.

He led me through a door at the end that opened onto a second staircase, one I hadn't seen before. The staircase I'd walked down on my way to breakfast had been broad and grand, with a marble banister and massive paintings hanging above the steps. This one was narrow and dark, with only one tiny window set high above to light our way and keep us from tripping on the dirty steps.

"The servants' staircase," said Mr. Gregson. "I assure you, Lydia, I mean no offense by choosing this direction. I merely thought it would be best, all in all, for us not to be seen in conversation just now . . . particularly if, as I surmise, our hostess does not yet know of your arrival?"

Oh, Lord. My mind flashed ahead to what would come next: greetings with Lady Graves, gossip about mutual friends I'd never met, and a room assigned to "Lady Fotherington," while my sisters and Stepmama searched for me throughout the house, creating gossip about my absence . . . and then, when the notice of this house party was inevitably placed into the gossip columns of the London newspapers, the real Lady Fotherington's reaction to the news that she had supposedly been a guest here.

I started down the narrow, dingy staircase with alacrity. "Excellent choice," I said. "I fully understand and agree with you." As more and more hideous possibilities occurred to me, I picked up my skirts to run faster and faster, finally clattering down the staircase at full speed. I had to wait for Mr. Gregson at the bottom of the stairs, before another closed door. He caught up a moment later, frowning at me.

I smiled weakly through the darkness. "No time to waste, is there?" I said.

"Mm," said Mr. Gregson. "Let me check." He pressed his cheek against the door and closed his eyes. "Ah. We're safe, for the moment at least. We'll have to be quick, though." He opened his eyes, and his frown deepened as he turned his gaze to where I waited, still holding my skirts above my ankles for speed. I dropped them hastily and smoothed down my gown.

"Well, I do hope you know what you're doing this time," I said, giving my best Lady Fotherington sneer.

"I hope so as well," Mr. Gregson said mildly. "But for now . . ."

He opened the door and waited for me to pass. I didn't like brushing past him. It put all my senses on alert. I could actually feel him analyzing me.

I clenched my hands into fists to keep them from trembling and giving me away.

We passed into a narrow corridor. No one was inside, but I heard bustling noises and clanging pots; the kitchen must be nearby.

"I think," Mr. Gregson said, and paused. "Yes. Yes, it would certainly be safest to conduct this conversation outside." He nodded to a side door I hadn't spotted. "Shall we?"

"Of course," I said. I was so eager to escape, I pushed the door open myself instead of waiting to let him open it for me.

The fresh air tasted like freedom, brushing coolly against my face and overexposed bosom. We had emerged on the hill just above and behind the main bulk of the manor house. If the ground hadn't been so rocky and bare around us, with no possible hiding places in sight, I might have given in to my impulse and simply run away, as fast as I could. But there was nowhere to go, so instead I lifted my chin and waited, trying to look bored rather than horribly afraid.

Mr. Gregson scanned the hill and looked equally dissatisfied with it. "Perhaps . . . inside the ruins of the abbey?" he suggested.

I followed him down around the side of the sprawling house, into the remains of the great stone abbey. He strode through the exposed nearer sections and into a grand, enclosed hall, safe from watching eyes. Grass poked up between the stone tiles of the floor, and the roof was missing overhead, but the ivy-encrusted walls still rose high on every side, topped by giant, open arches. Sunshine flooded down on us. I could hear birds close by, their calls carried on the fresh breeze as they flew past. But I couldn't see any chances for my own escape.

Mr. Gregson paced across the stone tiles for a minute without speaking. Then he turned on me. "I am surprised," he said. "I am most surprised by your decision. And not a little displeased, as well."

"Displeased?" I repeated, as contemptuously as I

could. "I make my own decisions. And I would not have come had I not thought you might need my help."

"I assure you, I am perfectly capable of handling this problem myself—and I must confess to being absolutely astonished that you chose to follow without even alerting me first. Did you have so little faith in my abilities?"

I was flailing for ideas. How well did they know each other, anyway? Now I wished I had let Mr. Gregson tell me more about their Order. It would have helped me bluff. Angeline would have known what to say, and how to carry this off. But Angeline wasn't here.

I said, "You can hardly blame me for being curious. I didn't plan to stay, only—"

"And what were you doing in that room, anyway? I felt the magic all the way through the house and knew that a Guardian was present. If I could feel it, I'm sure that others could as well."

I sneered. "Who? I'm not concerned with—" How would she speak of me? I ended weakly, "With that . . . girl, or her family."

"No? Well, what of Sir Neville Collingwood, then?"

I blinked. "I beg your pardon?" My voice came out as a near squeak.

"Yes, I thought you might not have known that he was here. You would do well to shield your magic when he is nearby."

"I—" I stopped, trying to collect myself. "You think he's truly dangerous?"

"You don't?" Mr. Gregson stared at me. "You are not yourself today, Lydia. What came over you in that bedroom?"

"Nothing," I said. "I only—"

"You fell." Mr. Gregson regarded me closely. "After performing some act of magic. Whose room? Ah, yes, one of the Stephenson girls. Not Katherine, though, I think. One of her sisters."

"It was a mistake," I said. "I'd thought that it was Katherine's room. I thought I might find the magic books there, hidden by a spell."

"I could have told you which room was hers, if you'd asked me." Mr. Gregson sighed. "So you found nothing useful there?"

"Only"—I threw all my confidence into the words—"that her sisters are protected by her as well. It was Katherine's spell that knocked me over. Witchcraft, of course. Horrid girl."

To my surprise, Mr. Gregson was smiling. "I told you she had potential. As soon as we can persuade her to exercise her talents in a better direction—"

I groaned. "Do give up!"

"I beg your pardon?" His smile dropped.

"I mean," I said hastily, "she won't do, I'm sure of it. We might as well forget about her."

"We've discussed this before. Your completely irrational dislike of her mother—"

I could feel my hands start to clench automatically. I

unfisted them before he could notice. "That has nothing to do with it," I said. "I merely think—"

"It has everything to do with it, as you well know. Once and for all, Lydia—"

A gasp sounded behind us. We both spun around.

"Oh, I do beg your pardon," said Elissa. She stood in the doorway, wearing her new straw bonnet and looking beautifully flushed. "I was only looking for my sister. I did not mean to interrupt. If you'll excuse me . . ."

"Wait," said Mr. Gregson.

He crossed the uneven stone tiles with quick steps; I trailed reluctantly behind, keeping my face averted. How well did Elissa really know me? Would she recognize my expressions on another woman's face? My manner of speaking, from another woman's mouth?

"Miss Stephenson, is it not?" Mr. Gregson bowed elegantly as he closed the distance between them. "Can we be of any assistance? You said you were looking for your sister—you have two sisters, do you not?"

"Yes . . ." Elissa bit her lip. I could see her looking between us doubtfully before she spoke again. "I was looking for my youngest sister, Kat—Katherine, I mean. I don't know if you met her last night? She looks—"

"I have met her," Mr. Gregson said, and glanced back at me.

I gave a horrible start. Then I realized he was being conspiratorial, rather than accusing. But it was too late for me to take the motion back, and his eyes were already widening behind his spectacles.

"You say she has gone missing?" he asked Elissa.

Elissa gave a nervous, deprecating laugh. "I shouldn't put it quite so dramatically, sir. She ate breakfast before us, and she may have grown tired of waiting for us to return, that's all. She likes the ruins very much, so I thought I might find her here, exploring them. She's very active and lively, you see."

"I see," said Mr. Gregson. His eyes were still fixed on me.

"We haven't seen anyone," I blurted. I turned and looked around pointedly. "I'm sure we would have noticed her."

"Thank you," Elissa murmured. Her cheeks flushed pinker; she was looking at the ground, not at either of us, and all of a sudden, I realized how compromising our position must seem to her, a single gentleman and a lady all alone in the ruins for a secret tryst. I felt my cheeks heat up.

"Indeed we would have," Mr. Gregson murmured. "I was just showing Lady Fotherington some architectural details of the ruins—her late husband was quite an expert in the field of medieval architecture, you know, so she takes a great interest in the matter. Have you two ladies met?"

We both shook our heads. I felt like a fool.

"Lady Fotherington," Mr. Gregson said, "may I present Miss Stephenson."

Elissa's cheeks were still flushed with embarrassment, but she smiled politely, curtsied, and held out her hand to me. We brushed fingers; I dropped my hand as quickly as possible.

"Charmed," I murmured, in the same dry tone Lady Fotherington had used for my own introduction several days ago. I looked pointedly away from her as I spoke.

Elissa blinked and stepped back, dropping her own hand and losing her smile. But her voice remained as soft as ever. "I must go," she said. "My sister Angeline—ah, here she comes now. I must tell her that Katherine wasn't here after all."

I spotted Angeline's dark head and figure coming down the hill toward us, every line of her body vibrating with outrage. She must have discovered the chaos in her room. For the first time, I was actually glad to be hidden in Lady Fotherington's body. Perhaps I wouldn't change back yet, after all. Perhaps not until I'd given Angeline plenty of time to simmer down. Then again, that might take weeks. Or years.

"Good luck!" I said to Elissa, with false cheer.

"Indeed," Mr. Gregson echoed. "Do tell us if we can be of any further assistance."

"I'm sure that won't be necessary," Elissa said. "But thank you." She turned and hurried up the hill to meet Angeline.

I looked at Mr. Gregson. He looked back at me.

"Well?" I said. "Where do you think she is?" The words

felt tangled in my throat, under his watchful gaze. "I hope she isn't spying on us."

"One can always hope," he said. "And yet . . ."

He stepped back, farther into the safety of the high abbey walls. I followed him with slow, dragging steps.

"There is another possibility," he said. "One I had not properly considered until this moment."

"Oh?" I moistened my lips. "It all seems fairly obvious to me. She grew tired of waiting for her sisters and went off to explore, just as Eliss—just as Miss Stephenson said. For all we know, she could be in these ruins, listening to us, right now. Or—her magic is very powerful, you know, it knocked me down earlier—she might not even need to be here to be listening to us, she might only—"

"She might," Mr. Gregson said, "be here already. Talking to me at this very moment."

Curses. I picked up my skirts and lunged for the doorway.

His small hand closed around my arm with a surprisingly strong grip. "I think not. In fact—"

I yanked my arm free and ran. The stone tiles were bumpy and uneven beneath my feet, and I was still wearing Lady Fotherington's cursed, flimsy evening slippers. He could catch me at any moment now. . . .

But I couldn't hear him running after me. Instead I felt something much more unsettling.

A great wave of air billowed in from the great, open doorway of the abbey and swept across the courtyard, pushing me back like a wall closing in. I threw myself forward. The wave of air pushed me back. In the distance, I saw Elissa and Angeline disappearing into the house, too far away to call for help.

With all my strength, I twisted my shoulders around to face Mr. Gregson. His lips curved into a satisfied smile. He lifted one hand to beckon me. The massed air picked me up in midair and lifted me toward him.

My head throbbed. It was too much. It was all too much.

"Enough!" I shouted.

The world seemed to flip inside out around me.

I landed on the ground with a clatter, gasping for breath. The world settled back again. The air was still and clear. The magic-working had disappeared—and so had my spell. My gown was white again. My chest was almost flat. I had never been so grateful to see it before.

Mr. Gregson was staring at me, his mouth wide open.

I turned and ran. Up the hill, past the house, stumbling over rocky outcroppings. Twice I fell and had to pick myself up with bleeding hands, skinned by the rocks that pushed up out of the grass. My breath came hard, burning against my chest. My vision narrowed into a tiny, bright tunnel ahead of me. I didn't care where I was running. I just had to get away. I had to—

I ran straight into a man's hard chest. He staggered. Strong hands rose to grip my arms and keep me upright.

I blinked and looked up, panting. "I'm so sorry," I began.

The words dried up in my throat.

Sir Neville Collingwood smiled down at me. "Not at all," he said. "It is a great pleasure, Miss Katherine. In fact, I have been looking for you."

Thirteen

"*Your sisters are most concerned,*" Sir Neville said.

"My—oh!" Relief pushed my breath out in a rush. "My sisters told you I was missing. I see. Thank you." I stepped back as his hands fell away from my arms. "I saw them go inside the house just a moment ago. I'll follow them straightaway."

"Not quite yet, I think," said Sir Neville.

"I beg your pardon?"

His lips drew back over his teeth as he smiled. "You must reassure me first, I fear. You see, I was most concerned as well."

At the look in his eyes, I took another step backward. Suddenly the bleak, rocky hillside felt far too empty around us. The cool breeze sent goose bumps skittering across my skin. I took a quick look behind me. No one else was in sight, or in calling distance. The massive stone walls of the manor house, below us, were so thick that no one would hear if I cried out.

I moistened my lips and raised my chin as I turned back to Sir Neville. "I'm afraid I don't quite take your meaning, sir."

"No?" He raised his thick, dark eyebrows. "You surprise me. In fact . . ." He stepped forward, forcing me to step back again. The breeze ruffled the black hair across his sloping forehead. His gaze fixed upon me like a hawk intent on mesmerizing his prey. "You surprise me a great deal, Miss Katherine. You are not what I'd expected."

"I don't know what you're talking about," I said.

"Then pray allow me to enlighten you."

His hand shot out and caught my wrist. I stumbled, preparing to twist away and escape—but he only tucked my hand into the curve of his forearm like any gentleman might, courteously giving a lady his arm for support. But his touch did not feel at all courteous. It tingled in all the wrong ways, like a thick, smothering cloak sweeping around me, muffling my breath.

A smoky, bitter scent flooded my nostrils, like burned meat. I would have turned to look for the source of the smell, but I didn't want to look away from Sir Neville. As his strong, hot fingers pressed against mine, I shivered and swallowed down sickness.

"It is cold, is it not?" Sir Neville said. "Do let me persuade you to take a turn around the house with me. Exercise is very warming. And it is always so much easier to have a proper discussion as one walks."

I dug in my heels and strained my ears, listening for any sound in the distance. Even Mr. Gregson would be welcome right now—at least he and Sir Neville might distract each other long enough for me to escape. What would Angeline do in this situation? What would Mama have done?

Not magic, that was for certain. *You would do well to shield your magic when he is nearby,* Mr. Gregson had said, and I believed him. Not that I knew enough magic to get away anyway. Somehow, I didn't think Sir Neville would be fooled if I suddenly turned back into Lady Fotherington right in front of him.

So I was on my own.

"I should go back," I said. "My sisters are looking for me, as you said. And—"

"And?" Sir Neville asked. His smile curved unpleasantly. "And—having listened to a bit of vulgar gossip, perhaps, about my past—you are afraid to be alone with me?"

That did it. "I am not afraid," I said, and met his eyes with a glare. "Not of you or of anybody else!"

"I am very pleased to hear it," said Sir Neville. "In that case, your sisters can wait for just a few minutes longer."

He walked forward, pulling me by my trapped hand and guiding me the rest of the way up the rocky hillside. Seething, I followed his direction.

No one could call me a coward.

But I had a nasty feeling that my sisters might call me a fool, for letting myself be tricked so easily.

Never mind, I told myself. After all, no matter what Sir Neville thought he was up to, this ought to be a perfect opportunity for advancing my own schemes. If I wanted to find a way to save Elissa from him, what could be better than a private conversation, to find out what he really wanted?

"Rumors," Sir Neville said reflectively, as we reached the top of the hill, "can be so deceptive, can they not?"

"Um . . . I suppose so?" I said. This was starting to sound like one of my least favorite kinds of conversation— Elissa's reflections on Morality in Private and Public Life.

As we walked along the long, rambling top of the hill above Grantham Abbey, the whole countryside stretched underneath us—the great stone manor leading down to the stone ruins, empty now, and the wild river beyond. The woods across the river looked thick and impenetrable, and I remembered the discussion of highwaymen at dinner last night. At least that had been interesting. Shouldn't a private conversation with a dangerous wife-murderer be even more exciting?

"My past, for instance, has garnered the most remarkable set of rumors," Sir Neville said. "Rather amusing, actually, in their absurdity. And even yours . . ."

"Mine?" I blinked back into full attention. "There aren't any rumors about my past. I don't have any."

"No past at all? Or no rumors? My dear young lady . . ." I didn't like Sir Neville's smile. It looked like he had scored a point in a game I didn't know how to play. "Everyone has a past," he said. "And even when our own lives are too short, or too secluded, to garner gossip, we are inevitably drawn into those of our parents."

"Parents," I repeated. *Oh.* I felt my heartbeat speed up. I tried to look as calm and fashionably bored as possible. "My father is a clergyman, sir. He could hardly—"

"Your father, yes, an excellent man, I'm sure. And yet . . ." Sir Neville trailed the words as delicately as a fishing lure. "He did make one grave mistake, did he not? In his choice of wife?"

"He did not!" I said, and stopped walking to glare at him. "There was nothing wrong with Mama."

"No?" Sir Neville's smile deepened. If he'd scored one point before, he looked now as if he'd scored at least twenty. "I see you thought first of your own mother. How charming. Of course, for all you know, I might well have been referring to your stepmother."

"Stepmama?" I stared at him. "No one disapproves of Stepmama." Well, apart from me, obviously. But I didn't think I should say that.

"Perhaps not," Sir Neville said. "And yet, admirable as she may undeniably be, she might, perhaps, be considered not entirely qualified for her particular position."

"As Papa's wife?"

"As your mother, my dear."

I gritted my teeth. "She is not my mother."

"Indeed not. And I would wager . . ." Sir Neville cocked one eyebrow. "She has no idea how to handle you, does she?"

Curses. He must have seen me tear fish-faced Mrs. Banfield's dress and break all those wineglasses last night.

"I don't know what you mean," I said, and looked away from him. "Anyway, last night was an accident. I didn't fall over on purpose."

"I beg your pardon?" For the first time in the conversation, he sounded startled. "I wasn't referring to that little incident in the gallery, Miss Katherine. I was referring to who you are, by birth and nature."

"Oh," I said. *Oh, Lord!* I had to restrain myself from groaning.

Not another lecture! We were high above the manor house now, much too far for a quick escape. I calculated distances anyway. Which was worse: to stay and be lectured on propriety by a wife-murderer, or to go back inside and be lectured on my disappearance by my sisters? Perhaps—

"You see," said Sir Neville, "very few people in good society understand how to cope with an unruly magical talent in their midst. And when that talent extends beyond mere witchcraft, into higher realms and unsavory secret Orders—"

I jerked away. His arm felt as if it had turned to steel,

trapping my hand against his body. I pulled as hard as I could, but I couldn't escape his grip.

He stood perfectly still and spoke as calmly as if I weren't struggling with all my strength to pull away from him. "Did you think no one would notice your fireworks in the house earlier? Or just now? Or last night?"

"Last night?" I repeated. My mind was whirling so quickly, I could hardly stand. But I hadn't done any magic last night. Had I? All I'd done was talk to Angeline and Mr. Carlyle and then—

He kept talking as if I hadn't even spoken. "The use of magic emits a particular sort of vibration in the aether, you know, to those who know how to recognize it. There are many different variations. A mere hedge-witch's spell is one thing; a more powerful witch's spell is another. And when it comes to the workings of an untrained and highly dangerous Guardian . . . I wondered why Aloysius Gregson was here at this house party. Has he bothered to tell you yet what his Order does to witches like your own lovely sister Angeline? I wonder how long it will take him to recognize what she is."

"Let me go or I'll kick you," I said. I was breathing hard. I could hear my heartbeat thumping in my ears.

"A dangerous threat indeed," said Sir Neville. "And yet I wouldn't, if I were you. For one thing, it would be remarkably uncivilized—and everyone agrees that your mother, for all her flaws, was never less than charmingly civilized. Perhaps even more importantly, though, your stepmother is actually watching us at this very moment, and you wouldn't want to scandalize her, would you?" He pointed with his free hand to the house below us.

I turned, my hand still trapped in Sir Neville's arm, and saw that he was right. Stepmama stood outside the far corner of the house, shading her eyes as she looked up at us. For once, I felt nothing but sheer relief at the sight of her familiar figure.

"Well, then," I said brightly. "I really should be going. So if you'll only let me go—"

"Your stepmother doesn't know you've been practicing witchcraft, does she? Or even more secretive Guardian magic?" Sir Neville watched me, smiling. "No? I thought not." He shook his head. "What a pity. To have to disillusion such an admirable woman . . ."

"I am not practicing witchcraft," I said. "I told you—I don't know what you're talking about! And I'm not a Guardian, either, whatever that is." Stepmama was hurrying toward us now, still out of hearing, but only barely. I said urgently, "I don't know what you've heard or imagined about my mother, but—"

"Oh, I know a great deal about your mother," Sir Neville murmured. "Probably more than you do, in fact. It's a pity you didn't inherit her ability to tell a good lie— by all accounts, she was quite an accomplished deceiver, while you, on the other hand, are quite, quite unconvincing in your attempts. Somehow I don't think your stepmother will have much difficulty in accepting my version of events, rather than your own. I wonder how surprised she will be by the news? Not very, perhaps. After all, it was only to be expected, from your mother's daughters."

"Please!" I hissed. Stepmama was only fifty feet below us now, and I could see from the rigidity of her smile (aimed, of course, straight at Sir Neville) that she was already furious. "You don't need to tell her anything. There is nothing to tell."

"If there is nothing to tell, then surely there can be no danger in repeating it. Perhaps, after all, she may not mind. Perhaps she would be proud to tell your father that—"

"No!" I said. It came out as a croak.

I could tell immediately that I had made a mistake. Satisfaction lit up Sir Neville's face until he looked almost demonic. I didn't have time to make it right or think of anything clever. All I could do was whisper, "Please. Please don't tell her. Please."

"Hmm." Sir Neville patted my trapped hand. "For your sake, I shall consider the matter. But we must talk again, later. In detail." He raised his voice. "Mrs. Stephenson! What a charming day it is for a walk, don't you think? Your stepdaughter was kind enough to join me on a morning constitutional to tell me all about her fascinating oldest sister."

"How very . . . enterprising of her," Stepmama said, and bared her teeth at me. I could tell she was trying not to pant from the exertion of her climb. "Katherine, you were very silly not to tell us where you were going. Your sisters were distressed."

"I'm sorry, ma'am," I said. "I'll come back now."

I darted a look up at Sir Neville, wondering what I would do if he refused to let me go. But he stepped away, bowing over my hand as he released it.

"Charming, Miss Katherine. If your sisters have anything like your talents . . ." I saw the teeth in his smile. "I shall be even more impressed by them."

Sickness roiled in my stomach. Stepmama tsked behind me.

"For heaven's sake, Kat!" she hissed. "Curtsy!"

I curtsied. My head felt thick and numb. I couldn't think of anything to say to combat the victory in Sir Neville's eyes. And the warning.

I shall be even more impressed by them . . .

I remembered Mrs. Watson's story about his first wife. I didn't believe it anymore. Looking into Sir Neville's hard, dark eyes, I couldn't believe for an instant that he had killed his first wife out of jealousy, or for any other reason as simple as that. But I was absolutely certain that he had murdered her. He couldn't be allowed to marry Elissa.

I had no idea how I could stop him. The worst part was, I could tell he knew exactly how helpless I was feeling— and he was enjoying it. Deeply.

He bowed to Stepmama. "Madam. Please do pass my compliments along to your oldest daughter. I can hardly wait to see her again later."

Then he turned and walked away, every line of his body radiating smug, inexorable power.

Stepmama had to tug my arm twice to start me moving. "Whatever is the matter with you this morning?"

"Helpless," I said dully. I could barely move my tongue to say the words. My gaze followed Sir Neville's retreating figure. I couldn't make myself look away.

Oh, I'd heard of helplessness before, but I'd never truly felt it. Now that I'd discovered the feeling, I didn't like it one bit.

But how could I possibly fight him?

"'Helpless'?" Stepmama repeated. "What nonsense are you spouting now? Speak sense!"

I took a deep breath and wrenched my eyes off Sir Neville. "You're right," I said. "It is nonsense. I was wrong."

"I beg your pardon?" Stepmama peered into my eyes. "Are you quite well, Kat? Perhaps you've spent too long in the sun today. Although, heaven knows, you ought to be inured to that by now, after all the days you've spent running wild in the fields around our own house. But you cannot behave like such a feral creature here! Disappearing without a word to any of us, forcing your poor sisters to tramp up and down the manor and the abbey in search of you before they finally came to me for maternal assistance. . . ."

You mean, before you finally nosed out for yourself what they were up to, I thought—but it wasn't worth arguing the point. Not now.

I let the rest of Stepmama's lecture wash over me as

we walked back down the hill to the manor house. A gold and brown carriage rattled down the drive ahead, no doubt carrying even more guests to gossip and stare at my behavior, but I ignored it. I didn't have time to care about trivialities anymore. If there was one thing I knew for sure, it was that I was not a helpless person. So the answer to my problems was very simple.

I would just have to find a weapon I could use against Sir Neville. No matter how difficult that might be, it had to be better than letting him hurt my oldest sister. But what that weapon might be . . .

"Stop gnawing your lip, Kat!" Stepmama hissed as we stepped inside the house. Footmen bowed as they held the great doors open for us, and Stepmama put on a social smile as she whispered through her teeth, "It is unladylike, and it looks ridiculous!"

"Yes, Stepmama," I muttered. With an effort, I kept myself from rolling my eyes at her. No doubt that would be unladylike too.

"You may think yourself very clever," she added, as we walked toward the main staircase at a tired turtle's pace, "but your scheme to turn Sir Neville against your sister has obviously had no effect. I don't know what you chose to tell him about poor, sweet Elissa—"

"Nothing that didn't make him happy," I said, and scowled.

"You will kindly remove that expression from your face at once," Stepmama said. "And in the future—"

But I never managed to hear what the future had in store for me. Just as we started up the staircase, the front doors swung open behind us once again, with a bustle of footmen snapping to new attention. At the very same moment, Lady Graves appeared at the top of the stairs and came running down them, far too quickly to be considered truly ladylike. A maid trailed behind her, still holding an open letter. Lady Graves barely spared either Stepmama or me a glance as she rushed past us, toward the open front doors.

I started to turn around to see what was happening, but Stepmama caught my elbow with a grip of steel and propelled me up the next step of the staircase.

"Ladies do not stare!" she hissed. "Just keep walking, Kat, and later, I am certain—"

Her instructions were cut off by an all-too-familiar voice speaking from the doorway.

"My dear Lady Graves."

"And my dear Lady Fotherington," Lady Graves answered. "How delighted I am that you could come, after all."

Fourteen

I had to grab the marble banister of the staircase for balance. My mind spun wildly. Had my spell not vanished, after all? Had I split into two, back in the abbey ruins? Was that me down there, talking to Lady Graves, at the very same time that—

"Of course I had to come," Lady Fotherington purred. "How could I stay away from such a gathering? Especially with so many charming gentlemen among your company?"

Well, that proved it wasn't me, at least. I would never say anything so disgusting, no matter how many spells had been placed upon me.

Unfortunately, that left me with only one conclusion: Lady Fotherington really was standing right below me.

Right below . . . Oh, Lord. I'd frozen on the third step of the grand staircase, in full view of the open front doors. The moment Lady Fotherington looked away from her hostess, she'd see me standing as still as a stick, just waiting for her.

I lunged forward, up to the next step. But Stepmama's grip was still tight on my arm, and she didn't follow me. To my horror, I could feel her starting to turn back.

"No!" I hissed. I yanked hard, pulling her up, stumbling, to join me on my higher step. "You said a lady never stares," I whispered. "You said—"

"Don't be absurd, Katherine," Stepmama said, in a horribly normal, horribly loud voice. She let go of my arm and shook her head. "We mustn't rush away now, just when a new guest is arriving!"

There was a sudden, startled silence behind us. I cringed. Stepmama swung around, beaming.

"Why, my dear Lady Fotherington," she trilled. "I do hope you remember me. We met at the Whitelaws' ball in Grosvenor Street ten years ago, and—oh, good, you do remember. But I had no idea you would be attending Rosemary's little house party!"

I clung to the banister. I couldn't bring myself to turn around. Maybe, if all Lady Fotherington could see was the back of my head, she might not—

"Why, Margaret Stephenson," Lady Fotherington said. "As I live and breathe. Of course I remember meeting you—you were still Margaret Havisham then, were you not? What a charming surprise to see you here. And is that one of your stepdaughters I see beside you?"

I gritted my teeth and turned around as slowly as I could. The front doorway came slowly into view before me: Lady Fotherington resplendent in a fashionable green morning gown, with her dark hair arranged in an elegant trailing style; Lady Graves with her hands still held out in warm welcome; and all the footmen trying to look as if they didn't have eyes or ears or brains, only uniforms. The very worst part came when Lady Fotherington deliberately met my eyes and smiled. She didn't have to speak. I could read her triumph even from fifteen feet away. And her nose, just as Mr. Gregson had told me, was as perfectly straight as if I had never even touched it.

"My youngest stepdaughter, Miss Katherine," Stepmama said, and put one hand behind my back. From the doorway, it must have looked like a loving gesture. I knew better. I curtsied before she could remind me of my manners with a pinch.

"Charming," Lady Fotherington murmured. "But . . ." She turned her gaze back to Stepmama. "Isn't she a trifle young for house parties, Margaret? She looks—"

"She *is* rather young to be allowed in public," Stepmama said. "Indeed, I would have kept her in the nursery myself, where she belongs, but dear Rosemary did choose to insist—"

That did it. I smiled brilliantly at Lady Fotherington and

cut straight across Stepmama. "But don't you remember, Lady Fotherington? We've already met."

"I beg your pardon?" Lady Fotherington blinked rapidly, losing her smile.

"Don't be ridiculous, Katherine!" Stepmama glared at me. "Of course you haven't met. Lady Fotherington has only just arrived. There is no possible way in which—"

"But we have met, Stepmama," I said, in my most innocent voice. I widened my eyes for added effect— not for Stepmama's sake, of course; she would never be fooled by that—but for the benefit of our observers below. "And Lady Fotherington can't have just arrived, because I met her this morning in the abbey ruins. She was with that pleasant gentleman we met yesterday— Lady Graves's cousin from town. Mr. Gregson, I think his name is?"

I heard the hissing sound of Lady Fotherington's indrawn breath all the way across the foyer. But she didn't say a word. She didn't have to—Stepmama was bristling enough for three.

"That is quite enough out of you, young lady. Making up absurd stories to tease our hostess's guests—"

"But it isn't a story, Stepmama," I said sweetly. "It really happened. If you don't trust me, you can ask Elissa. She met the two of them there, as well. You wouldn't accuse Elissa of making up stories, would you?"

Stepmama looked like a startled frog, blowing up her cheeks with air and stuttering instead of speaking. But our hostess, Lady Graves, let out a low, delighted laugh.

"My, my, Lydia," Lady Graves said to Lady Fotherington. "From the mouths of innocents, eh?"

"Innocents . . . ," Lady Fotherington repeated.

She might have been trying for a light tone. But I could almost feel the steam that rose from her rigid figure all the way to where I stood on the stairs, looking down on both of them with my most harmless and puzzled look.

"I do beg your pardon, Lady Fotherington," I said. "Have I said something wrong?"

The look in Lady Fotherington's eyes was worth everything I'd suffered in the last few hours. I tried to memorize it, so I could enjoy it again later, during my sisters' inevitable lectures.

"I would never have mentioned seeing you and Mr. Gregson in the abbey ruins if I'd had any idea that you wouldn't like it," I said, and then stopped, biting down hard on my lower lip, before I could ruin the effect by laughing.

"Now, now. You can hardly blame the poor girl for not knowing better than to let your little secret out." Lady Graves took Lady Fotherington's arm. "My dear, you must tell me all about it. I want all the delicious details. I would never have guessed Aloysius to be your sort. You two have been cunning, haven't you?"

"Someone certainly has been," Lady Fotherington said coolly. "I must admit, I should quite like to talk to him right now." She shot me a meaningful glare.

"I imagine you would," Lady Graves said. "But just now, I am going to spirit you away for a proper interrogation, before you can agree on any stories with him. Margaret, won't you join us for tea and a spot of gossip in my dressing room?"

"Ah . . ." Stepmama hesitated, glancing between me and the two ladies.

It must have been an excruciating dilemma for her—whether to indulge herself in a towering scold over my behavior, or to be included in a private gossip with two fashionable women from the high society she longed for. I wondered if the effort of choice would turn her cheeks purple. Perhaps she would even explode. I watched her with interest to see what would happen.

"Now, Margaret, I am sure that Miss Katherine is old enough to find her way back to her own room by herself," Lady Graves said.

"Indeed," Lady Fotherington said, and smiled thinly. "One certainly does receive the impression that Miss Katherine is capable of anything."

I smiled back as enchantingly as possible, just to make her seethe. "That is very kind of you to say, Lady Fotherington."

Lady Graves glanced between us. Her lips twitched. "As I said. Margaret? Lydia? Shall we retire to my dressing room?"

"I would be delighted," Stepmama said. But before she stepped away, she leaned in to whisper in my ear. "You will go directly to your room, Kat. Or else!"

"Yes, Stepmama," I said, and batted my eyelashes at her.

She couldn't let out any shrieks of rage in public, not in front of Lady Graves and Lady Fotherington. But the look on her face was enough for me.

I smiled all the way up the stairs.

I might have kept my smile even longer if Angeline hadn't caught me.

"Aha!" She swooped down on me as I turned into the corridor that led to our bedrooms. "I thought I heard your voice."

I tried out my innocent, wide-eyed look on her. "Were you looking for me? I'm so sorry. If I'd had any idea—"

"Very amusing," Angeline said. "Now stop blinking like a fish, Kat. It won't have any effect on me. Or on Elissa, once I'm finished with you." She took my arm and started hauling me down the corridor as she spoke.

I said, "Stepmama's already given me a tedious, long lecture, so—"

"So that would be a good beginning, then," said Angeline. "Just you wait."

She swept me past the door to Elissa's room, past my door, and on to hers. She swung it open and pushed me inside. "You see?"

"Ah . . ." I stared at the irrefutable evidence. The closet door stood open. Mama's magic books sat in full view on top of the bed. The four valises that had been neatly stacked in the corner by the closet were scattered across the floor, knocked open and trailing clothes.

Angeline crossed her arms and leaned back against the closed bedroom door. There was no escape. "Now do you see why I'm so furious?" she said.

The best defense is a good offense, I thought. "What a mess," I said. "Has Stepmama seen how you keep your room tidy?" I shook my head portentously. "And that certainly doesn't look like a safe hiding place for Mama's books."

Angeline's glare should have burned my skin. I had to force myself not to step back.

"No?" she said. "Well, then, it's a good thing that isn't where I left them. But when I came back to the room after breakfast, they were lying on the floor, underneath the bed, which isn't where I left them either. And the rest of the room"—she waved at the scattered luggage—"was as you see it."

I put on my most offended voice. "And you think I did this?" I asked.

"No, you ninny, of course I don't." Angeline rolled her eyes. "If you knew anything about magic, you would be able to feel all the magical residue and know that I'd left a spell here—a strong one—and someone else broke it. Someone truly powerful. Trust me, you wouldn't have been remotely capable of doing it."

"Oh." I slumped with relief. "Well. That's all right, then." I sat down on the bed. "I'm glad you realized that. Because of course I would never—"

Angeline's eyes narrowed. "But I think you know who did."

"What?" I straightened with a start. "What are you talking about? Why would I know anything about it? That's absurd!"

Angeline ticked off the points on her fingers. "One: You're babbling. You never babble unless you're nervous—which means that you do know who did this, and you don't want to tell me. Two: Last night you asked me where Mama's magic books were. I assumed you were only after them for yourself. But you kept asking if they were safe. So." She advanced on me like the Angel of Vengeance. "You knew that someone would come looking for them."

"No, I didn't," I said. "You're leaping to conclusions. Papa would tell you that that is very bad logic, and—"

"The question is," Angeline said inexorably, "how did you know that they were in danger? The only answer I could come up with is that you told someone about Mama's magic books. Someone who should never have been trusted with that information. So, Kat." She stood over me, her hands on her hips. "Whom did you tell?"

I squirmed, pinned under her glare like a butterfly under glass. I knew perfectly well, and believed with all my heart, that I did not have to obey Angeline in anything. But sometimes it was difficult to remember that . . . especially when she was so convinced of the exact opposite.

It was patently unfair. She was only five years older than me.

"I didn't tell anybody," I said, and jerked my chin up to return her glare with interest. "Now stop interrogating me. I haven't done anything wrong!"

"Now, there's a likely story." Angeline laughed. "I don't think—"

A knock sounded at the door behind her. "Angeline?" It was Elissa's voice. *Saved.* I relaxed and grinned up at Angeline as cheekily as I could. "I think we're finished now," I said. "Don't you?"

She sneered down at me. "Don't even imagine it. Elissa is just as unhappy about your disappearance as I was."

"And how does she feel about these?" I scooped Mama's magic books off the bed. "Have you told her about them yet?"

"Give me those!" Angeline grabbed them, but I didn't let them go. "Kat, if you don't—"

The doorknob turned. Then it hit the lock and stopped. It turned again.

"I can hear Kat inside with you," Elissa called. "Why have you locked the door?"

"Yes, Angeline," I said. "Why have you locked the door?" I batted my eyelashes at her. "Could you possibly be keeping secrets from our sister?"

"That's it." Angeline snatched the books from my hands. "Don't even imagine that you're safe now, Kat. I will find out the truth."

I sneered back at her. "Fine. Then maybe Elissa can find out the truth about you, too."

The doorknob rattled. "This is absurd," Elissa hissed through the door. "What is going on in there?"

"It's not my fault," I called out. "I want to let you in. It's Angeline who—ow!"

Angeline straightened. Her cheeks were flushed from bending over to shove the books under the bed. Her eyes were glowing—no doubt from the pleasure of kicking me hard on the way. She crossed the room and threw open the door.

"Elissa," she said. "Come in."

Elissa's cheeks were flushed too.

"Do you have any notion of how embarrassing that was?" she said. "I was passed by two people while you made me stand out there, rapping. Two people! The looks they gave me—"

"Good God, it must have been a fate worse than death," Angeline said, and closed the door behind Elissa with a bang.

"Must you be so vulgar?" Elissa swept across the room and stopped, staring at the wreckage beyond the bed. "What on earth has happened to your bedroom?" She swung around and looked back and forth between me and Angeline. "Have you two been fighting again?"

I opened my mouth. But before I could say a word, Angeline said, "Yes. We have." She crossed her arms and gave me a sardonic look. "Kat started it."

"I did not! Elissa—"

"Never mind." Elissa sank onto the bed beside me. "I don't even want to know the particulars."

"Just as well," Angeline murmured, and crossed the room to throw herself down across the pillows on her bed. "So. What have you come for, darling sister?"

"Really, Angeline." Elissa glared at her. "You are in the oddest humor today."

"I wonder why," said Angeline, and darted me a malevolent look. I stuck my tongue out at her, behind Elissa's back.

I had to pull it back in fast when Elissa turned to look at me. "I looked everywhere for you this morning, Kat. You really mustn't disappear without telling anybody."

"This is my third lecture," I said. "Please, please, may I finally be forgiven now? I didn't mean any harm."

Angeline snorted. Elissa sighed.

"I know it must seem very tedious to stay cooped up in your room when the abbey and the manor house are here to explore, but you are old enough by now to understand the rules of propriety. Lady Graves has been very generous in letting you be a part of the house party despite all of Stepmama's arguments. If you embarrass her now by doing something foolish and immature—"

"I won't," I said. "I won't, I won't, I won't! Now, please, can the lectures finally be over?"

Elissa put her hand on mine. "Do you promise not to go exploring again without telling one of us first?"

"Yes," I said. "At least, I will if I can find any of you to tell."

"Fair enough," said Angeline, and swept her legs off the bed, preparing to stand up. "You two can stay and weep and forgive each other all day long if you like, but I won't. I'm going down to the drawing room to—"

"Keep an eye on Mr. Carlyle?" I supplied. I braced myself for possible flight, watching Angeline's face get more and more flushed as I spoke. "Monitor his flirtations? Sigh if he—" I leaped backward as Angeline lunged for me.

"Angeline, don't!" Elissa snapped, and Angeline subsided back onto the pillows, even though I could still see murder in her eyes. "Kat, behave," Elissa added, keeping a wary eye on our sister. "Both of you, be still." She took a deep breath. "Honestly. I came up here to tell you something, and you drove it completely out of my head."

"Honestly, Angeline," I said.

She narrowed her eyes at me in a way that meant: *Revenge.*

Elissa said quickly, "We're going out tomorrow night, all of us, on an expedition to the local assembly ball. Kat, we'll have to look through your gowns and see if we can quickly make something up a little finer for you. Angeline, I thought perhaps the rose. . . ."

Angeline shrugged her shoulders and, for once, escaped a lecture from Elissa on how unladylike it was to shrug. I didn't blame Elissa for letting the gesture pass unremarked—even I was starting to wonder if I'd pushed Angeline too far.

"I'll find something to wear," Angeline said. "Don't worry about me."

"Good." Elissa looked warily between us. "Kat, perhaps you should come with me."

"Wait," I said. I had only just realized. "We can't go out anywhere tomorrow night, can we?"

"Whyever not?" Elissa blinked. "I just told you—"

Angeline's smile made prickles of fear run up my spine. "Let me guess. Kat's hatched some new scheme for tomorrow night, and going out would ruin it? What a tragedy that would be, and yet—"

"No," I said. "It's nothing like that. But it isn't safe to leave the house at night. Is it?"

"I beg your pardon?" Elissa stared at me. "What are you talking about?"

I stared right back at her. Hadn't either of them had a decent gossip with their dinner companions last night? Surely I wasn't the only one who had heard the news.

"But what about the highwayman?" I said.

Fifteen

For once, I didn't actually mind being overruled. As I waited to step into Lady Graves's sixth carriage the next night, holding my battered reticule in one hand and lifting my skirts up off the ground with the other, I felt a delicious thrill of anticipation.

Highwayman, I thought.

Of course, I knew we might not be lucky that night. There would be carriages driving to this assembly from all across this part of Yorkshire, so the chances of the highwayman actually attacking our particular carriage were perishingly slim. But he had to attack someone, surely. Otherwise it would be a wasted night for him. Even the simple act of driving to the assembly and back, when such an attack might happen at any moment, had to be a better adventure than another night spent smothered in Lady Graves's drawing room, making inane small talk and listening to Sir Neville drop horrible veiled threats while Lady Fotherington and Mr. Gregson watched me from opposite sides of the room. Last night I'd felt like a mouse being stalked by three great cats. It was not a comfortable feeling.

Much to Stepmama's surprise, I'd actually leaped at the prospect of spending all day today until now sitting safely with her in her bedroom to sew extra ruffles and a new neckline and sleeve caps onto my best gown for the ball. I'd even managed to listen to her usual lectures on ladylike deportment and propriety without exploding from sheer boredom. I'd had tonight to look forward to, after all.

"Come along, Kat!" Stepmama said. "You're making everyone wait for you."

I followed her into the carriage and pressed myself as close to the window as possible. The cushions in Lady Graves's carriage were thick and comfortable, and it would have been easy to rest back against the padded seats and close my eyes. But I didn't want to miss a second of the preparations.

The sky was only just starting to fade into twilight now, so the torches the footmen carried had not been lit. But I could see something else as I looked through the window. Two more men swung up to sit beside our driver—and both of them were carrying rifles. I sucked in my breath.

"Is something wrong, Kat?" Elissa asked.

I shook my head. "Nothing at all," I said happily. I peered through the window, twisting my head to try to see all the way up to the driver's seat on top of the carriage. No luck. "I wonder if they would let me sit with them on the way back," I said. "I could hold one of the rifles for them."

"Heaven forbid," said Elissa, and she and Angeline and Stepmama all exchanged a meaningful look.

I ignored it. "I told you it was dangerous," I said. "You should have believed me."

"It is not dangerous," Stepmama said. "Rosemary has taken all reasonable precautions. No highwayman would dare to attack a line of six carriages—particularly not when each of the carriages is armed."

"Mm," I said, and angled my head farther to try to see the other carriages. "Perhaps if we were separated, though—"

"That is quite enough!" Stepmama said. "You will kindly refrain from any more speculations on the matter. Especially—" She cut herself off as a fifth figure stepped into the carriage.

"I do hope you'll pardon the squeeze," Frederick Carlyle said, and grinned at all of us. "I'm afraid all the carriages are equally packed, so I thought, if it wouldn't be too much of an imposition . . ."

I looked at Angeline, waiting for her to say something sharp about rakish flirtation. Instead she blinked rapidly and looked away from him. I saw color rising on her cheeks. She must have been too angry to speak. So I smiled brilliantly at him.

"You can sit next to me," I said. "There's plenty of space." At least there would be if Stepmama moved over.

"Thank you, Miss Katherine," Mr. Carlyle said, and made me a sweeping bow. "You are very kind," he added solemnly, and winked at me.

"Thank you," I said primly, and winked back.

I didn't mind shoving myself even closer to the window to make space for him. "Have you seen the rifles the footmen are carrying to protect us from the highwayman?" I asked. I pointed out the window to where the other carriages were being loaded.

"Katherine," Stepmama said in an undertone, behind Mr. Carlyle's back.

"I have indeed," Mr. Carlyle said. "Have you ever shot a rifle yourself, Miss Katherine?"

"Not yet," I said.

"Not ever," Angeline amended. "For which we are all eternally grateful."

Mr. Carlyle's lips twitched. "I'll teach you when you're older, if you like," he said. I saw him glance surreptitiously at Angeline from the corner of his eyes. Leaning closer to me, he added in a stage whisper, "I do believe your sister Angeline might be an excellent shot too. She does have the temperament for it, don't you think?"

"Now that would be far too dangerous," I whispered back, with great satisfaction.

The carriage door closed. I heard the crack of the driver's whip.

"Thank goodness," Stepmama said. "We're on our way."

The carriage rolled smoothly down the drive and into the deep green overhang of the woods. As the sky darkened, the woods on our right looked more and more ominous, full of tantalizing shadows, and the river on our left became a deep, dark mystery.

But still, the highwayman didn't appear. By the time we arrived at the local assembly room, an hour later, I was completely disgruntled.

You would think he would have noticed that Lady Graves had visitors. You would think, if he wanted to make a good picking, he would aim for the top.

If I found out that he had wasted his time attacking some completely impoverished family in full moonlight while we were driving down that whole long, shadowy road full of possibilities, I would . . . well, I would be seriously displeased.

At least Angeline seemed to have finally gotten over her temper—with Mr. Carlyle, at least. Elissa had engaged him in polite conversation at first, and then Angeline had gradually unbent. By the time the carriage ride ended, she and Mr. Carlyle were actually laughing at each other's jokes and trading stories like old friends.

Until we stepped out of the carriage.

"Mr. Carlyle!"

"Oh, Mr. Carlyle!"

"Oh, there you are, Mr. Carlyle!"

The three young ladies who'd breakfasted with him for the past two mornings fluttered toward us in a cooing flock from the next carriage over. In the darkness, I couldn't make out the exact shades of their gowns, but they were all wearing light pastels that matched their fair hair and skin, and their fans flapped madly in front of their faces.

"Isn't this exciting?"

"I feel so giddy with nerves, I vow, I positively cannot breathe!"

"Only look at my hand, see how it's trembling, Mr. Carlyle!"

"Humph," said Angeline, and turned away pointedly.

I couldn't take my eyes off them. They were just like birds, but person-shaped. As they clustered around Mr. Carlyle, their fans fluttering, they let out cheeping sounds of glee, and I had to bite down hard on my lower lip to keep myself from laughing out loud.

"Ladies, if you'll excuse me . . ." Mr. Carlyle was grinning. He met my eyes across their fair heads for a moment, and we shared a look of perfect understanding. I bit my lip harder as I watched him try to disentangle himself from all the fans and clinging hands. It didn't work. But I was impressed by the ingenuity of his next attempt. "If you'll pardon me," he said to them, straight-faced, "I had actually promised to be Miss Angeline Stephenson's escort to the ball, so—"

"Oh, no!"

"Oh, Mr. Carlyle—"

"But Mr. Carlyle, please—"

"You needn't worry yourself about it, sir," Angeline said. Her voice cracked through their chirps like a whip through feathers. "I am sure I am perfectly happy to excuse you."

I made a face at her. Hadn't she even noticed her cue?

"Come now, Miss Angeline," Mr. Carlyle said. He looked across the flock of pastels to where she stood by the carriage, her chin up high like an angry queen, and his voice shivered with laughter. "I really must insist on fulfilling my obligations. What kind of gentleman should I be otherwise?"

"I would never desire to be considered an obligation."

"Not even a charming one?" he asked.

"Good evening to you," Angeline said frigidly, and swept past the flock, head held high.

Elissa and I followed in her wake. I could have pointed out that it was a waste of effort—Stepmama had just been gathered into a low-voiced conversation with two older women from the next carriage, and it was clear she wouldn't be ready to move inside the assembly rooms for at least five more minutes—but when I opened my mouth to tell Angeline so, Elissa touched my arm and shook her head.

Later, she mouthed.

I sighed. Behind me I could hear Mr. Carlyle's laugh mingle with the flock's chirps and giggles. At least he wasn't suffering too badly. Stepmama and her cronies looked as if they'd settled in for a full round of vigorous, pre-ball gossip. I settled myself in for a tedious wait.

We might still have been in Yorkshire, but the local assembly rooms were in a small, round-roofed building that looked like it wanted to be in ancient Greece. It had arrived about two thousand years too late. Marble pillars rose up to support the overhang, but they just looked silly beside the plain, low-roofed stone butcher's shop on its left and the pastrycook on its right.

Lights shone through the windows, and music and voices filtered through the closed doors. The rest of the party from Grantham Abbey shuffled around in a genteel confusion behind and around us, trying to avoid the horse pats on the ground and the lean dogs scavenging in the street nearby. In the confusion, I almost didn't notice the light, insistent tug at my arm. No, not at my arm itself, I realized—at the reticule that hung off it.

I clapped my hand to the cord it hung by, just before it could snap. "Careful—," I began.

Then I saw who it was.

"I thought so," said Sir Neville, and let the reticule go. He smiled. In the shadows, he seemed even taller, and I had to resist the urge to back away from him. "You couldn't leave it behind even for one night, could you?" he asked softly.

I licked my lips, trying to think of what I could say. *"I don't know what you're talking about"* had been used up in our conversation the day before. Anyway, it wouldn't work. Not now.

The reticule was warm against my fingers, the mirror's heat burning through the thin, beaded cloth. Obviously, Sir Neville had felt that heat. Equally obviously—and much worse—he knew exactly what it meant.

"I—that is—," I began.

But Elissa turned around before I could think of what to say. "Sir Neville!" She curtsied hastily. "I am sorry. I didn't hear you approach."

Angeline turned too at the sound of Elissa's voice. Her gaze flicked first, razor sharp, to the flock of giggling, chirping females behind us. Then she looked back to our own group.

"Sir Neville," she said, and bared her teeth in a smile as she curtsied. "What a delightful surprise."

"Delightful for myself, indeed," said Sir Neville. "But surely no surprise." He took Elissa's hand and raised it to his lips. "I could hardly stay away."

Elissa's cheeks flushed, and her eyelashes swept down to cover her eyes. I gritted my teeth. Heat rose from my reticule, warming my hands. The heat of magical power . . . completely useless in this situation. What could I do, apart from snatching Elissa and vanishing with her into the Golden Hall? That would be no use at all. Firstly, I would have to listen to her lectures there for hours, even if Mr. Gregson or Lady Fotherington didn't appear as well, to make up a horrible magical party. And secondly, hiding in the Golden Hall could hardly be considered a long-term solution.

So I just stood there, choking on rage and that hideous, unbearable feeling I'd discovered earlier. *Helplessness.* I breathed in the smell of charred meat and almost gagged. Someone in a nearby house must have let their dinner burn.

I could actually feel Sir Neville's power circling through the air around him. It prickled against my skin like a thousand tiny needles. It made me want to sink to the ground like a coward and give up.

Weapon, I thought. All I had to do was find the right weapon to use against him.

It was so laughable, I couldn't even pretend to believe it. All I could do was clench my jaw to hold myself back. Even if I didn't know how to fight Sir Neville in a way I could win, I did know that launching myself at him with my fists in public would do nobody any good at all.

Although it would feel satisfying. . . .

A discreet cough sounded behind me. "Sir Neville," Mr. Gregson said.

For once, his voice came as a welcome interruption. I looked back and found him standing just behind me, his spectacles glinting oddly in the shadows. He smiled faintly but didn't look at me.

"Gregson." Sir Neville turned away from Elissa, focusing his hard gaze on my would-be tutor. "I hadn't expected to see you here."

"No?" Mr. Gregson said mildly. "You know I enjoy observing local customs. Especially when something worthwhile is at stake."

"You know I enjoy winning," said Sir Neville, and his stare hardened into a fierce glare. "You might as well have stayed at home."

"My, you're both acting mysterious," Angeline said, and yawned behind her fan. "Might the rest of us be included in your conversation, please, or must we all start speaking enthusiastically about the weather?"

"I . . . beg your pardon, Miss Angeline," Sir Neville said. It looked like it took a real effort for him to yank his gaze away from Mr. Gregson's calm face and assume an unconvincing smile. "Gregson and I are old friends, you see. We sometimes forget our company and lapse into childish banter when we are together."

Mr. Gregson coughed. It was not a sound of agreement. But when Sir Neville turned sharply to look at him, Mr. Gregson was smiling charmingly . . . at me.

"And how are you enjoying your first ball, Miss Katherine?" he asked. "Are you terribly excited by it?"

I narrowed my eyes at him. "I might be, if we ever went inside."

Dangerous as Mr. Gregson might be, at least I could breathe when I was around him. Ever since he'd arrived, the tight knot of tension—*helplessness*—in my throat had disappeared. The horrible smell of burned meat was gone. Even the prickles against my skin had eased. So I was happy to throw myself into battle against him once more.

"You must be very bored, though, after all those elegant London balls you usually attend," I said. "Sometimes," I added, looking him in the eye and thinking of the first night we'd met, "you probably don't even return to your townhouse until dawn. It must be exhausting."

Amusement glinted in his eyes. "It is a bit exhausting. And yet, I expect you might enjoy it too, if you gave the London life a chance."

Sir Neville muttered something under his breath.

"I beg your pardon, Sir Neville?" Mr. Gregson said.

Sir Neville bared his teeth. "I wouldn't recommend it, Miss Katherine," he said loudly. "I have known many young ladies who found that life more dangerous than they had expected. Some of them even lost their lives to it."

"Lost their lives to too much dancing?" Angeline said dryly. "My goodness. What pitiful young ladies you must have known, Sir Neville."

It wasn't until she'd finished saying it that I realized— and she did too, I could see it in her face—exactly which young lady Sir Neville had known.

His first wife, to be specific.

Angeline's face tightened into something sharp and dangerous. I clenched my hands around my skirts, feeling that choking sensation start up again.

Elissa flicked her fan out with a jerky, nervous gesture. "We shall all have to hope we may manage some dancing tonight, at least." Her voice sounded tight, almost as choked as I felt. "And look—here comes Stepmama. Perhaps we won't be out until dawn after all."

"Perhaps not," Mr. Gregson murmured, and faded back into the crowd as Stepmama approached.

Now that all the older women had broken up their gossip group, the rest of the crowd prepared for action. As Stepmama sailed toward us, the crowd pressed close, pushing us forward.

"Sir Neville!" she said brightly. "How delightful to see you. I hope you come prepared for dancing tonight."

"Indeed I do, Mrs. Stephenson," Sir Neville said. "I hope to dance with all three of your daughters tonight."

I gritted my teeth even harder and wished Mr. Gregson were still there to tarnish the smug arrogance on Sir Neville's face.

"Miss Stephenson, may I escort you into the ball?" Sir Neville asked, holding out his arm.

"She would be delighted," Stepmama answered for her, and Elissa took his arm.

She looked wistfully over his shoulder as she did it, and I looked too, but Mr. Collingwood was nowhere to be seen. *Poor Elissa*, I thought. She'd probably spent all day dreaming of dancing with Sir Neville's younger brother and enjoying the tragic bitterness of hopeless love.

The thought of it irritated me so much that it loosened the knot in my throat and let me speak. "Where is Mr. Collingwood tonight?" I asked Sir Neville.

"My brother?" He blinked. "I'm afraid he felt unwell and could not come."

"Oh, no!" Elissa said. Then she caught herself, looking guiltily up at her escort. "I mean—do please give him our condolences. It is terrible to miss a ball."

"Terrible indeed," said Sir Neville. His gaze had sharpened, but he didn't look displeased. "Those who miss it must be pitied," he added, and smiled.

I thought if I ever heard a double meaning again in my life, I might be violently sick.

I was still simmering as we all finally filed into the main assembly room and heard ourselves announced like kings and queens to the locals. And I was ready to throttle myself out of sheer boredom by the end of the first hour of the ball, when I'd sat on the sidelines with my hands folded, listening to Stepmama gossip, for longer than any reasonable creature could possibly stand.

But I was surprised when the orchestra drew to a sudden, screeching halt. The dancers in the middle of the floor stopped too, and the patterns broke into confusion as they all turned around, looking for the source of the interruption. Whispers and high-pitched speculation rose to fill the room.

A shot exploded in the center of the dance floor. Plaster rained down on the heads of the dancers. Screaming, they scattered toward the sidelines.

A man's confident voice rang out and silenced even the most panicked screams.

"Ladies and gentlemen," he called. "I am sorry to break up such a charming party, but I really must insist. My associates are here to assist me in asking you all to make a choice, and I beg you each to consider the question carefully: your money . . . or your life?"

The highwayman had arrived after all.

Sixteen

As the dancers scattered in a panicked rush, a man in a cloak and black half mask stood revealed in the center of the floor. His first pistol, now empty, was still aimed at the ceiling, where a large chunk of molded plaster was missing. Somehow, none of it had fallen on him.

He was smiling underneath the half mask, and he held a second loaded pistol ready in his right hand.

"You may form two lines, ladies and gentlemen," he said. "As quickly as possible, if you please."

"This is absurd!" It was the burly man who'd sat next to Mrs. Banfield on our first night, the one who'd told her not to worry about the highwayman. "It's only one impudent rascal. We can all—"

The second loaded pistol was suddenly aimed directly

at him across the room, and the burly man's neighbors were clearing away from him as rapidly as they had from the highwayman.

"I must request that no one does anything rash," the highwayman said. "Not even you, Major Connors."

The burly man's face flushed brick red. "How the devil do you know my name?"

"That, I'm afraid, is my own concern," said the highwayman. "Meanwhile . . ." He turned his head, and his gaze swept the room. "I think I really must keep one of you with me to help maintain order. But which one . . ."

I jumped up from my chair. "I'll come!" I said.

"Get down, Kat!" Stepmama hissed, and grabbed my arm. She flung her own fan, stretched wide, across my face to hide me from the highwayman's gaze. I batted it away with my free hand.

The highwayman met my eyes and laughed. "Very generously done," he said. "But I think perhaps . . ." He circled. It looked aimless, but I was suddenly strangely certain that it wasn't. The way his gaze searched the crowd . . . He pivoted to point. "There. You, please. Miss Stephenson."

It took a moment, through my excitement, for the name to penetrate. Then I lurched forward, and Stepmama fell back.

Elissa stepped away from her dancing partner. I could see her pallor from across the room.

"No!" I said. I pulled forward, but Stepmama wouldn't let go. "Not her!" I yelled. "Don't make her—"

"It's all right, Kat," said Elissa. "Better me than either of my sisters."

She walked across the dance floor, looking pale and saintly. I glanced around wildly and glimpsed Angeline among the watchers. Her eyes were squeezed shut, and she was muttering something. If she planned on any sort of magical attack, I hoped she'd found more useful spells in Mama's magic books than I ever had.

"Ah, Miss Stephenson. Very brave and kind of you. If you'll just stand here . . ." The highwayman gestured for her to stand beside him. He was remarkably fussy about it, adjusting her until she was in just the position he wanted, at a slight angle facing away from him.

Wait. My eyes focused more sharply. He wasn't only adjusting her position. He was whispering in her ear as he did it. The rascal! If he was embarrassing her, or making her unhappy . . .

Elissa blinked rapidly. Her eyes flicked to his face and away. I clenched my hands into fists . . . then loosened them as I recognized the emotions flitting across her face.

She wasn't frightened or embarrassed. She was shocked, surprised, relieved . . . and then absolutely furious in a way I knew only too well. For a moment I was actually tempted to feel sorry for the highwayman. I wondered if she would start lecturing him on his behavior in front of all of us. What a way to spend his greatest robbery ever—being ranted at about propriety by the one young lady he'd chosen for looking most sweet tempered.

I could have told him a great deal about my angelic-looking oldest sister's temper. But there wasn't any time for that now.

She started to speak, then stopped when he whispered something urgently in her ear. Obediently, she pressed her lips together. But I saw the angry flush rising on her cheeks, and I knew he'd hear more about it later . . . if there was a later.

Someone was moving quietly through the crowd, as stealthily as a wolf stalking his prey. I couldn't see who it was, but I felt the shift of people around me, making way. Then I felt the sparks brush against my skin. *Sir Neville.*

I coughed loudly. The highwayman jerked around, abandoning the whispered argument with my sister. His eyes narrowed, and his right arm swung out, pointing the loaded pistol. "Ah, Sir Neville," he said. "Have a care, please. I'd prefer not to shoot anyone tonight."

"I'm sure you would," Sir Neville growled. "But I will personally make certain you hang for tonight's work anyway."

"My, you are bloodthirsty." The highwayman nodded to someone behind Sir Neville. "But you might be interested to know that I am not the only one aiming a pistol at you just now."

I swung my head around, along with everyone else in the crowd. But the press of people was too thick for me to see anything.

"My associates are positioned around the room rather carefully," said the highwayman. "So I'd advise you to restrain yourself. You may distract yourself by planning your revenge, if you'd like."

"I will," said Sir Neville, and I believed him.

"In that case, we may begin," the highwayman said, and beside him, Elissa gave an audible sniff of disapproval.

It was a sniff I knew all too well. Even the highwayman's confident smile faltered for a moment as he turned to look at her. He looked like a puppy who'd brought her a brand-new bone as a gift, only to be told that it was horrid. I'd seen that expression on another man's face just two nights ago, when he'd seen Sir Neville escort Elissa into dinner.

And suddenly I knew.

"Oh, my Lord!" I muttered, and fell back into my chair.

"Language, Kat," Stepmama whispered. She was fanning herself rapidly and taking deep breaths.

I wished I could calm myself as easily. But everything was suddenly much too complicated for me. The idea of a highwayman—even one holding my sister hostage—had been exciting. But this was just ridiculous.

I looked at Sir Neville's angry face and felt my stomach sink. He obviously hadn't recognized the voice behind the mask. But somehow, I didn't think it would make him any more forgiving when he realized he was facing his own brother.

I couldn't let him find out. It was bad enough for Elissa to be in love with a penniless younger brother. But for her to have to watch him be captured, arrested, and hanged . . .

Well, if that happened, I would never persuade her out of her belief in gothic romances. She would be a confirmed tragic heroine for life.

I took a deep breath, yanked my arm free from Stepmama's grip, and started through the crowd toward Sir Neville.

"Kat!" Stepmama hissed. "Get back here!"

I ignored her. The closer I came to Sir Neville, the stronger the prickles against my skin became. They felt like burning needles, pushing me back, trying to form that choking, helpless feeling in my throat again. It made me want to go back to my seat and fold my hands like a proper young lady, and not even try to avert impending disaster.

I hated that feeling.

I swallowed hard against it and charged onward. I couldn't push straight through the people in my way, unfortunately; that would have created too much of a commotion. But I squeezed my way through the gaps in the crowd. Sir Neville hadn't noticed my approach; his scowl was still fixed on the highwayman in the center of the room. His whole body was braced to lunge. *Oh, Lord,* indeed. I hurried up my pace.

"Ladies and gentlemen," the highwayman called. "If you will kindly form two lines . . ."

The crowd began to separate obediently. Sir Neville tensed. I could see it in his eyes: This was it. His opportunity to attack.

I flung myself forward to get in his way.

And that was when Angeline's magic took effect.

I smelled the flowery scent in the air before I realized what it meant. Then the gasps I heard made me turn my head, even as I flung myself toward Sir Neville.

I tripped. I didn't care. Even as I fell to the ground, I kept on staring.

The loaded pistol had lifted directly out of the highwayman's right hand. It floated in the air just above his head. He lunged for it and missed. It floated an enticing inch higher up. He glanced hastily at the flabbergasted crowd and jumped for it, dropping his empty pistol to reach out with both hands. His fingers brushed the butt of the loaded pistol and fell away without taking hold.

The sound of the crowd changed. A high, nervous titter rang out behind me. The fearful whispering all around turned into a dangerous, low mutter of anticipation. I looked up at Sir Neville's face and saw fierce satisfaction spread across it.

"You fool, Angeline!" I muttered. Across the crowd, her face was filled with virtuous disinterest. But I wasn't fooled. That flowery smell was unmistakable.

"Ah . . . ladies and gentlemen," the highwayman began.

He licked his lips and made one more lunge for the loaded pistol before giving up on it and crossing his arms defensively. "If you will recall, I am not alone here in this room, and—"

"Indeed you are not," Sir Neville said, and smiled wolfishly. He began to stroll forward, at a rolling, predatory pace, stalking the highwayman from across the room. "Your associates don't seem to be in any hurry to rescue you, though, do they?"

"Er—," the highwayman began. He looked across the room at Sir Neville's face and thrust Elissa protectively behind his back.

I let out a groan of sheer frustration. Trust Elissa to fall in love with such a fool! Yes, certainly he was being a chivalrous fool—and Sir Neville did look dangerous, it was true—but now the highwayman didn't have a hostage to guarantee his own protection. Unless . . .

Aha. Realization struck me. There was no time to think my plan through. So I just launched myself across the room.

"Elissa!" I shrieked, at the top of my lungs. "I'll rescue you!"

I made out her horrified face behind the highwayman's shoulder. Then I rolled straight into both of them, nearly knocking them over. I steadied myself on the shoulder of the highwayman's black cloak.

"Go!" I urged Elissa, and shoved her aside. She stumbled back. I fell against the highwayman's side.

"Oh!" I cried out to the watching crowd. I flung a hand up to my brow for proper dramatic emphasis. "Oh! He has a knife! Please don't hurt me, sir! I beg you!"

The highwayman swallowed. "Miss Katherine," he whispered in my ear. "I hardly—"

"Play along, you fool!" I hissed through my teeth. I kept my expression as tragic as any gothic heroine's, for the sake of the horrified crowd around us. I whispered, "Do you want to get out of here, or do you want your brother to expose you right now in front of everyone?"

The highwayman gave a jerk of surprise against my back. "How did you—?"

"Quickly!" I hissed. Sir Neville wasn't alone now. A group of other men had stepped away from the crowd to join him, including Frederick Carlyle, who looked surprisingly dangerous with a scowl on his handsome face.

The highwayman stiffened his shoulders, put one hand behind my back, and swept his cloak out commandingly. "Stand back!" he bellowed to Sir Neville and all the other men. "If you don't want to see her hurt."

Stepmama let out a scream and fainted. I was so pleased, I could have hugged her. A crowd of older women fluttered to her side, trying to revive her. It was almost as much diversion as we needed.

"Clear a path!" the highwayman barked. "I'll let the girl go only after you've let me past and safely to my horse."

Elissa let out a small, choked sound behind us. I peeked

past the highwayman's shoulder and saw her face nearly purple with emotion. She sat on the floor staring at us.

Don't worry, I mouthed to her.

The blur of emotions on her face resolved into sheer exasperation. There was no chance at all that I would escape a lecture later, even if I did save the day.

But we weren't free yet.

"Step aside, I said!" the highwayman called. "Or I'll—"

"Ouch!" I shrieked, and jumped as if I'd felt the point of a knife. Gasps sounded in the crowd.

Sir Neville started forward. Frederick Carlyle flung out an arm to hold him back.

"No," he said. "Let them past. It's too dangerous to interfere now." He turned to meet the highwayman's gaze full-on. His dark blue eyes looked colder than I'd ever seen them. "But if you don't let her go the very moment you're free . . ."

"Oh, I shall," said the highwayman, more quickly than he should have. "Don't worry about that!"

I gritted my teeth and restrained myself from rolling my eyes. Instead I just squirmed as if I felt the knife still against me. "Please!" I said. "Do hurry, before he hurts me!"

Something glinted in the corner of my vision. I turned to look. It was Mr. Gregson's spectacles, catching the light from the chandeliers. Mr. Gregson himself was watching me with what looked alarmingly like full understanding in his eyes . . . and a fair share of amusement, too. I bit my lip and looked away quickly.

Just in time. The flowery smell suddenly got stronger. I saw Angeline's lips moving in a silent whisper. I *felt* her spell arrowing toward us across the room. I could almost see it when I squinted, glimmering in the corner of my eyes, coming to pull apart everything I'd worked for.

I couldn't bear it. It was too much, too idiotic of her when I'd worked so hard, and with so little help from my co-conspirators. I could feel the pressure mounting in my head, until I could have exploded with sheer frustration. Then I recognized the arrogant satisfaction in Angeline's face—*saving Kat from herself, as usual*—and I broke.

"No!" I shouted.

Pressure rocked through the air and shattered in a silent boom. I staggered. Something clattered behind me. Angeline fell back and was caught by her neighbors, who bent over her solicitously. My head was clear and ringing. Sir Neville was suddenly staring only at me.

The flowery scent was gone from the air. Angeline's magical attack had disappeared.

I licked my lips, looking around the room. Who had realized the truth, apart from Sir Neville?

Wait. That clattering sound I'd heard . . . I twisted around to peek over the highwayman's shoulder. Then I wished I hadn't.

It was his loaded pistol. It had fallen from the air onto the empty dance floor, twelve feet behind us. Twelve feet behind us . . . and only six feet from the closest of the spectators. I couldn't breathe. If we ran for the pistol, someone else would get there first. If we ran for the door and didn't make it out in time, the highwayman might be shot down trying to escape, before anyone even knew who he really was.

My horrified gaze met Elissa's across the space between us. She was still sitting staring after us, looking ready to swoon at any moment. But when she followed my gaze to the pistol, color flooded her cheeks.

"The pistol!" someone shouted in the crowd. "Get it!"

A concerted rush started across the floor.

"Stand back!" the highwayman bellowed. But his voice cracked on the command.

I whirled back around, trying to pull the highwayman with me. No one *should* shoot at him when he was holding me close. If we ran for the door—if we could make it past all the people who stood between us and it, and if—

A shot rang out behind us. I jumped. The highwayman staggered. *Oh, no.*

"I am so sorry," Elissa's soft voice said behind us. "It went off by accident."

I turned, slowed by dread. My sweet, gentle oldest sister was standing in the middle of the dance floor, covered in plaster. She was holding the pistol—now empty—in her hand, and another piece of molding had come off the ceiling above her.

"Horrid thing," she said, and shuddered, shaking flakes of plaster off her fair hair. "I can't bear how dangerous it is!" She turned, as if carelessly, to toss it away from her. It flew straight across the room and out the window, in a crash of shattered glass.

Charles had taught Elissa to throw like a boy for our family cricket games, before Stepmama had married Papa and banned the practice. I wondered if he had taught her to shoot, too.

But I didn't have time to gloat over her cleverness. The crowd of men who'd been aiming for the pistol had all turned back to us, now, along with Sir Neville's original group.

"Hurry!" I urged, and the highwayman nodded against my hair.

"Out of my way, or the girl bleeds!" he snarled loudly, and the crowd around us fell back.

It was hard to walk quickly when I had to stay just one step ahead of him, so close that no one could see the lack of a knife between us. Prickles burned against my skin as we shuffle-walked past Sir Neville. He didn't speak. He didn't have to. His silence was more frightening.

He'd seen me defeat Angeline's magic. He knew now that I'd been helping the highwayman. And as for how in the world I was going to defend myself against him . . .

Well, there wasn't time to worry about that now. We shuffled out of the assembly room and down the hall, out the door, and down the broad marble steps of the displaced Greece-in-Yorkshire building. Coachmen stared at us. The dogs ignored us, concentrating on their scavenging. A single horse stood tethered to a tree outside.

The highwayman let go of me with visible relief. "I do beg your pardon, Miss Katherine. And I thank you with all my heart. But—"

"No time!" I said. "Where are your associates? They can—"

"What associates?"

"'What associates?'" I repeated. I stared at him through the dark. "You know who I mean! Your associates in the ballroom, who were holding pistols on the other guests and—"

"I'm afraid I made those up," the highwayman said, and smiled ruefully beneath his mask. "It seemed like a good precaution."

"But—" I cut myself off, gritting my teeth. Curse Elissa's taste in men. There was no time to tell him how stupid he had been. That would have to wait until later. "You have to go now, as fast as you can, and—oh, Lord, it's too late."

The crowd of men had already followed us, surging onto the top steps. They all stood there, watching us silently. *Waiting.* As soon as the highwayman jumped up onto his horse and I was out of danger, they would be after him. Once they caught him . . .

I sighed. The adventure wasn't over yet after all. And I would have a great deal of explaining to do for my sisters later.

"Come on," I said. "Help me onto your horse."

"What are you talking about?" He glanced back and forth between the ominously silent, watching crowd and my face, which seemed to frighten him even more. "Miss Katherine, you mustn't—we couldn't possibly—"

"Do you want to survive tonight or not?" I said, and backed away from him, toward his horse, trying to look reluctant, as if I were under threat. I injected an expression of terror onto my face for the sake of our pursuers. It had a bad effect on my highwayman, though—I was afraid he would swoon at any moment. "Don't be foolish," I said briskly between my teeth. "There's no other choice. You have to take me with you."

"I—I don't know—I'm afraid Miss Stephenson might—"

"Elissa would much rather have you escape a hanging," I said firmly. "She is very attached to propriety, in case you hadn't noticed. A hanging would be far too scandalous for her sensibilities. So." I undid the knot that tethered the horse to the tree and scrambled up onto its back. There was no lady's sidesaddle there, of course, so I had to swing my leg straight across like a man and forget all about my own modesty and proper sensibilities. I yanked my skirts down to cover as much of my stockinged legs as possible. "Are you coming or not?" I said.

He glanced back at the silent crowd of men one more time. Then he gave in. "Oh, very well." He jumped up behind me and swirled out his cloak. As the crowd surged toward us, he raised his voice to a dangerous roar.

"No one dare follow if you want her returned to Grantham Abbey unharmed!"

He wheeled the horse around in a fast circle, and it whinnied with excitement.

"I already know that I'll regret this," the highwayman said.

We tore down the long road, into the moonlight.

Seventeen

The wind blew through my short hair, and the highwayman's cloak billowed around me. I laughed out loud with sheer exhilaration.

The highwayman let out a pitiful groan.

"How can you laugh?" he called. He was sitting just behind me, but I could barely hear his voice over the sound of the horse's pounding hooves and the wind in my ears. "This is a disaster!"

I shook my head against his chest. "That's not it," I shouted back. I spread my arms out, scooping up the rushing wind before me. "I've never ridden this fast in my life!"

He only groaned again in answer. I decided to ignore him for the rest of the ride.

I'd never be allowed to ride like a man again, straddling the horse and riding at full gallop. Poor Papa didn't even own any horses that could run this quickly. I wouldn't waste the rest of my thrilling ride by worrying about Elissa's mooning suitor.

But I had to turn my attention back to him when he slowed the horse and guided it into the dark woods that bordered the river. Tree branches poked into my face and eyes. I batted them away, slumping down to keep as safe from them as possible.

"What are you doing?" I said.

"We have to hide." Now that we'd slowed to a trudge, to pick our way among the thickly clustered trees, the highwayman's voice had settled back from despair into glum resignation. "Even if they follow us, we'll have a chance if we're far enough into the woods."

"Mm," I said doubtfully, and peered through the darkness that surrounded us. The canopy of leaves above us was so full that only the thinnest strands of moonlight filtered through it, leaving the trees around us in deep shadow. With my vision dulled, my hearing intensified until I could hear my own breathing loud in my ears. I heard low, hooting bird cries and insects, and the crunch of the horse's hooves through the undergrowth. It would be hard to pursue us here, it was true, but if the horse turned an ankle, we'd all be stuck. And then—

"No!" I said, and straightened up so fast, the top of my

head slammed into the highwayman's chin. He yelped with pain. I said, "We can't!"

"I know this can't be pleasant for you," the highwayman said in a muffled voice. He'd dropped one of his hands from the reins to clutch his jaw. "But I did try to warn you, and you will be perfectly safe. You needn't be afraid of—"

"I'm not," I said. "You don't understand. We have to get back to Grantham Abbey right now!"

"Miss Katherine, every man from the assembly ball will be chasing down that road at full speed. If they catch us—"

"If they reach Grantham Abbey before us," I said grimly, "then Sir Neville will go straight to your room to tell you what's happened and roust you up for the manhunt. And what will he find there?"

Sir Neville's younger brother swallowed audibly. "Ah. I hadn't thought of that."

"I'm not surprised." I sighed. "Now do you understand why we have to hurry back?"

"All right. Yes. Yes, I do see that." His shoulders rose and fell behind me. "This is all much more complicated than I'd expected." He tugged at the reins, and the horse turned back obediently, picking his way back toward the moonlit opening to the road.

"You didn't expect it to be complicated?" I said. "I know you've been robbing carriages for a long time now, but surely you must have known it would be more difficult to rob a whole ballroom full of people."

"But I haven't been," the highwayman said.

"I beg your pardon?" I twisted around in his arms to stare at him. "I saw you."

"I tried to rob a ballroom," he said. "I've never robbed a carriage in my life."

"But—but—" I slammed my mouth shut to stop stammering.

"I'd heard people talking at dinner two nights ago," he said. "All about the highwayman and how dangerous he was. So I thought, there's a way to get enough fortune to marry."

"Oh, my Lord," I said. "Are you telling me you put on a cloak and mask, shot out the ceiling of the assembly rooms, and risked a hanging, only so you could afford to offer marriage to my sister?"

Mr. Collingwood pulled off his mask. His face shone in the moonlight as we neared the road, pale and dreamy against his jet-black hair. "Well," he said, "it was the only thing I could think of."

"But—," I started again. Then I stopped. I jerked around. "Did you hear that?"

"What?" Mr. Collingwood didn't bother to look back. He was already pointing the horse's nose at the road ahead. "We'll have to hurry."

"No," I said. My voice sounded strange and choked, as if it belonged to someone else. "I don't think we will. I think you should stop the horse right now."

"You know I can't—"

A click sounded in the darkness. It was the click of a pistol being cocked. Mr. Collingwood must have known that sound. He yanked the horse to a halt and turned to stare in the same direction as I was, at the pistol pointing directly at us.

"I think you had better listen to the young lady's advice," a deep voice growled from the darkness. "Now, put your hands up and ask yourself: your money . . . or your life?"

Swathed in a great black cloak, the highwayman was nearly invisible in the darkness. I had to squint to pick out the deeper shadow of his silhouette between the trees, and the outline of the big black horse he sat on. I could only catch the glimmer of the horse's eyes as it watched us, and hear its steady breath. But I had no difficulty at all in picking out the gleam of the highwayman's single pistol, which never wavered from my chest. I couldn't look away from it.

"You'll want to turn your horse around," the highwayman said, "and come back away from the road, so we can be more comfortable."

"I—I don't think I do want that, actually," Mr. Collingwood said. His voice sounded rather higher-pitched than normal.

"I think you do," said the highwayman. "And so does the young lady. Don't you, *Miss Katherine?*"

"How—?" I started. Then I realized. "You were

listening to us! Eavesdropping on our conversation! That's outrageous!"

"As outrageous as playing a highwayman to try to steal your fine friends' jewels? That's a hanging offense, that is."

"Well, you can hardly be offended by that," I said. "I mean, you of all people—"

"You think not?" The highwayman's voice hardened. "Get back under the trees, miss. Now. Before I show you both just how offended I can be."

I began, "Well, really—"

"Yes, sir," Mr. Collingwood said hastily. "We will." In my ear, as he lowered his hands to the reins of his horse, he hissed, "Please, Miss Katherine. Be quiet!"

I closed my lips and pressed them together to hold back the rest of my remarks. We were all silent as Mr. Collingwood's horse stepped slowly into the darkness. The woods wrapped around us like a blanket, cutting us off from the moonlit road, and from safety.

Through the darkness, I could hear the highwayman breathing. His breaths sounded quick and strained with nerves . . . or with excitement. I swallowed hard and told myself that I was not afraid.

I had wanted to be held up by a highwayman for ages. This ought to be the most thrilling moment of my entire life.

"Off the horse," the highwayman ordered. "Now."

"Sir," Mr. Collingwood said. "I'd be happy to get off

the horse myself, for your convenience, but couldn't my companion please keep her place? You can see she's very young, and—"

"I said, off the horse!"

Mr. Collingwood slid off. When I started to follow him, though, he put one hand up to stop me. The highwayman's pistol shifted to aim at him. "Please," said Mr. Collingwood. "If you would only consider—"

The highwayman's pistol shifted again. "She can get off the horse now on her own," he said, "or I can put a bullet through its head and let it fall down underneath her."

I scrambled off the horse. I wasn't used to having to get off a horse without a sidesaddle; I couldn't just slide easily down the way I usually would. I swung one leg over and slipped. I would have fallen straight onto my backside on the forest floor if Mr. Collingwood hadn't caught me in his arms. Mr. Collingwood's horse whickered and danced backward, out of reach. I couldn't blame him.

"There now," the highwayman said, and eased his horse closer to us through the dark. I could hear him breathing hard above me. He held the pistol less than a foot away from my head, now. "Isn't this more comfortable?"

I let go of Mr. Collingwood as I found my feet on the forest floor. He squared his shoulders and patted my back comfortingly. "All will be well, Miss Katherine," he whispered. "I promise."

I could hear the shiver in his voice. It might have been enough to really frighten me if I had been the kind of simpering female who actually needed comforting.

The highwayman was a dark shadow looming over us in the blackness. I cursed myself for leaving Mr. Collingwood's pistol behind on the ground outside the assembly hall, where it could be of no use to anyone. If only Elissa had thrown it straight to us, instead of out the window, we could have reloaded it. If only . . .

"Purses first," the highwayman said. "Now."

"I don't—," Mr. Collingwood began.

The pistol slammed into the side of my head, so hard I staggered. Tears of pain started in my eyes. I choked back the cry that wanted to come out.

"Now," said the highwayman.

"Look!" Mr. Collingwood stripped off his cloak and opened his jacket. He turned the pockets inside out. "You see?" he said. "They're empty. That's what I was trying to tell you. I don't have a purse on me. I didn't bring any money."

"Don't try to play me for a fool," the highwayman snarled. "You just robbed a whole ballroom. I heard the girl."

"I tried to rob a ballroom," Mr. Collingwood said. "It didn't work."

"Oh, so you just gave up and rode away empty-handed? I don't think so. Anyway, I can hear your accent, and I know what it means. You've got money, whether it's enough for you or not. So hand it over!"

"He's telling you the truth," I said. I straightened carefully. My head throbbed with every movement, but I lifted my chin and glared up at him through the darkness. "If you were less of a fool, you'd listen to him and realize—"

The muzzle of the pistol was suddenly pressing directly against my head. My breath stopped in my throat. The cold of the metal radiated through my hair and across my skin, freezing me in place.

"That's better," the highwayman said. "Now, you listen to me, *Miss* Katherine. Interesting thing about highway robbery you ought to know. It's a hanging offense." He paused. The pistol shifted infinitesimally against my scalp. "I *said*, it's a hanging offense," he repeated. "Did you hear me?"

"Yes, sir," I whispered. I breathed in and out as lightly as I could, straining not to move an inch. Every nerve in my body was focused on the circle of cold metal.

"Good," he said. "Then you understand. I can do anything I like to you now. What's the worst that could happen to me? I might be hanged. Well, that'll happen anyway. So what's to stop me murdering you right now, where you stand?"

Another pause.

Mr. Collingwood spoke, his voice stifled. "Please, sir—I beg of you, don't—"

"Quiet!" said the highwayman. "I was speaking to the young lady. I want to hear her answer. So? What's to stop me from shooting you in the head right this moment, Miss Katherine?"

I licked my lips. "Nothing," I whispered.

"That's right," he said. "Nothing at all. So maybe you'd better keep that in mind, and keep a civil tongue in your mouth. Because you don't want me to go losing my temper now, do you?"

"No, sir," I whispered.

The pistol didn't move. My legs were trembling now with the effort of standing perfectly still against it.

"I thought not," the highwayman said. "In that case, Miss Katherine, I'd recommend your friend here turn over his purse, and yours, before I start to get irritated. Because it's a good deal easier to take a purse off a dead body than a live one."

"Yes, sir," I whispered. "But—"

"Here," Mr. Collingwood said hastily. "I don't have any money, but I have this pocket watch. It's on a gold chain, you see? And, um . . . my card case! You can have my card case, it's made of silver, and it's—"

Even with a pistol to my head, I had to speak. "You brought your card case on a robbery? What were you planning to do, hand out your calling cards before you left, so they could return the favor at your house next week?"

"Well . . ." He paused. "I didn't mean to, it just happened to be in my pocket, so—"

"Trinkets," the highwayman said. "You're standing unprotected in the dark while I hold a pistol to the young lady's head, and you still want to fob me off with trinkets?"

"No!" said Mr. Collingwood. "That is, I don't want to fob

you off with anything, sir, but these truly are all I have, and—"

"Do I need to shoot her right now to get your attention?"

"No, sir!"

"Good. Then listen carefully. I will shoot her if you don't hand over something of real value. Something to make this godforsaken half hour worth my time."

"I have something," I said hastily. My teeth wanted to chatter, even though it wasn't cold. I had to grit them together to speak. "My reticule. I have a golden mirror inside."

"A golden what?"

"A mirror," I said. "It was my mother's. It's made of gold."

"Hand it over," the highwayman said. "No, not you. Him. Take it out of her bag and hand it to me."

"Yes, sir."

Mr. Collingwood fumbled with the cords around my wrist, in the darkness. There was a moment of silence, except for the sounds of the night birds in the woods around us and the highwayman's heavy breathing. The pistol shivered against my head. His hand must be trembling. He was nervous too.

I wondered how hard it would be for the pistol to go off, if his fingers slipped. I stood still and unmoving, with my jaw clamped tight to keep my teeth from chattering and bumping the pistol. I wondered what Angeline and

Elissa would think if I didn't come back that night. I wondered what Mama would have done in my situation. Well, she would have cast a spell, obviously, but I didn't know any . . . or at least any that would be useful.

"Here," said Mr. Collingwood, and the reticule slid off my wrist. I heard movement in the darkness, and saw the silhouette of Mr. Collingwood's hands reaching up to the highwayman on his horse. The pistol jiggled against my head as the highwayman accepted the mirror and Mr. Collingwood's own offerings.

I had to bite back an unexpected pang of loss. Mama's mirror had brought me nothing but trouble, but still . . . I breathed in deeply. It wasn't as if it would be gone for long. It never—

"What the devil?"

The highwayman's curse came just as I felt a familiar, smooth metal circle appear in my left hand. The mirror had returned sooner than I'd expected. Too soon.

"Here," I said. "It fell into my hand. You can have it back."

"What do you think you're playing at?" He snatched it out of my hand. The pistol was definitely trembling against my head now. "That did not fall. Are you trying to make a fool out of me?"

"No!" I said. "I'm so sorry, it only—oh, the devil!"

It was back in my hand again, and glowing with warmth. I could actually see the light radiating out of it now, illuminating my hand in the darkness for both men to see.

"What's happening?" Mr. Collingwood said. "I don't understand."

"Please," I said. I thrust the mirror back up to the highwayman. "I can explain. It only—"

"Fell?" the highwayman said. His voice sounded hoarse. "I don't think so."

"Look," I said. "I know this is going to be hard to believe, but—"

"Shut your mouth!" He grabbed the mirror, closing his hand tightly around it. The light glowed between his fingers. "I don't want to hear another word out of you or else—"

"Oh, Lord," I whispered. The mirror was back in my hand again.

The highwayman stared at his empty fingers. Then he turned to me. The mirror was glowing brightly in my hand. I couldn't hide it.

"That's it," he said, and grabbed hold of my shoulder with one meaty hand as he steadied the pistol against my head. "They can't hang me twice."

"No!" Mr. Collingwood said. He lunged toward us.

There was only one last thing to try.

I flicked open the mirror.

The shot went off as the world turned inside out around me.

Eighteen

I landed on my backside on a smooth, hard floor.
When the world stopped spinning, I opened my eyes. A
familiar rounded golden ceiling arched high above me.
Golden walls rose to each side. My head still ached horribly, but I didn't feel as if I'd been shot. I would be able
to tell, wouldn't I? Unless I'd gone into shock and just
couldn't feel the pain . . . .

I patted my head and arms, just to make sure. Then I
let out a sigh of sheer relief. I absolutely, definitely had
not been shot. I could still feel the memory of cold on my
head, where the muzzle of the pistol had rested, but that
was all.

I was in the Golden Hall, and I was safe. Now, all I had
to do—

A familiar voice spoke just behind me.

"Where the devil have you brought me?" the highwayman snarled.

*

Oh, Lord.

I turned around, taking a deep breath for courage.

In the golden light of the hall, the highwayman looked different. Even bigger, if possible, with bulkier, heavier shoulders than I'd imagined in the darkness. His broad, weathered face looked older than I'd expected too—he must have been at least as old as Stepmama. And I mean Stepmama's true age, not the age she claimed to be.

But he didn't look any less dangerous out of the forest, especially as he swung around to face me, his pale green eyes wide and wild in the golden light. "I asked you a question," he growled. *"What have you done?"*

"Nothing bad," I said. His hands were hidden underneath his threadbare black greatcoat; I kept my eyes on where they ought to be, searching for the telltale shape of his pistol underneath the cloth. "I couldn't just stand there and let you shoot me, could I?"

He started toward me. He walked like I imagined a prizefighter might walk, or a tiger out in the jungles of Asia: with a predatory, rolling stride that made goose bumps rise on the back of my neck. "I'm the one asking the questions, Miss Katherine," he said. "Not you. And I'd strongly suggest you answer me."

I backed away from him. My thin evening slippers

whispered against the golden floor. Thank goodness the hall was so big; at least he couldn't back me against a wall. I was smaller and lighter than him. Maybe I could outrun him . . . but I didn't want to test it.

I smiled at him as innocently and sweetly as I could. "Don't be angry," I said. "We can go back any time you want, I promise. All you have to do is—"

"Don't you tell me what I have to do!"

He leaped for me, and I bolted. I was halfway across the hall before it hit me.

"Your pistol's empty!" I panted. I stopped, balancing on my toes. He was still ten feet away, closing in fast. I put out my hands in a *wait* gesture. His eyes narrowed, and he slowed but didn't stop. "I heard you fire the shot."

"So?" he said. "I don't need a pistol. Not against a slip of a girl like you."

"I brought you all the way here by magic," I said. I jerked my chin up to look as haughty as I could. "That means I'm a witch. A very powerful witch," I added. "So what do you think you can possibly do against me without a pistol?"

He snorted. "If I'm no danger to you, lass, then why were you running?"

"Ummm . . ." I blinked.

"Thought as much," he said.

"Did you indeed?" another voice said mildly.

We both spun around to face the new arrival. Mr. Gregson polished his spectacles as he smiled at us.

"I rather thought you might arrive here in the end, Katherine," he said. "But I must confess to being rather curious: Where did you find this gentleman? A second highwayman, I presume?"

"Ah . . . ," I began.

"Who the devil are you?" the highwayman said. His huge fists clenched menacingly. The sight made me wince, but Mr. Gregson didn't seem to notice.

"So," he said to me, "I believe this leaves us with two questions to resolve. What have you done with Sir Neville's foolish younger brother, and what exactly do you intend to do now?"

"Um," I said. I looked from one to the other of the two men. "That is to say . . ."

"I don't know what the devil you two are on about," the highwayman began, "but—"

"I can, of course, take care of this little matter for you," Mr. Gregson told me, "but only if I know that we are both on the same page, so to speak. If you asked me, as your new tutor, to step in and help you—"

"I think not!" I said.

"Are you threatening me?" the highwayman said to Mr. Gregson. "You puny little—"

"I hope you're aware that time passes differently here than in the more ordinary world," Mr. Gregson said to me. "So while you may think you have plenty of time before your followers arrive at Grantham Abbey, you might be surprised to learn—"

"Oh, Lord!" I said. When they found Mr. Collingwood missing . . .

"Precisely," Mr. Gregson said. He put his spectacles neatly into place and smiled indulgently at me. "It has been quite an amusing little struggle, Katherine, but I think it's finally time to accept the truth, don't you? All you need to do is agree—"

"Never," I said. "I'll take care of this myself."

He blinked. "And how, might I ask—"

"Like this," I said, and reached for that still point inside me, the point I'd found by accident the first time I ever had to escape from the Golden Hall.

The last sight I had was of Mr. Gregson's shaking head. The expression on his face made my teeth grind together.

I was not running away, no matter what he might think. I would take care of the highwayman later. But first I had to save Mr. Collingwood and my sister's future happiness.

I prepared to land in the dark forest.

Instead I hit a hard stone floor, arms first.

"Miss Katherine!" Mr. Collingwood's voice came out between a whisper and a squeak behind me. "Where did you come from?"

"Magic," I said. My voice came out as a groan. My elbows throbbed with pain. I pulled myself up carefully, massaging them and peering through the smothering darkness. The air smelled stuffy and confined. I reached out and felt cool stone walls on either side, barely three feet apart. "Where are we?"

"Inside the manor," he said. "But you—where—how—?"

"I know," I said. "I disappeared. But I'm back now. You must have brought my mirror with you."

He held it out to me, glimmering in the darkness. "I picked it up from the ground when you vanished. But Miss Katherine, you—look here, it isn't possible, but I actually saw you—"

"I'm fine now," I said, as I took the mirror. "I'll explain it all later. But this can't be the manor. Unless—" A horrible thought struck me. "You haven't been thrown into the dungeon, have you? Is there a dungeon in Grantham Abbey?"

"I—I don't know," Mr. Collingwood said. "But no, I haven't been. We're in the servants' corridor, behind the walls of the third floor. Hiding. I haven't been taken prisoner. Not yet."

"Then you won't be," I said, and brushed the dust from my white evening dress with a few brisk strokes. "I'm here now. I'll take care of everything."

"Er . . ." I couldn't see his face, but his voice positively dripped with doubt.

I sighed. "You were so brave when you were wearing the highwayman's mask. Don't you remember?"

"Please don't mention that," Mr. Collingwood said. "I don't know what came over me. Your sister was most shocked by my behavior. If you had heard what she said to me when she realized who I was—"

"Oh, I can imagine," I said. "But don't worry about that.

She's not here now, so just pretend you've put the mask back on, and—"

"But that's exactly the problem!" Mr. Collingwood said. "She is here now. They're all here now!"

"So? All you need to do is take off your cloak and greet them as if nothing was amiss, and no one will—"

"You don't understand," Mr. Collingwood said. "I was coming up through the back staircase to make my way back into my room undetected and pretend I'd been here all along. When I opened the door, I saw Neville coming out of my room, with two other gentlemen behind him, looking grim. And Neville said"—Mr. Collingwood's voice deepened into his brother's unmistakable growl—"'We'll have him when he finally slinks back here to hide.'"

"Oh," I said. That did sound bad. I started to frown, but it hurt my aching head too much, so I stopped. "I don't understand. How did they get here so quickly? Even after we were held up, we should have been faster—"

"Miss Katherine, it has been two full hours since we were held up," Mr. Collingwood said. "I didn't arrive at Grantham Abbey until just twenty minutes ago."

"What on earth were you doing, to take so long?"

"Searching for you, of course!" he shouted, straight into my ears.

"Ouch!" I said, and stepped away.

"Forgive me," said Mr. Collingwood more quietly. "I should not have spoken so to you. But it was not a pleasant experience. The idea of telling Miss Stephenson that I'd lost you—"

"I wasn't lost," I said. "I left. You didn't have to worry about me."

"You vanished before my eyes with a highwayman who meant to murder you."

"Oh, well, I took care of him," I said, and tried not to think about where the highwayman was right now. At least he couldn't do any damage in an empty hall without any weapons, no matter how angry he might be. I couldn't imagine that Mr. Gregson would let him. Of course, Mr. Gregson was probably on his way here himself to give me a piece of his mind. So all in all, it was best not to think about him, either.

I sighed. "Do you think Sir Neville will be forgiving, since you are his brother?"

"You must be joking," Mr. Collingwood said.

"Why? Of course, I know brothers can be annoying from time to time," I said, in a true masterpiece of lady-like understatement. I thought of Charles's gambling debts, and my teeth ground together. I forced them apart. "But still, family is family. He might be as angry as anything, but he can hardly call for his own brother to be hanged."

"I think nothing would give him greater pleasure," Mr. Collingwood said.

"But—"

"Miss Katherine, did you not think it was odd that he

didn't recognize me in my disguise? That my own brother could not recognize my voice behind the mask?"

"Well . . ." I shrugged in the darkness. "*I* recognized you."

"Quite," said Mr. Collingwood. "Because you had—forgive me—paid some attention to me in the first two days of our acquaintance."

"I had to," I said. "You were mooning over Elissa, and she was mooning back. I couldn't ignore you after that."

"Neville can," Mr. Collingwood said. "He's spent his entire life trying to pretend I don't exist. He was fifteen years old when I was born, and our mother died only four weeks later. I always thought he blamed me for her death, but lately, I've wondered if it was more than that. And Sarah said—"

"Who?"

"Sarah," Mr. Collingwood said. "Neville's wife." He paused, and coughed uncomfortably. "Neville's late wife, that is. Neville said she had to be kept secluded in the house because of the scandals she would have created if he allowed her out in Society, but if you had known her sweetness and goodness, and then seen the monstrous way he treated her—"

"Yes, yes, I've heard about all that," I said. "But what did she say?"

Mr. Collingwood lowered his voice. "Miss Katherine, what I'm about to tell you is the most horrifying of rumors, and if it is untrue, then merely mentioning it is a terrible slander of my brother's good name."

"Never mind that," I said. "Slander away. What did she say?"

Mr. Collingwood's whisper was so soft I had to strain to hear it. "Sarah said that she had come across my mother's will, hidden in Neville's own dressing gown, while he slept. She said he carried it with him everywhere, because he was so afraid of the servants coming across it in any other hiding place."

"Your mother's will?" I repeated. "But I thought—Elissa told me the whole reason you were penniless was—"

"Miss Katherine, as far as I or anyone else is aware, our mother did not leave any will at all!" Mr. Collingwood hissed. "Neville's estate was inherited from our father. But the money to run it all came from our mother's dowry, which my grandfather ordered in such a radical manner that she had a right to will nearly all of it away as she chose. Because no one ever found a will, everything went to Neville."

"Oh," I said. "*Oh*. But Sarah said . . . ?"

"Sarah said she saw the will," Mr. Collingwood said. His voice was rising now in agitation. "She said it was properly witnessed and signed, and it left me half of my mother's funds. That would be a fortune! The money she left—all of which passed automatically to Neville—makes him one of the wealthiest men in the country. Even half of such an amount would be more than most men ever dream of."

"But . . ." I gripped the mirror hard in my hand, trying to think clearly. "That makes no sense! If such a will existed, and Sir Neville found it—well, yes, I can see why he would have kept it secret from everyone else. But why wouldn't he have destroyed it? Carrying it around everywhere might be safer than hiding it in the house for someone else to find, but it would be far, far safer to have burned it."

"Perhaps he felt guilty," Mr. Collingwood offered. "Perhaps it still burns at his conscience, and he cannot bring himself to—"

"Have you been reading Elissa's gothic novels?" I said. "Because that doesn't sound like Sir Neville to me."

Mr. Collingwood's sigh ruffled my hair. "No," he said. "It doesn't sound like Neville to me, either."

There was a glum silence.

"It could still be true," I said. "Perhaps we just don't know the whole story. There could be some reason—"

"No," said Mr. Collingwood. "No, you were right to rebuke me. It is a romantic, unlikely tale. It's only . . ." He paused. "Neville never cared for me, never found me anything but an irritation and an inconvenience to him. I spent my childhood with tutors and then at school, rarely seeing my own brother, and knowing that I always disappointed him. Since I came of age, he's kept me on a meager allowance—the merest pittance—and acted as though he were granting me the highest of favors. He only summons me to accompany him for large house parties such as this one so he can maintain the appearance of family loyalty without ever having to talk to me. I suppose . . . I suppose I wanted to believe it was for some reason that would reflect badly on him, and not on me, for being such an unlikable brother."

"Don't be absurd," I said. "You are not an unlikable brother. Trust me. My brother is far worse than you, and we still like him. You weren't sent down from Oxford for too much drinking and carousing, were you? And you haven't run your entire family into debt with hopeless gambling, have you?"

"Er . . . no," Mr. Collingwood said. "But—"

"Well, then. If we can like Charles despite everything he's done, then Sir Neville is certainly capable of liking you, if he wanted to," I said. "It's his own fault if he doesn't."

"But our mother's death—"

"My mother died," I said, and felt the words catch in my throat. "She died when I was born too. Just like you and your mother. But my sisters never, ever said it was my fault."

"Oh." Mr. Collingwood's voice sounded strangled. "Miss Katherine, please forgive me. I never meant to bring up bad memories, or—"

"Never mind," I said, and took a deep, steadying breath. "The point remains. There is nothing inherently wrong with you as a brother, but if Sir Neville won't protect you from the gallows, then we had better make sure you don't get anywhere near them. I think the first thing to do is for me to distract everyone."

"How?"

"By escaping from the highwayman, of course," I said. His eyes widened in sudden horror, and his mouth fell open; I kept talking, before faintheartedness could over-whelm him completely. "I'll creep down to the back of the house, then come racing around screaming from the front. Everyone should come running, and I'll gather a crowd. Meanwhile, you can come yawning down from the roof, where you've been stargazing for the past few hours. Sir Neville may be suspicious, but he can't have any proof—all he knows is that you're missing. If I tell everybody that I've been in the woods with the highway-man until just ten minutes ago, and you come down from the top floor of the house . . ."

"Miss Katherine—"

"Just act confident, as if you have nothing to worry about," I said. "Pretend you're wearing that mask again, and you can say or do anything. Be a highwayman in ordi-nary dress."

"Miss Katherine!" This time, Mr. Collingwood's voice came out as a high-pitched squeak of terror.

"Don't worry," I said, as warmly and reassuringly as I could. Really, Elissa could have picked a braver hero to fall in love with . . . but since she hadn't, I would have to be brave for him. "What could possibly go wrong?"

"Well, let me think about that," Sir Neville's voice said behind me.

I spun around. A door stood open twenty feet behind me, leaking light into the dark servants' corridor. Behind Sir Neville stood two of my dinner companions from our first night's meal, Major Connors and the red-faced, wine-guzzling man. They were both staring at me as if I were the devil incarnate.

Sir Neville's face creased into a grin of pure satisfaction. "You tell me, Miss Katherine," he said. "What exactly could go wrong?"

Nineteen

They marched us out of the corridor and down the grand staircase. The foyer at the bottom of the stairs was empty, except for the footmen by the main doors, who looked more stone-faced than ever when they saw us. I looked longingly at the closed doors, but I didn't even try to break away from the men around me. There was no place left to go.

Even from the staircase, I could hear the roar of agitated gossip coming from the salon. As we approached it, flanked by our captors, I looked up at Mr. Collingwood's pale face. He looked back at me and gave me a twisted grimace. After a moment, I realized it was meant to be a smile.

Two footmen swung the doors to the salon open. The conversations went suddenly silent as we stepped inside.

Then they exploded into a cloud of whispers, broken by Stepmama's trembling voice.

"You found her!" she cried. She broke through the crowd to come running toward us. "Oh, Kat, you horrid, wicked girl. I am so glad you're safe!"

I'd never seen Stepmama run in public before. Elissa and Angeline were close behind her, followed by Mr. Carlyle. Neither of my sisters looked as thrilled as Stepmama to see me. They must have known better.

Elissa's face looked white as chalk as she looked from me to Mr. Collingwood. When her gaze passed to Sir Neville behind us, she put one hand on her chest and swayed as if she might fall over in a swoon. Angeline grabbed Elissa's arm to hold her up and watched us with wary eyes.

"Kat!" Stepmama said again as she reached us. She took my hand to pull me away from the others.

Sir Neville's voice stopped her. "Not yet," he said. His voice was low, but I knew everyone in the room could hear it. "I'm afraid we must talk in private, Mrs. Stephenson."

She fell back, dropping my hand. "What do you mean? Surely—"

I could hear Sir Neville's smile in his voice. "You may trust me, ma'am, when I say that your stepdaughters would prefer the truth of this matter not to be made public knowledge."

Stepmama's face paled. Then it flushed bright red. "Katherine!" she hissed. "What in heaven's name have you done this time?"

"Have no fear," said Sir Neville. "You'll find out soon enough, I promise. Lady Graves?" He raised his voice to call across the room. "Might I beg the use of your library for a private discussion?"

Lady Graves hurried toward us. "Of course," she said. "But perhaps it might wait just a short while, Neville? Miss Katherine must be famished with hunger by now, and weary from all her excitement. Perhaps a few refreshments first—"

"I am afraid not," Sir Neville said. "The matter is too grave to wait."

Stepmama drew herself up to her full height, until she looked like a battleship ready to charge. "To the library, then," she said. "And I wish to hear everything."

She swept past us, leading the way. As I turned, I spotted Lady Fotherington watching us from the crowd. She raised one eyebrow at me in a mocking question. Her lips curved into a smile. She leaned close to whisper something to fish-faced Mrs. Banfield, her neighbor, and both of them burst into laughter.

My fingernails bit into the palms of my fisted hands.

It wasn't until we reached the library door that anyone spoke. "Major Connors, Mr. Green . . ." Sir Neville nodded to the two men who had helped him, as a footman hurried past to light the candles inside the room. "You needn't accompany us inside. But if you wouldn't mind standing guard outside the doors . . ."

"Of course," Mr Green said. He looked at me and then

yanked his gaze away, as if I were too outrageous to focus on. "We'll be here if you need us, Sir Neville."

"Call if you want us, and we'll come straight in," said Major Connors. Now that he wasn't bellowing about hunting, as he had at dinner that first night, his voice was a low mutter. But he looked as sturdy as the highwayman I'd left in the Golden Hall. I didn't fancy my chances of escaping through the library doors.

"'Standing guard'?" Angeline repeated. "Really, Sir Neville, is that absolutely necessary?"

"I'm afraid it is," said Sir Neville. "Now, ladies, if you would step inside . . . ah, Mr. Carlyle." He frowned. "You need hardly come with us. Not being a member of the family . . ."

Angeline took Mr. Carlyle's arm and stepped close to him. She met Sir Neville's gaze without flinching. "Mr. Carlyle is a good friend of the family, and he is entirely welcome to join us."

"Thank you, Miss Angeline," Mr. Carlyle said, and put his hand over hers. "I think I'd better, if you don't mind."

"I'm not sure . . . ," Stepmama began.

"Come now, Stepmama," Angeline said. "You know Mr. Carlyle was sent here as Papa's representative. You could hardly think that Papa himself should not be represented at any family meeting—especially one so grave as Sir Neville has been promising us."

I was impressed by how reasonable she made it sound . . . especially considering that Papa had never once been included in any family meetings, grave or otherwise, unless Stepmama had dragged him inside to parrot her words back at us for added emphasis. But Stepmama could hardly admit any such thing in front of Sir Neville.

So she said, "Yes, well, I suppose, if we really must," and walked ahead of us into the library without further complaint.

Elissa followed her, darting a frightened glance back at Mr. Collingwood as she passed. The rest of us waited at the open doorway.

Sir Neville regarded Angeline with what looked suspiciously like the beginnings of a nasty grin. "Are you quite certain that was a wise decision, Miss Angeline?"

"Oddly enough, I don't believe I need you to approve my decisions for me, Sir Neville," she said, and glared back at him, backed by Mr. Carlyle's broad shoulders.

"Mm," Sir Neville said, and his lips curved the rest of the way into a full and unpleasant smirk aimed at both of them. "Well, if that truly is what you'd prefer . . ." He waited for them to pass, arm in arm, and then gestured me and Mr. Collingwood after them.

He followed us inside, and the footman shut the door behind him. The library was a long, rectangular room filled with books, comfortable-looking couches, and high windows, and at any other time, I might have liked it. But Sir Neville's presence filled the room as the door closed behind him, and the familiar prickles of discomfort clouded the air around him, biting against my arms, forcing helplessness down my throat until I nearly choked on it.

I forced the words out anyway. "There's been a mistake."

"Indeed there has," Sir Neville said. "Will you confess the truth to your poor stepmother, or shall I tell her myself?"

"Someone tell me what has happened!" Stepmama said. She turned to Sir Neville's brother. "Mr. Collingwood, I take it that you rescued Kat from the dreadful highwayman. I am so sorry if she has misled you into any—"

Sir Neville laughed. At the sound, the prickles intensified against my skin until it burned. "I'm afraid you have quite mistaken the matter, Mrs. Stephenson. You see, Miss Katherine never did require rescuing."

"I beg your pardon?" Stepmama collapsed onto the closest couch. "I don't understand. I saw—"

"You saw, as we all saw, the results of a despicable ruse, and one that has brought dishonor on both our families."

"Neville—," Mr. Collingwood began, in a strangled tone.

Sir Neville ignored him. "I'm sure you must have thought your stepdaughter admirably brave when she rushed to save her oldest sister from the highwayman's clutches. But what neither you nor I realized at the time, ma'am, was that Miss Katherine never stood in any danger from him. You see, she had been his collaborator all along."

"What?" Stepmama's mouth dropped open. If I'd ever looked at her with such an expression, she would have told me off sharply for such unladylike gaping. "But that can't be."

"That is an utter lie!" I said. "I didn't even know who he was until—" Standing behind Stepmama, Angeline closed her eyes with a look of pure agony, and I stopped myself too late. "I mean—that is to say—"

"How could you have met such a person?" Stepmama wailed. "I know I've allowed you too much freedom, but still—"

"She met him in Lady Graves's own gallery, at the same moment that you yourself made his acquaintance," Sir Neville said. "I told you, did I not, that tonight has brought dishonor on both our families?" He stepped aside to point directly at his brother. "Behold the highwayman. I may safely say that I have never felt such bitter shame in my life."

"Ohh!" Elissa staggered and fell onto the couch beside Stepmama. It was as if the only thing holding her up until now had been her hope that Sir Neville might not know the full truth.

Angeline gripped the top of the couch with white knuckles. "What a very dramatic scenario you've concocted for our entertainment, Sir Neville," she said. Her voice was as dry and amused as I had ever heard it, but I could see her knuckles, and I wasn't fooled. "I daresay you must have some evidence to back up this wild story?"

"Indeed I do," Sir Neville said. "Your sister's own confession, overheard as she made plans with her collaborator to return him to the house unsuspected."

"Overheard by you," said Angeline. "And you expect us to believe—"

"Overheard by myself, certainly," Sir Neville said, "and also by Major Connors and Mr. Green, two highly respectable gentlemen. Will you try next to tell us we imagined everything? Or shall you attempt to use witchcraft on me? That is your usual method of persuasion, is it not?"

Angeline stiffened. Elissa's eyes flashed open.

Stepmama let out a muffled shriek. "Has everyone gone mad?"

"Why, have your stepdaughters kept it secret from you, ma'am? Miss Angeline has been a practicing witch for some time."

"Angeline," Elissa whispered.

"That can't be," Stepmama repeated helplessly.

"I say, Neville," Mr. Collingwood began.

"Stop it!" I cried.

But it was Mr. Carlyle's voice that cut through it all. "That is more than enough, Sir Neville," he said. He stepped forward, so that he stood partly shielding Angeline from Sir Neville's gaze. "We have all listened to your story about tonight's robbery, and if you do have the others' words of honor on what you overheard, then we'll deal with that matter as we must. But you go too far when you start flinging around wild accusations without proof. Once you've apologized to Miss Angeline, we can—"

"What a forgiving attitude," said Sir Neville. "You set an example to us all, Mr. Carlyle. Have you forgiven her so quickly for what she did to you?"

Angeline made a choked noise. Elissa looked as if she might be ill. Stepmama's eyes widened with a look of horrified realization.

I said, "Stop it! You can arrest me. I don't mind. Just don't—"

"Miss Angeline hasn't done anything to me," Mr. Carlyle said. "And if you continue to slander her in this fashion—"

"No? Then tell me: How much of the last week do you remember?" Sir Neville asked.

Mr. Carlyle blinked. "How did you know—?"

"Has no one told you what a fool you made of yourself, following her everywhere, even to Grantham Abbey, to propose marriage at every turn?"

"I—," Mr. Carlyle began. I could see his chest rise and fall with his breath. When he spoke again, his voice sounded lost. "I did no such thing. Did I?"

Stepmama's voice sounded more helpless than I'd ever heard her. "He said he'd walked all the way across the country to find us. But that was to study with my husband, not—"

"Oh?" said Sir Neville. "And was it your husband he was most anxious to meet? Tell me, how long after his arrival did he wait before proposing marriage to Miss Angeline, whom he'd never met before in his life?"

"Please!" I said. "Can't we just—"

"He didn't wait at all," Stepmama said blankly. "He proposed the very moment he first saw her."

Her words dropped into the air and were swallowed by it. I felt the pressure mount around us, like a storm gathering. It took all of my strength to look across the room at Mr. Carlyle's face as he turned to stare at Angeline.

"You wouldn't—tell me you didn't—"

Angeline's dark eyes glittered with tears. Her voice cracked as she spoke. "I'm so sorry," she said. "I didn't mean to—"

"She didn't accept any of your proposals," I said. "No matter how often you asked, she never took advantage of you, she said it would be too ridiculous—"

Elissa shook her head sharply at me, and I stopped. Mr. Carlyle was still staring at Angeline.

"You never took advantage of me," he repeated flatly. "How grateful I must be. I wonder why nobody told me until now what a fool I'd made of myself over you."

"You didn't make a fool of yourself," Angeline said. "It was me. I was the fool."

"Apparently not the only one," Mr. Carlyle said. He backed away from her, shaking his head. "And I thought—" He cut himself off as he jerked his gaze off her to look at the rest of us. "All of you saw, and knew. . . ."

"It wasn't your fault," I said. "Honestly, it wasn't even all that bad. It was quite funny, really, if you just—"

"Kat!" Elissa hissed.

Angeline's tears brimmed over and slid down her cheeks in a silent stream. Mr. Carlyle swung back to face her.

"So you all thought I was ridiculous," he said. "A proper laughingstock, following you around and making a nuisance of myself. You must have enjoyed yourself so much as you laughed about me."

"Angeline didn't laugh," I said. "She thought it was terrible. It was only—"

"Thank you, Miss Katherine," Mr. Carlyle said coldly. He didn't even look in my direction as he spoke. "I think you've clarified everything quite nicely now."

"Oh, don't think too hardly of Miss Katherine," Sir Neville said. "If it weren't for her intervention, you'd be under Miss Angeline's love spell even now. It was Miss Katherine who set you free with her own magic."

"I did not!" I said. "I mean, I suppose I did . . . but that wasn't proper witchcraft with spells, that was only—"

"Far more powerful magic," Sir Neville finished for me. "You see, mere witches like Miss Angeline require spoken spells to enchant a man. You, on the other hand, are something far more dangerous and uncontrollable, and you require no spoken spells for your magic. Have you not found that to be the case, in your numerous experiments over the past few days?"

"I believe I am going to swoon," Stepmama announced. "Katherine—Angeline—"

"I shall leave you to your privacy," Mr. Carlyle said. "This is a family matter, after all. Ma'am. Sir Neville Collingwood. Miss Stephenson, Miss Katherine . . . Miss Angeline." He bowed stiffly to her. "I can only give you my most heartfelt apologies and promise not to bother you again. You must be very tired of my attentions by now. Please convey my apologies to your father. I shall leave for Oxford immediately. If you would be kind enough to see that my belongings are packaged, I shall send for them by post, and then you needn't be inconvenienced by my presence any longer."

He pivoted on his heel and stalked out of the room. The door swung closed behind him.

A sob escaped Angeline's throat. I started toward her.

"We are not yet finished, Miss Katherine," Sir Neville said. "As regrettable as that little interlude may have been . . ." His lips curved into a smile. "We come now to the crux of the matter."

"What, more?" Stepmama gestured limply. "What could be worse?"

"Nothing," Sir Neville said, "could be worse than the behavior of two of your daughters, and of my own brother. But it remains to be decided how we shall deal with the matter. As I see it, we have two choices."

Angeline opened her mouth, as if she were about to

speak. But only a sob came out. She pressed her lips tightly together and turned away to hide her face.

"What can be done?" Stepmama said. "The scandal— oh, my heavens, what people will say and think of us!"

"Precisely," said Sir Neville. "Our first option is to follow the course of strict justice, which will entail enormous scandal. My brother shall be sent, as is only right, to the gallows for his crime; Miss Katherine must be tried as his accomplice; and the truth of both her and her sister's shocking magical proclivities must be made public knowledge as protection against the entrapment of any other unfortunate gentlemen."

"No," said Elissa. She was staring outright at Mr. Collingwood now, her blue eyes swimming with tears. "You cannot—you must not—"

"No?" Sir Neville said. "Well, perhaps not, after all. I should hate to bring distress to such a charming young lady, especially when she has done nothing to deserve the suffering her sisters' actions would heap upon her. So there is one other option we could take."

"Oh?" Stepmama sat up straighter.

"Indeed," Sir Neville said. "If all the conditions of my second option were met, I might choose to rescue my wretched younger brother from his well-deserved punishment and merely banish him to the Continent to avoid embarrassing my new wife further."

"Yes!" Elissa said. "Please, Sir Neville. Please do rescue him. No matter what conditions there might be—"

I interrupted her. "Your new wife?" I said. "What new wife?"

"If Miss Elissa Stephenson will do me the honor of accepting my hand in marriage," Sir Neville said, "as her husband, I should assume full responsibility for her two younger sisters." His smile at Stepmama showed all his teeth. "Under my protection, ma'am, I believe I may safely promise that they shall give us no more trouble."

Twenty

"*No!*"

Three of us spoke the same word at once: Angeline, me, and Mr. Collingwood, whose shouted "No!" overpowered all the rest.

"You must not, Miss Stephenson," he said. "I beg you. You cannot sacrifice yourself for me!"

"Not even for Kat," Angeline said. "We'll find another solution."

"There is no other solution," Sir Neville said. "Unless you wish me to go back into the salon now and announce the truth of this sorry matter to the rest of the assembled company? In which case, I may safely promise you that not only will my brother lose his life, but none of you will ever find a husband, much less pay off your brother's debts. Miss Katherine may go to Newgate prison for her crime, your father will certainly lose his position for the scandal, and the rest of your family will end together in debtors' prison."

"That's blackmail!" I said.

"Katherine," Stepmama began. Her voice sounded unusually tentative. "If Sir Neville really thinks it best . . ."

I ignored her. "Elissa, you can't listen to him! He's only trying to bully you."

"But there's no need," Stepmama said. "He was going to marry Elissa anyway—that is, as soon as he made the offer—"

"I think you've missed the vital point, ma'am," Angeline said. "He doesn't want only Elissa. He wants all of us." Her eyes narrowed. "All of Mama's daughters, in fact. And perhaps even—"

"The magic books!" I said. "You were the one who ordered the burglary, not Mr. Gregson after all!"

"Why on earth should Mr. Gregson burgle our house?" Stepmama said. "We had never even met him when it happened!"

"I just said it wasn't him," I said impatiently. "I only thought it was. But it was actually Sir Neville. I can see that now. Mr. Gregson was right. The magic books are in danger!"

"Don't be absurd. Sir Neville is one of the wealthiest gentlemen in England. He hardly needs to go about burgling houses!"

"He would if he wanted Mama's magic books," I said. "And the spells she wrote inside them." I frowned at him. "But what did you want them for?"

"Her *spells?*" Stepmama's voice spiraled up to a wail. "But—"

"Pray don't worry yourself about such nonsense, ma'am," Sir Neville said. "Your stepdaughters only need a firm hand on the reins. I shall make certain no rumors of their activities reach the public, and you will feel much more comfortable with all their mother's leftover belongings safely out of your house at last."

"I don't understand!" Stepmama said. "Why would you even want such dreadful things?"

Mr. Collingwood shoved past Sir Neville to drop down on his knees before Elissa. "You must not marry my brother," he said. "Forget me—choose someone, anyone else to make you happy—but you cannot marry Neville. If you had seen the way he treated poor Sarah, only for the scandals he imagined she might somehow cause . . ."

"Poor Sarah," Angeline murmured. "Let me hazard a wild guess, Sir Neville. Was poor Sarah from a family of witches as well?"

"How very clever you are, Miss Angeline," Sir Neville said. "I am not at all surprised at how much trouble you have caused for your poor stepmother. You and I shall deal very well together."

"Sarah was from a family of witches," I said, thinking

it through. "And Elissa is from a family of witches. That's why you were interested in her, despite the lack of dowry. Wasn't it?"

"But . . ." Mr. Collingwood frowned. "That can't be right. *Our* mother—"

"As charming as this conversation may be for the rest of you," said Sir Neville, "it grows tiresome to me. Miss Stephenson," he said to Elissa, "I'm afraid I must press you for an answer. Which shall it be? Will you give in to your sisters' stubbornness, or will you save your entire family from debt and despair as well as saving my worthless brother's life?"

"Don't do it, Elissa!" I said.

"Don't be a fool, Elissa," said Angeline. "Of course she won't do it," she said to Sir Neville. "We won't allow it."

"As close as you may be to your sister, I'm afraid it is hardly your decision to make," Sir Neville said. "The only person in this room who could force your sister in this matter is your stepmother, who would hardly be so foolish as to oppose my offer. Would you, ma'am?"

Stepmama opened her mouth. Then she shut it again. For the first time since I'd met her five years ago, she looked positively haggard.

"I don't know," she said. "I don't understand any of this!"

"You will not stand against me, then," Sir Neville said.

Stepmama looked from Sir Neville to Mr. Collingwood

to Elissa. "I don't understand!" she repeated.

"Indeed." Sir Neville yawned. "As I said. Your stepmother desires you to accept my offer. Now—"

"No!" Stepmama said. Then she blinked, as if she'd startled herself as well as the rest of us.

"I beg your pardon?" Sir Neville said.

"I said no," Stepmama repeated. She turned to face Elissa. "I will not make this choice for you."

Sir Neville's voice hardened. "Perhaps you do not yet understand the position your family is in. But if I might clarify the consequences for you—"

"Debtors' prison," Stepmama said. "Yes. I heard you. But I never believed the rumors about your first wife, and now your brother says they were true. I owe a duty to my stepdaughters no matter how ill they might behave." She took a deep breath. "You must make your own decision, Elissa."

"Thank you!" Angeline said. "You've done the right thing, ma'am."

Stepmama ignored Angeline. She took Elissa's hand and looked into her eyes. "Listen to me, child," she said. "You must do what you truly think is best for your family, and not let any of us change your mind."

"No!" I said. "Don't listen to her, Elissa!"

"Oh, *damnation*," Angeline said. "Elissa, don't—"

"I shall," Elissa said. She lifted her chin. Her pale face looked exalted, like a holy martyr. "I shall do what is best for my family."

"Miss Stephenson, I beg you!" Mr. Collingwood said. He snatched her free hand. "If you care even the slightest bit for me—"

Elissa pulled away from Stepmama and rose to her feet. She gazed down at Mr. Collingwood's tormented face and smoothed back the jet-black hair from his forehead. I could have sworn I saw a glowing halo rise around her as she spoke. "You must forgive me, my love, and learn to forget me, for my sake."

"Oh, my Lord," I said. "You've been waiting your whole life for this, haven't you?"

"Can you doubt it?" said Angeline. "Look at the two of them! He's as bad as she is."

They both ignored us as if we hadn't spoken.

"I would gladly sacrifice my life for your happiness," Mr. Collingwood said.

"Do you think I could live with such a burden on my soul?" Elissa asked.

"I am going to be sick!" I announced.

"I am both honored and delighted by your decision," said Sir Neville. "Miss Stephenson, if you would give me your hand . . ." He held out his arm, ignoring his brother, who knelt between them. "Shall we repair to the salon to announce our betrothal?"

"No!" I shouted.

The doors were closed and guarded. It didn't matter. Like it or not, there was only one option left.

"Grab Elissa's hand!" I said to Angeline, and I lunged

across the room. I shoved past Mr. Collingwood and grabbed Elissa's arm.

"Kat, what on earth—?" she began.

"What is going on?" Stepmama demanded. "Katherine—"

"Got her," Angeline said. "Now what?"

"Miss Stephenson!" said Mr. Collingwood, and grabbed for Elissa. "You must reconsider."

"I think not," Sir Neville said. "Whatever you may be planning, Miss Katherine—"

I tightened my grip on Elissa's arm and clicked the mirror open.

"That's Mama's mirror!" Elissa gasped. "How did you get—ohhh!"

Her gasp turned into a scream as the world flipped inside out around us.

We landed in a tumble of arms and legs and moans of pain.

"Ouch!"

"Get off!"

"You're sitting on my head!"

"Miss Stephenson, where are you?" Mr. Collingwood's voice came out muffled by yards of muslin across his face. He spat it out and sat up, wild-eyed. "Miss Stephenson!"

Stepmama's voice rose above all the rest in a shriek of pure outrage as she yanked the skirts of her dress back down over her legs. "Kat, what have you done this time?"

"It's all right, ma'am," I said, as I disentangled myself and shoved Angeline's elbow off my throat. "You weren't meant to come with us, but since you have, you might as well—"

"Did you truly mean to leave your own stepmother behind?" Sir Neville drawled behind me. "How deplorably inconsiderate of you, Miss Katherine. And how fortunate for me that I managed to see through your rather transparent ploy and take a firm hold of your sister myself. I should have hated to be left behind and miss this experience. I have heard of the Guardians' Golden Hall many times, of course, but the reality . . ." He rose to his feet and scanned the room with cool authority. "Truly astounding. I shall enjoy exploring it further, with your sisterly assistance."

"Where are we?" Elissa whispered.

I stood up. My knees were trembling. I had to hold out my arms for balance. *Curses.* I'd really thought I'd managed to find the perfect escape. Of course, it wouldn't have solved our larger problems, but I'd thought I could at least keep Elissa safe and secluded until I had time to think of a real solution.

It looked like I didn't have any more time after all.

"Clearly, Kat's been playing with Mama's belongings," said Angeline. "That must be why she went through Mama's cabinet back home." Her voice was more level than I would have expected; perhaps her anger at Sir Neville was balancing out her outrage at me.

"You did what?" Stepmama's bellow echoed around the Golden Hall, bouncing off the walls around us. "How dare you?!"

"Could everyone please concentrate?" I said. "You can all shout at me later, if you like, but—"

"Give me the mirror now," Angeline said, "and we'll pretend you never took it."

"I can't," I said. "First of all, it's not here with me—it's back in Lady Graves's library—but mainly, it won't let me. It's mine now."

"It belonged to Mama."

"I know. But when I found it—"

"You broke almost everything else in her cupboard. How can you claim one of the only things that's left?"

"I know," I said. "It was an accident. But—"

"You've been after her magic books ever since you first saw I had them," said Angeline. "You're trying to take away everything that was hers. How can you be so selfish?"

"I am not!" I said. "But she was my mother too, not just yours. You can't pretend—"

"You never even met her!"

"You—"

"Be quiet!" Elissa shrieked. She leaped to her feet. Her cheeks were flushed, and her eyes sparked with rage. Mr. Collingwood gazed up at her in awe from the floor by her feet, and I had to admit, she did look exactly like an avenging goddess. "I cannot believe you two are squabbling right now!"

"It wasn't me!" I said. "I was only trying to explain how—"

"Are you saying you don't even mind that Kat stole Mama's mirror?" Angeline demanded.

"I did not—"

"You must have known you were in the wrong. Otherwise you wouldn't have kept it hidden from us!"

"You mean, the way you kept Mama's magic books hidden from Elissa?" I said.

"This is all utterly fascinating," Sir Neville said. "And you shall both have plenty of time to debate all these points further in the future . . . although not within hearing range of the rest of us, if at all possible. Once Miss Stephenson and I are married and the two of you safely ensconced at Collingwood Hall—"

"That is not going to happen," I said.

"No?" Sir Neville raised one eyebrow. "May I ask exactly how you plan to prevent it, now that your sophisticated and complex strategy of running away has failed?"

"I did not—," I began, and then I stopped. There was no point in denying it. This time, I really had just tried to run away.

This time . . .

I swung around. The Golden Hall was empty. The highwayman was nowhere to be seen. Mr. Gregson was gone.

But he had set a magical alarm to notify him whenever I arrived, hadn't he? He'd said so the second time I came here. He must still be able to tell, or else he couldn't have arrived so quickly when I'd come with the highwayman.

So where was he this time? If he'd finally decided to be reasonable and give me uninterrupted time alone in the Golden Hall for exploration, I would simply have to throttle him.

The point was, I was on my own. I took a deep breath and tried to think. What did I know how to do? I could turn myself into someone else; well, that wouldn't help right now, not in full view of everyone. I hadn't learned a single other magic spell.

But Guardians didn't require spoken spells. And I had performed magic several times now, magic powerful enough to shatter Angeline's spells from Mama's own magic book and even Mr. Gregson's magic. All I had to do . . .

I squeezed my eyes shut, forcing the pressure to mount inside my head and into the air around me.

"NO!" I bellowed.

The air did not implode around me. Instead, it gave a quiet *pop* and went limp. I stumbled.

"Very entertaining," said Sir Neville. "If I had been foolish enough to try to cast a spell on you, I'm sure that would have deflated it nicely. Unfortunately, powerful though your spell-breaking abilities might be, they are not actually enough to change anyone's natural, nonmagical mind about you or anything else in the world." He laughed, then whispered something under his breath. I was just as glad not to be able to hear it.

"Oh," I said. I swallowed hard.

The choking sensation was back in my throat. Along with it came that horrible new feeling I'd discovered: *helplessness*. Prickles raced along my skin, pushing me tight in upon myself. The smell of burning meat made me sick to my stomach. I wrapped my arms around my chest and let the misery overwhelm me.

What was the use of fighting anymore? Sir Neville was right. There was nothing I could do. I couldn't cast a single useful spell. I couldn't even use my Guardian magic to break his spells if he didn't bother to cast any— and why should he bother? He didn't need to. He had the whole weight of Society behind him, promising scandal and poverty and disgrace to everyone I loved, and all I had was an old mirror. I was completely alone. I might as well give up now, before—

Wait. The word felt almost like a tangible breath against my ear. I blinked and spun around, but I didn't see anyone except my family, all staring at me in various attitudes of despair or outrage. *Wait for what?* I thought. I was on my own. Nobody else was coming to help.

That's it. I shook myself like a dog. The prickling, creeping, choking feelings clustered back around me, biting at my skin, but I ignored them. What I'd been thinking wasn't true. That was the helplessness talking, in Sir Neville's voice. And it was completely mad.

I had never been alone in my entire life. Perhaps Sir

Neville and his brother had grown up apart, like only children, but I certainly hadn't.

And there was something else I would gamble on just as high as Charles had ever gambled on a round of cards: that prickling, choking sensation that surrounded me was no more natural than the color of fish-faced Mrs. Banfield's hair. Sir Neville had attacked when I was off my guard.

I didn't even have to try to summon up the pressure in my head this time. It came naturally.

"NO!" I shouted again, and the air imploded around us.

Sir Neville blinked. "Well, that was certainly unusual."

"Don't cast another spell on me," I said. "Because I won't be fooled again, no matter how powerful a witch you might be. I am not a helpless person."

I turned to my sisters. "Elissa," I said, "Sir Neville's first wife came from a family of witches. He locked her up, and she died."

"It's true," Mr. Collingwood said from the floor below us. "He didn't murder her, as everyone said, but she simply faded away."

"Exactly," I said. "She faded away. Why did he want someone from a witch's family? Why does he want all of us? Because we have magical powers."

"Kat, you mustn't speak about—," Elissa began.

"We'll be proper later," I said. "Right now we need to think. Angeline! I know you're angry at me, but you have to help me now. Why would he want all of us and our powers locked away in his house in the country?"

"Well, that's simple enough," Angeline said. "He must want to use our powers for himself somehow. As he used his wife's powers." Her eyes narrowed. "And she faded away when he'd used her up."

"This is ridiculous," Sir Neville said, and laughed as he turned to Stepmama. "Really, ma'am, are you going to let your stepdaughters natter on in this vulgar fashion?"

Stepmama laughed too. Her laugh sounded much sharper and less humorous. "Really, Sir Neville," she replied, "I have never been able to stop them before in my life, so I don't see how I could possibly stop them now."

"Thank you, ma'am," I said. "Now, Elissa." I swung back around and took her hand. "Your fiancé is planning to lock us up in his house and use up our powers until we die. Do you really, truly believe that agreeing to that will save the family?"

"Well," Elissa began. Her eyes darted back and forth. "But he couldn't truly mean to do that. It's so—"

"Improper?" I suggested. "Vulgar? Not the actions of a gentleman you could bring yourself to marry?"

"Pray recall, Miss Stephenson," Sir Neville snapped, "that you are not only saving your family by accepting my hand in marriage. You are also saving the life of my younger brother."

"Ohh!" Elissa pulled away from me and put her hand to her mouth. "I cannot—"

"Let me die!" Mr. Collingwood said, and rose to his

knees to grab her other hand. "Gladly would I give up—"

"That is quite enough from both of you," I said. "No one is going to die!"

"My brother will hang if your sister refuses me," said Sir Neville. His voice had hoarsened; he was glaring at me as the veneer of gentlemanly polish dropped away.

"My love," Elissa began.

"My darling," Mr. Collingwood said, raising her hand to his lips.

"He will not hang," I said.

"When I bring my two witnesses to testify to his guilt—," Sir Neville began.

"It won't do you a jot of good," I said. "Because he'll still be here. He can't leave without me. None of you can. Haven't you realized that yet?" I looked around the group. "We came here through my magic mirror."

"Mama's magic mirror," Angeline said.

"It was Mama's," I said, "but I inherited it, and now it belongs to me."

"Don't talk nonsense," said Angeline. "I don't know what stories you've been telling yourself, but—"

"Oh, she isn't talking nonsense, Miss Angeline," Mr. Gregson said mildly from behind me. "She is, in fact, your mother's heir, as I have been telling her for some time . . . and I am most gratified to hear that she has finally accepted it."

Twenty-one

"So there you are," I said. I turned around. "I wondered when you would arrive."

"Your highwayman took some time to dispose of," Mr. Gregson said. "However, you may be happy to know that he is safely on a transport ship to Australia now. You do take up with the most unlikely personages, Miss Katherine."

"Will someone please explain to me what's going on?" Stepmama wailed. "Kat? What highwayman?"

"The real one," I said. "Not Mr. Collingwood, as anyone with any sense would know."

"Ma'am," Mr. Gregson said, and bowed to Stepmama, and then to my sisters. "Miss Stephenson. Miss Angeline. Mr. Collingwood." He straightened, and his eyes met Sir Neville's. "Sir Neville."

"Gregson," Sir Neville growled. "You had better leave now."

"Does everyone but me know about this place?" Stepmama said. "Who should we expect to arrive next? Lady Graves?"

Mr. Gregson's lips twitched. "I profoundly hope not," he said. "But perhaps . . ." He glanced my way. "One more person could come, if you required more aid than I alone could give."

"*Not* Lady Fotherington," I said. "I don't care how much help she could give."

Stepmama swayed and put one hand to her head. "Are you genuinely telling me that Lady Fotherington herself— one of the most fashionable women in London society— spends time here too?"

"Not when I can help it," I said.

"Would everyone please *be quiet*?" Sir Neville's voice rose to a roar. "You all seem to have forgotten, but the point remains: Miss Stephenson must marry me, and her sisters must come to live with us, or else my brother will hang!"

"Ah, Neville," Mr. Gregson said, and sighed. "You never were any good at admitting when you'd been beaten."

Sir Neville fisted his hands. "You think you can beat me, Gregson?"

"No," said Mr. Gregson. "I think Miss Katherine already has. Or hadn't you understood what she said ear- lier?" He turned to me. "So, I take it, the plan is to leave

Mr. Collingwood safely here until you're well away from Grantham Abbey, and then—"

"No," I said. "Not anymore."

"I beg your pardon?" Mr. Gregson raised his eyebrows—both of them at once, I was glad to see. I would have had to go mad if everyone I knew could raise a single eyebrow at a time except for me.

"That was my plan," I said, "but then I thought of something better." I turned around. "Mr. Collingwood," I said. "Earlier, when we were talking about how Sarah came from a family of witches, you started to say something, and Sir Neville cut you off. What was it?"

Mr. Collingwood blinked up at me. "I'm afraid I don't quite recall—"

"Who cares?" Sir Neville interrupted. "There's no point in asking him about anything important."

"That's it," said Mr. Collingwood. He rose to his feet, still holding Elissa's hand. "You were talking about families of witches, and it occurred to me—did you not know? Our mother was a witch too."

"What?" Stepmama said. *"What?"*

"She was no such thing," Sir Neville snapped. "You wouldn't know anyway. She was dead before you could—"

"I do know," Mr. Collingwood said, "and she was my mother as well as yours. The servants told me."

"Servants' gossip," said Sir Neville, "means nothing."

"Oh, it means something," I said, and smiled. "It means

I finally understand what's going on and what to do about it. Angeline?"

"Kat?" She looked measuringly back at me.

"If you need assistance, Miss Katherine, as your tutor—," Mr. Gregson began.

"No, thank you," I said. It was time to take a calculated risk. I was almost sure I had figured out the truth about Mr. Gregson, as well as Sir Neville. Now was the time for me to find out for certain, while my sisters and I could stand together. "My family can take care of this ourselves." I reached out my hand to Angeline. "Help me?"

"Don't be a fool," Sir Neville said to Angeline. "Didn't you hear what she was gabbling on about earlier? Calling herself your mother's heir, taking away what belonged to you . . ."

Angeline rolled her eyes. "I am so relieved that you are not going to be my brother-in-law after all," she said. "You do have a great deal to learn about families." Her hand slipped into mine, strong and warm. "Now don't get cocky, Kat," she said. "I'm still going to throttle you later."

"I understand," I said. "But right now, I need you to do something else."

I leaned up to whisper in her ear. She sighed.

"I hope you're not making fools out of both of us," she said.

"It wouldn't be for the first time," Elissa muttered, and shook her head. But she stepped up to stand beside me anyway and took my other hand. As the warmth of both of my sisters pressed against me, I lifted my chin to meet Sir Neville's gaze full-on.

"Now!" I said, and Angeline cast her spell. The scent of flowers filled the Golden Hall.

Sir Neville's shirtfront bulged and rippled. He gave a start. Then he flung his hand up to press it down. His lips began to move in a fast, whispered chant. Burnt meat mingled with the flowers. Out of the corner of my eye, I saw Mr. Gregson start forward.

"No!" I said. "I'll take care of this myself."

I narrowed my eyes into thin slits, until all I could feel was Sir Neville's spell flying toward Angeline. There . . . closer . . . *got it*.

"*NO!*" I bellowed, and the air imploded around us.

Sir Neville fell back. His shirt ripped open. A white envelope flew out of it, through the air, straight into my hands.

"What on earth—?" Stepmama began.

"How intriguing," said Mr. Gregson. "And may I ask—?"

"What is it, Kat?" Elissa said.

I held it out to Mr. Collingwood. "This belongs to you, I think."

He tore it open with trembling hands. "I—Miss Katherine, I—I—"

His face changed color. He sat down abruptly on the golden floor and put his head in his hands. His shoulders rose and fell. Elissa flew to his side.

I said, "What is it? Was I wrong? Is it—?"

He lifted his face from his hands. He was laughing helplessly, and he had his reckless highwayman grin on his face. "It is my inheritance," he said. "I am a wealthy man. I could—I could buy and sell Grantham Abbey twice over!"

"You may not—don't you dare—!" Sir Neville began.

"Fascinating," said Mr. Gregson. "And how, exactly, did you discover this, Miss Katherine?"

"I'd heard of the will," I said. "But I didn't believe in it until just now. You see, I thought Sir Neville would have burned it if it had existed. I didn't understand why he would have kept it until—"

"Until you realized his mother had been a witch," said Angeline. A smile spread slowly across her face as she shook her head. "My, my, Sir Neville. Perhaps you do understand something about families after all. No matter how hard you try, you simply cannot leave them behind."

"She cast a spell on the will before she died," I said. "It protected the will—and Mr. Collingwood's inheritance—even after her death. Even when Sir Neville used up his first wife's magic—and her life—trying to defeat his mother's spell. That's why Sir Neville wanted Mama's magic books—in case she had created a spell of her own that could defeat the protection on his mother's will. And that's why he wanted all three of us."

"Aha," Mr. Gregson murmured. "And I believe you may

have discovered by now that a strong enough Guardian can break any spell or magic-working."

I nodded. "So if he'd managed to use my Guardian magic against the spell on his mother's will . . ."

Stepmama waved away the talk of magic with a shudder. But she had a predatory gleam in her eye as she asked her own question: "Do you mean to say that Mr. Collingwood is now the wealthier brother?"

"Not exactly," I said. "The money was divided in half. But since Sir Neville must use his half to keep up all his vast estates, and Mr. Collingwood has no properties of his own to tie him down . . ."

"I believe Sir Neville may be tied very closely to his estates, from now on," Mr. Gregson said. "And there is very little likelihood of his creating any trouble for the rest of you, is there?" His voice hardened. "Especially with the eyes of the Order fixed firmly upon him. We had only suspicions before—but now we have evidence. If he shows even a hint of trying to harm another innocent through magic . . ."

Sir Neville let out a growl, like a cornered wolf. "I'll destroy all your reputations in an instant. When Society finds out the scandalous magic that all of you have been doing—"

"*If* Society finds out the scandalous and murderous magic you have been doing," Stepmama said, her voice dagger sharp, "then I think it is you whose reputation will be destroyed. And, more than that, my future son-in-law has every right to take you to court and strip you of every possession you own in recompense for the heinous crime you committed by stealing his inheritance!"

I blinked. Sir Neville took a step back.

"Oh, I say," Mr. Collingwood said. "I wouldn't—" He gave a start and looked up at Elissa. Her face was as angelic as ever, but I was ready to swear by his look that she had pinched him.

He drew himself up and squared his shoulders. "That is to say, Neville," he said, "I shall certainly do exactly that if I ever hear of you threatening my new family again. So you had better stay very close to your estates from now on, and leave innocent young women alone!"

"As I thought," Stepmama said, and smiled at him. "Welcome to the family, Mr. Collingwood. We are very pleased to have you."

⁖✱⁖

Mr. Gregson was the first to leave the Golden Hall, transporting Sir Neville with him. While Stepmama drew Mr. Collingwood to one side to fuss over him—and over his mother's will, which she was eyeing with avid curiosity— my two sisters and I were left with a moment of solitude. But not of peace.

I eyed them nervously. Of course, we had just won . . . and yet . . .

Elissa said, "Is this where you were that night I found you next to Mama's cabinet?"

"Well . . . yes," I admitted. "But I didn't destroy her

things on purpose, I swear! That first time I opened her mirror, the magic came like a hurricane. I didn't know it was going to happen. There was nothing I could do to stop it."

"It was a terrible shock," said Elissa, "but we do understand now, truly, darling. You mustn't worry about it anymore. It was only a horrible accident."

"And yet it still didn't teach you to keep out of places you don't belong," Angeline said. Her words were sharp, but she half smiled, shaking her head. "I suppose that was probably a lost cause from the start, wasn't it? Never mind, Kat. You've suffered enough by now, I think."

I could have left it there, with my sisters' forgiveness. But I remembered the conversation between Mr. Collingwood and his own older brother just a few minutes before, and I took a deep, steadying breath. "I did belong there, at Mama's cabinet," I said. I met Angeline's gaze without backing down. "Just as much as either of you. She was my mother just as much as yours."

Angeline's eyes narrowed. "It's not the same at all. You didn't know her. You don't remember—"

"I don't remember her," I said. "You're right. I can't. I don't have any of your memories to hold on to. All I have of her is this." I pointed at the Golden Hall around us. "That's exactly why I need it."

Angeline opened her mouth to say something else. But before she could, Elissa spoke.

"I miss Mama every single day," she said softly. "And I

know she would have been proud of you tonight."

Her arms wrapped warmly around me, and I felt her tears fall on my hair. I blinked hard against my own as I hugged her back.

"Thank you, Kat," she whispered. "Thank you."

She straightened and looked over at Stepmama and Mr. Collingwood. The will had changed hands. Stepmama was reading it with sharp concentration while Mr. Collingwood looked on helplessly, tugging at his cravat. Elissa's eyes widened in alarm as she watched the beads of sweat gather on her new fiancé's forehead.

"Kat?" she said, "I think it may be time for you to take us back to Grantham Abbey and the rest of the party."

Angeline followed her gaze, and her lips twitched. "Yes," she said. "And quickly, too. We don't want Mr. Collingwood running away before we've even announced your betrothal. Do you think perhaps we ought to find him another highwayman's mask to wear for courage every time he faces Stepmama?"

"Angeline!" Elissa gasped. "Of all the outrageous suggestions—"

"Oh, don't listen to her," I said, and rolled my eyes at Angeline.

Angeline only smiled enigmatically in return. But her sidelong look at me, as we all linked hands, said as clearly as any spoken words could have: *We're not finished yet.*

Once we'd landed in the library, where Mr. Gregson stood with a glowering Sir Neville, Stepmama, Elissa, and Mr. Collingwood swept together into the salon to announce the betrothal and the unexpected discovery of Mr. Collingwood's fortune. Elissa was beaming as she left, looking less like a tragic heroine than I had ever seen her. Sir Neville stalked out of the house and straight to his carriage in a way I found most satisfying. Angeline stayed behind, waiting for the door to close behind our other relatives before she spoke.

"So you really think you're a—a 'Guardian,' did you call it?" she said.

I felt Mr. Gregson's eyes on me and sighed. "Yes," I said. "Mama was, and now I am too."

"And as a Guardian, you think you're more powerful than any witch," Angeline said.

"Erm . . ." I took a deep breath and looked into my older sister's dark eyes. "Not yet," I said. "But I can break a witch's spell. And I can fight the witches like Sir Neville who use their magic against innocent people."

"Ha." She raised a single eyebrow in the way she knew I hated. Then she looked down at Mama's mirror on the floor nearby. She picked it up. It appeared in my hand a moment later.

Angeline scowled. She muttered something under her breath. It flew back to her hand.

I felt its cool smoothness in my palm less than a second afterward.

"It's no good," I said. "I've tried not to keep it. It never works."

"Well." Angeline pressed her lips together as she looked hard at me. Then she sighed. "Do try not to get completely above yourself, Kat. If you can possibly help yourself, that is."

She leaned forward and gave me a quick, warm hug. Then she turned away. "I'm going up to my room now," she said. "Please tell Stepmama I have a headache."

"But don't you want to see Elissa and Mr. Collingwood be congratulated?"

"Not now," Angeline said. "Later I will. But . . ." She shook her head. I saw the lines of strain and unhappiness against her mouth. "Later," she said softly. She almost ran out the door.

I turned back to Mr. Gregson, who was watching me with mild eyes. "So," he said. "I take it you've finally come to the conclusion that you do want to join our Order, after all?"

"I think . . ." I took a deep breath. "I want to fight people like Sir Neville. I want to learn how to use all my powers, like Mama did. But . . ." I stopped, desperately trying to read his countenance. "You did see Angeline performing witchcraft, didn't you?"

His lips twitched. "As I have been neither struck blind nor entirely obtuse, yes, in fact, I was aware of what was happening."

I eyed him narrowly. "And you're not going to do anything horrible to her?"

He sighed. "I told you, Katherine, we reserve pacification only for those witches who present a genuine threat to Society—like Sir Neville, should he try any of his murderous tricks again. So far, nothing I have observed has given any hint of a threat presented by your sister."

"But . . ." My hands curled into fists. I had to know. "If Mama's love spell would have been considered a threat—"

"I beg your pardon?" Mr. Gregson stared at me.

I winced but continued. It couldn't hurt Mama for him to find out now. "I know Mama set a love spell on Papa, and that was why he—"

"My dear girl," Mr. Gregson said. "Your mother broke that very foolish spell herself. How could you know about the spell's existence, and not know how it ended?"

I stared at him. My chest felt tight. "I saw the spell in her book! She wrote down his name, and—"

Mr. Gregson put one hand on my shoulder. It felt warm and solid, anchoring me. "My dear girl," he said gently. "Your mother was very young when she met your father. She did cast that spell—indeed, I believe she may have turned to witchcraft in the first place through her love for him. She knew how very unlikely it was that he would choose to marry her with her lack of any dowry, and it was that which caused her to break her Guardian oaths and turn to such desperate methods. But when I spoke to her, just before she was exiled, she confessed it all to me. Not only did she release him from the betrothal, but she broke the spell before my eyes and of her own accord. She bitterly regretted the injustice she had done him by casting it."

"But—but—" I looked into his pale blue eyes. They were steady on mine. "But they still married! He still married her! He—"

"Perhaps," Mr. Gregson said, "you do not know everything about your father after all."

My mouth was hanging open. I closed it with a snap.

I remembered Mama's cabinets. All those scandalous magical items, all so carefully preserved. Papa hadn't let Stepmama destroy them, after all.

Perhaps there was far more to my parents' history than I had ever understood. But I was going to find out. And I was going to do something else, too.

"I will join your Order, after all," I said. It was a gamble as risky as any Charles had ever made, but the words felt right as I said them.

I was going to fight dangerous rogue witches like Sir Neville and keep them from hurting anybody else. But I wasn't going to stand by and let any of the Lady Fotheringtons in the Order persecute innocent witches, either. The whole Order was going to have to make some massive changes while I was a member—because, just like Mama before me, I wasn't going to let myself be bound by either ignorance or prejudice.

But it was too early to let anyone know about that. So I just smiled dazzlingly and said, "But don't expect me to become one of those students who never questions her tutor."

"Somehow, that does not surprise me," Mr. Gregson said, and sighed.

"And more than that," I said. "I have a full list of conditions to set out before I join. When I'm older, I'll marry whoever I want to marry—*if* I decide to get married at all. And no matter what, Lady Fotherington is never, ever going to be one of my teachers!"

"I doubt you could persuade her into it no matter how hard you tried," said Mr. Gregson. "I should warn you, Katherine, that you may not have an easy time of it. Lady Fotherington is not the only one in our Order who was appalled by your mother's decisions. You will have to expect some opposition, and even distrust, when you first begin your work with us. And I'm afraid you will also have to expect—"

"Oh, I can manage all that," I said. "I'm not afraid of being talked about. But I won't have anyone trying to work any magic on me. You can tell Lady Fotherington that too. Or rather, I'll tell her so myself, as soon as I'm finished with my business tonight. I know how to break her magic-workings now, and I shall, if she makes any more attempts."

"Understood," Mr. Gregson murmured. "So am I to understand that you are finally ready to accept me as your tutor?"

"For a while," I said. "I want to find out what Mama could do, and what I can become, if I work hard enough." I took a deep breath and looked out the library windows into the darkness over Grantham Abbey. "But I still have two more conditions."

"More?" Mr. Gregson sighed. "I knew you would be difficult, Katherine, but really—"

"Don't worry," I said. "These ones should be easy for you." I grinned as I turned to face him. "All that I still need tonight are a pistol and a horse."

I was dressed in my boys' clothes again, for speed, as the horse I rode astride tore down the long road in the moonlight. The wind ruffled the short hair against my neck. Mr. Gregson had retrieved Mr. Collingwood's horse for me from the stables, along with the pistol I'd required. There had been a glint in his eyes that looked like danger as he'd handed the horse's reins to me, and I had an uneasy feeling that things might not progress quite as easily from then onward. But the horse felt like an old friend underneath me, so I didn't let myself worry about the future. Instead I swung one leg across the saddle, like a boy, and let exhilaration fill me up like sparkling champagne as I rode away from Grantham Abbey.

When I glimpsed Sir Neville's carriage ahead, I leaned over my horse's neck and urged him on. We flew past the jet-black carriage and sent my laughter back to Sir Neville through the wind.

It took me only ten more minutes to spot the second carriage on the road—one of Lady Graves's green and gold traveling carriages, borrowed for the journey. It was traveling at a snail's pace, as if even the driver thought that leaving was a bad idea.

It was hardly even a challenge. The driver faced away from me, and no footman had accompanied this journey. Nobody even turned to note my arrival.

Until I drew the pistol from my jacket and fired it straight into the air.

The horses leaped straight up. The carriage jerked to a stop. The driver's full attention had to stay on the horses as he fought to control them; he could only throw one swift, wide-eyed look back at me, in my boys' clothing and full, swirling black cloak.

The carriage door jerked open. "What the devil—?" began Frederick Carlyle.

I rode straight up to his open door. "Stand and deliver!" I said, and grinned.

"Miss Katherine?" He stared at me and shook his head. "I don't know what you're playing at this time, but I can't—"

"Oh, yes, you can," I said, and pointed the pistol at him. "Your money or your life," I said. "And since I know you don't have any money on you . . ." I shrugged. "There's only one possible solution."

I could see him fighting not to laugh. "Is that pistol even loaded, or did you just fire the only bullet in it?"

I raised both eyebrows at him. "Does it matter?"

"Do you honestly believe you can make me—"

"I know one thing," I said. "My sister is up in her

bedroom crying her eyes out over you right now."

Mr. Carlyle went still. Then he shook his head. "No," he said. "Angeline Stephenson doesn't care a jot for me. I'm just—"

"You're her true love," I said. "That's what her magic spell was for: to summon her true love. And it worked, even if you haven't realized it yet."

"But . . ." He took a deep breath. "Listen to me, Kat," he said. "If you're making this up just to bring me back—"

"If I am," I said, "then you can go ahead and shoot me with this pistol, and then we'll find out for sure if it's loaded."

He began to laugh. "I sincerely hope it isn't," he said, "because you've been holding it all wrong for the past five minutes. With the way you live, you really do need someone to teach you how to point a pistol properly before you get much older."

"That's up to you," I said. "So? What's your decision?"

Frederick Carlyle shook his head. "Come," he said. "Get in the carriage, and you can tell me everything that happened after I left, and how you managed to defeat Sir Neville and probably bluff your way into a fortune or even a knighthood or kingship, too, in some scandalously rapscallion manner I can't even begin to imagine. It can be my bedtime story on the way back to Grantham Abbey." He reached up and banged the roof of the carriage. "Turn around!" he called to the driver, and he gestured me inside.

I looked at the safe, comfortable, cushioned seats of

Lady Graves's carriage, and I shook my head. "No, thank you," I said. "But I'll be waiting there when you arrive."

I rode back to Grantham Abbey in the moonlight, while the wind ruffled my hair and blew the cloak out around me, and the pistol bumped satisfyingly against my side, promising more adventures yet to come.

I was twelve years of age when I cut my hair short, became a highwayman, and captured husbands for both of my sisters.

I could hardly wait to find out what would happen next.

Acknowledgments

Huge thanks and love to my parents, Kathy and Richard Burgis, who introduced me to Jane Austen and shared their love of her books with me at a ridiculously early age, sparking a lifelong passion. And many thanks to my wonderful grandma, Sandra Burgis, for trading Georgette Heyer novels with me and forgiving me when I woke her up by giggling over them in the middle of the night!

Thanks so much to my brothers, Ben and Dave Burgis, for being my first readers, ever since we were little kids with a secret writing group. Every day I feel lucky to be your sister.

I owe my husband, Patrick Samphire, so many thanks that I couldn't fit them all onto one page. From cheerleading my work to giving me the best critiques to handling all the housework and taking on extra child care so that I could write . . . You are the best, and I am so very lucky to be your wife. You're not just my husband, you're my very best friend and favorite writer in the world.

I owe so much to Barry Goldblatt, officially known as The Best Agent In The World™. Thank you so much for your enthusiasm and support for Kat and for me. They have made all the difference. I also owe enormous thanks to my wonderful and perceptive editor, Namrata Tripathi.

Thank you so much for believing in Kat and in me! I have been very lucky to be able to work with you. I'm also truly grateful to Lindsay Schlegel, for her efficiency and generosity, and to Valerie Shea and Jeannie Ng, my copyeditors, for doing such beautiful work.

Thanks so much to all the generous people who read and critiqued various drafts of this book: Patrick Samphire, Lisa Mantchev, Sarah Prineas, Jenn Reese, Justina Robson, Ben Burgis, David Burgis, Richard Burgis, Jenna Waterford, Tiffany Trent, Samantha Ling, and Karen Healey. Lisa, thank you so much for our literary tea party, with its exchange of red-ribbon-wrapped manuscripts. Without it, I might never have had the courage to write that very first draft that had been calling to me for so long. And Jenn and Justina, thank you both so much for showing such total enthusiasm and commitment to Kat, above and beyond the call of friendship! There were so many times when I was feeling discouraged and you two saved me.

Thank you to Delia Sherman, who has provided invaluable advice and encouragement over the past few years, as well as being a wonderful role model. Thank you to Caitlin Blasdell for an incredibly useful and provocative discussion about Kat's world. Thank you to Caroline and E. R. Hooton for their generous help with research. And thank you to my community of friends on livejournal .com, who have cheered me on when I was nervous, comforted me when I was lost, and joined with me in all my celebrations. You guys are the best!